HER
DARK
PATH

A gripping crime mystery full of twists and turns

KEN OGILVIE

JOFFE

BOOKS

Published 2017 by Joffe Books, London.

www.joffebooks.com

ISBN- 9781979312875

This book is dedicated to Elizabeth, Linda, Gail and Janice.

Chapter 1

Ontario Provincial Police headquarters, Orillia, Ontario (July 1, 2007)

Rebecca Bradley charged up the two flights of stairs. At the top, she slowed her pace, took a deep breath and forced herself to calm down. The next few minutes would be crucial for her career. Her meeting with Regional Superintendent Jonathan Cartwright was due in a few seconds, just enough time to run a hand over her tightly pinned hair and flick a speck of lint off her uniform.

She arrived at Cartwright's office precisely on schedule and rapped on the imposing oak door. Strong and sturdy, like the man behind it — or so he liked to think. Rebecca swallowed.

Five seconds passed. She waited a while longer, and put her ear to the door. He must be in there. Only minutes ago she'd watched his Audi pull into its reserved parking spot. She straightened up and rapped again, more sharply. He could at least acknowledge her.

She glanced around the outer office, glad that no staff were on the second floor today, just a couple of duty officers on the floor below. It was Sunday, and better still,

Canada Day. No one who mattered would be around to see her asking for a personal favour, and breaking protocol to do so.

She faced the door again and banged harder. Still no response. Now she was worried. Surely he hadn't cancelled their meeting?

She called out. "It's Rebecca, sir. Please let me in." She held her breath and listened. Stone cold silence.

Finally she heard Cartwright's gravelly voice, thinly, as if it came from far away. "Enter."

Rebecca moved forward cautiously. She felt like a supplicant begging for an audience with the king. She almost tripped on the thick pile carpet — newly installed, smelling of chemicals, and royal blue, naturally. She conjured up an image of Cartwright with a bejewelled crown and sceptre, and stifled a nervous giggle.

He was standing at attention with his back to her, gaze directed out of the window towards the mid-afternoon sun. He had just returned from officiating at the celebrations in Orillia town centre. Dressed in his charcoal uniform, silhouetted against the bright sun, the kingly figure shrivelled to a burnt tree stump.

Rebecca waited for him to turn around. She knew he suffered from depression, and she wondered if he was having a difficult day. Maybe he'd forgotten to take his meds. She scanned the room, looking for pill bottles. Seeing none, she forged on. She was determined to get what she had come here for.

She came right out with it. "Let me have the McBride case, sir. I won't let you down." She knew she had no right to sneak in like this, asking for a favour - especially this one. It put them both at risk of censure, but she was counting on his devotion to her. Their relationship had broken up four years ago, ended by her. He still wanted to give things another try, had promised he would do anything for her. Now she was putting him to the test.

She knew she was being unfair, and she felt guilty. What kind of person was she turning into? Until today she had never imposed on anyone's goodwill in this way, and she was horrified at herself. But she had to have the McBride case, so similar to her mother's tragic murder sixteen years ago. Cartwright should know this. She'd told him about her mission in life, her vow to someday catch the perp. But she also feared that he might demand a price she wasn't willing to pay.

The blackened tree stump came to life, and Cartwright turned and strode across the room, his deep-set eyes boring into hers. Since his promotion to head up central region, his manner with subordinates had become standoffish, almost pompous. Was he going to start treating her like that?

He addressed her formally. "I did a thorough job on McBride, Constable Bradley. Top-notch work. I didn't solve the case, but I will."

Rebecca felt uneasy, aware she was on shaky ground. But then he shouldn't have said he would do anything for her. If he refused to give her the McBride case, he'd have to stop making that offer. She remained mute.

Cartwright snorted. "An infuriating investigation. Every line of inquiry was a dead end. I've never had a case so baffling. But I *will* solve it." His hands balled into fists, and he lapsed into a moody silence.

Rebecca wondered what was going on inside him. What really lay behind his angry words? This wasn't the first time she'd seen his disquiet over the case flare up. But today he seemed disoriented, almost unstable.

Waiting anxiously, Rebecca gazed at the impressive row of hardware pinned to his chest. His Medal for Police Bravery shone out in pride of place. Bestowed on him after he was wounded in a shootout, it gave him bragging rights, which he exercised too often. She raised her eyes to the pink scar that sliced across his left cheekbone, from a bullet that might have killed him. The upward angle of the scar puzzled her. Had the shot come from below? He bragged, but he was sensitive about the details.

Her thoughts shifted to Abigail McBride from Conroy, a small town about half an hour's drive west of Orillia. Abigail was a thirty-two-year-old housewife who had disappeared without a trace thirteen months ago, while out on her usual walk. Sixteen days later she was found returned to her home, strangled and propped upright on a kitchen chair, with no fingerprints or other evidence of who did it found after a thorough search of the house. At the time, Cartwright was leading the Criminal Investigation Branch. He'd failed to solve the murder and now, after a year, it was deemed a cold case.

He cleared his throat. "Why not ask Detective Inspector Sykes? He heads the CIB." Rebecca gaped in disbelief. Cartwright knew why.

He turned his head up to stare at the ceiling. "I suppose the case *could* use another look. Enough time may have passed to warrant it." His eyes angled down at her, his voice turning hard. "But that's a task for seasoned detectives. You're not ready, Constable Bradley. You need more training, more experience. You're too young."

Rebecca's back stiffened. He'd never spoken to her like this before. Moreover, *he* had joined the CIB at twenty-six, just two years older than she was now. He'd been the youngest homicide detective on the force. Five years later, at the age of thirty-one, he was heading up the branch. He clearly didn't want anyone to better his precious record, especially a woman. Namely, her. His chauvinism was another strike against him, enough to once and for all rule him out of her private life.

"It's a cold case, sir." Her voice was steely. "More than a year has passed. I've taken all the core detective courses and several more besides, and I stood first in most of them. I've assisted on four homicide investigations, all of them while *you* headed the CIB. I am ready. But not alone, I agree. You could guide me, be my mentor. DI

Sykes didn't touch the case while you were on senior management training. Let me have it. Anyway, you're still the lead investigator. You told me you held onto it, although I don't know why. Surely you don't have time to work on it now?"

Cartwright's jaw muscles bunched. "I kept the case, Constable Bradley, because Sykes talked me into it. Said it would erase the blot on my career. And I will solve it. You know my record."

Rebecca bit her lip. Despite his words, Abigail McBride stuck out like a flagpole on a sinking ship. Various top detectives had claimed DI Sykes could have solved the case in days, and Cartwright had heard these whispers. Rebecca wondered why Sykes hadn't taken over the case when Cartwright was promoted. He might have solved it, with the bonus of humiliating his former boss. Everyone on the force knew that no love was lost between them.

Cartwright made a show of buffing his bravery medal. "In any goddamn event, forget the stupid case. There's no need for *me* to erase anything. The investigation is under control. So the trail went cold? It happens, even to bloody Sykes."

Rebecca repressed a sigh and said nothing. When he railed on about Sykes, it was best to let him vent.

His face twisted into a scowl. "What I don't understand is why he was promoted to head up the CIB. On the very day I left. No consultation with me. Should've been my call." His scar flushed scarlet. "I could dump McBride on the bastard now, though. Why not? I've got more important things to work on. Let *him* lead the follow-up. See if *he* can do any better." His smile said he was already envisioning Sykes's failure.

Rebecca's knees went weak and impulsively she seized Cartwright's hands. "Please don't let Sykes have the case. You know how important it is to me. I will ask you just one more time. If you refuse, I won't mention it again. But think carefully, Jonathan. Remember what you told me." She looked into his eyes. "Give me McBride. Don't let Sykes solve it and get the credit. We can do it, you and me. Then we'll shove it in his smug face."

Cartwright was silent for a minute. Then he emitted a leaden sigh. "All right, Rebecca. I keep my promises. The McBride case is yours. Commissioner Hardy will kick my ass, and Sykes will be furious. But to hell with them."

Then his jaw softened, and his eyes beseeched her. "Please don't give up on us."

Suddenly Rebecca felt awful. He truly did love her. And now he'd made good on his do-anything offer. She moved closer to him and caressed his cheek.

"Thank you, Jonathan. This means everything to me." She took in a shallow breath. "When can I start?"

The question seemed to catch him by surprise, and he stuttered. "I'll . . . I'll let you know tomorrow, Constable Bradley. Officially, homicides are a CIB matter. DI Sykes still has to approve it. But don't worry. I'm sure he'll agree."

Rebecca's chest constricted. He had to fix the start date now. If he asked Sykes for permission, she was lost. Sykes didn't like her, and he avoided her whenever he could. He probably knew about her affair with Cartwright. Most likely the entire force did.

"You don't owe anything to Sykes, Jonathan. McBride is *your* case. It's your decision who works on it." She watched as his pupils darted around the room. There was fear in them. Sykes exerted some kind of perverse influence over him that she didn't understand. She had to do something dramatic to swing the situation back in her favour.

"You know Sykes set you up last year?" She moved even closer to him and peered up into his face. "Well, don't you?"

That worked. His scar blazed crimson. He slammed a fist into his palm.

"Damn right it's my decision. I head up the entire region, including the CIB. To hell with protocol. From this very moment, you're on the case. You have one week to solve it. Send me updates, and call when you need help. I'll guide you through it." He cleared his throat and added, "One more thing. I want you to assess the Conroy office, and the local constable, Jack O'Reilly. Advise me if I should close it, and fire him."

She agreed, without thinking twice about his addition, and then she almost hugged Cartwright, but quickly changed her mind. Instead, she backed off and thrust out her hand. Time to seal the deal and get out of there.

"Thank you, sir. I'll come in tomorrow and clean up loose ends. First thing Tuesday, I'll be in Conroy."

He folded his large hand around hers for a moment, then he let it drop. He crossed the room to gaze out of the window again.

Silence returned to the office.

Then Rebecca heard him mutter, "Watch out for O'Reilly."

Chapter 2

I loved Mom so much. She was, and still is, everything to me. Dad won't answer my questions about her. He doesn't understand. I need to know why she was killed, and who did it. He knows something that he won't tell me, I'm sure of it.
— The diary of Rebecca Sarah Bradley (1995)

Rebecca raced north on the Trans-Canada Highway in her sporty red Mercedes-Benz convertible, another lavish present from her father. It had arrived at her door a month after her twenty-fourth birthday. He probably felt guilty at forgetting the date, yet again. Her colleagues ribbed her about it in Orillia but she didn't care, she loved her Merc. Anyway, she couldn't ask for an unmarked car. DI Sykes would have to approve it, and she didn't want him to know about her assignment, not yet. Cartwright was to tell him this morning, when it would be too late to stop her.

She pressed on the accelerator and kept a sharp eye out for speed traps. The warm summer breeze buffeted her face and loose hair whipped about her head. She was free. It felt exhilarating.

Her SIG Sauer P229 rested snug in her hip holster. Since she was alone on the investigation, it was best not to take chances. Laying on the passenger seat, a black leather briefcase contained spare ammo and a thick file of notes on Abigail McBride, compiled last year by DI Cartwright during his month of fruitless investigation. No solid clues were found, in spite of diligent work by a world class forensics team and some of the finest detectives in the country. Abigail's death remained an enigma. But today she, Rebecca Bradley, was leading the case. She would put the murderer behind bars. Then she would get the CIB job she coveted, despite Sykes's opposition. And she might even learn something that would help her catch her mother's murderer.

Mind turning over the investigation, she nearly missed the sign to Conroy. Its weathered letters were hidden by a patch of scraggly bush, as though the town sought to remain anonymous after its spell of notoriety. Rebecca realized just in time and swerved onto the exit lane. The asphalt road leading her to the town centre was full of potholes. Conroy was a neglected town with a population of less than four hundred. It was isolated, far from the main tourist destinations of Georgian Bay to the west, Lake Simcoe to the east, and the sparkling lakes of the Canadian Shield that ran for hundreds of miles to the north. If the McBride homicide hadn't occurred, no one would know of its existence.

One by one, houses began to appear. She drove past lonely, sick-looking bungalows with paint peeling from weathered clapboard siding. Most had cheap lawn ornaments scattered out front, rusty cars dumped next to decrepit garages. The houses reminded Rebecca of her childhood in Prospect, a northern Ontario goldmining town that had more than its share of poor families. But Rebecca had always felt awkward around them. She had never needed to worry about money. Hers was by far the wealthiest family in Prospect and, after her mother was gone, the loneliest.

She slowed her car and cruised to a halt at the side of the road. Her watch showed 7:40 a.m., twenty minutes early for her meeting with Constable O'Reilly. Good. It gave her time to prepare herself. Straight ahead, the morning sun had crested a stand of white pine.

Her first lead on a homicide investigation. She quivered with anticipation. Much better than trailing behind senior constables, writing interview notes and fetching cups of coffee. *Will that be double cream and sugar, sir? Right away, sir. Two doughnuts? Of course, sir.* Tonight she would open a new diary.

She settled into the soft leather seat of her car and filled her lungs with clean country air, breathing in the aroma of freshly cut hay. Her thoughts turned to Jack O'Reilly, the last single-outpost constable in OPP Central Region. A sheriff in a cowboy town. But his private domain was about to be eliminated. Yesterday evening she had called Cartwright and reminded him to inform Sykes about her assignment. Cartwright was in a foul mood and ranted on about his mountain of problems. He told her he planned to concentrate central region staff in fewer centres, to save money or so he said. That didn't fool her. What he really wanted was to get rid of O'Reilly. He obviously detested the man, but wouldn't say why. Maybe he just needed someone to blame for his own failure on the investigation.

Rebecca closed her eyes and listened to the birds chirping. Doubt began to creep into her mind. Why did she think she could do better than the CIB detectives with all their experience? She'd done well on her detective courses, but she was still an amateur compared to them. She shook her head and told herself to stop. She would show everyone what she could do, now that she had the chance. Then she smiled to herself. She had already dug up one new piece of information that Cartwright seemed to have missed — that Abigail McBride was born to a wealthy family in the Netherlands, as Marijke van Rijn. At least, his case notes hadn't recorded it, and just maybe this detail could lead to a clue about her murderer. If so, it was an awful oversight by him, Rebecca thought, and an opportunity for her to prove her worth.

It was getting hot, and sweat had beaded on her forehead. She checked her watch — 7:55 a.m. Time to go. The GPS indicated one minute to O'Reilly's office. She wiped her face and pulled out, just as an old Buick blazed past from behind, almost sideswiping her Mercedes. She wrenched the steering wheel round and slewed into a shallow ditch. Shaken, she watched the Buick race towards Conroy, too fast for her to catch the licence number.

She slumped into her seat, breathing hard. It took her a few minutes to compose herself, and then she gunned the car, spraying mud. Now she'd be late for her meeting.

O'Reilly's office was in a red brick building with a corrugated metal roof, at the south end of town. Rebecca wheeled into the gravel parking lot and came to a halt in the shade of a giant sugar maple. She studied her face in the mirror, frowning at the sprinkle of freckles that made her look younger than her age. At least her sage-green skirt, matching blazer and white cotton blouse suited her detective role. Her new Cole Haan pumps were tight on her feet, but they looked the part.

Struggling to contain her excitement, she went up two steps to a door marked *Ontario Provincial Police*. She knocked, and then knocked again. She peered through a dusty side window. There was no movement inside. She twisted the latch and pulled but nothing happened. She recalled her lengthy wait for Cartwright two days ago and hammered on the door.

"Damn!" It dawned on her that the only car in the parking lot was her Mercedes.

"Okay, Rebecca, he'll be here soon enough," she reassured herself, and meandered about the lot. She soon tired of that. She brushed twigs and dirt off the chipped concrete steps, and sat on her handkerchief. She drummed her nails on her cheekbones and watched a crow flap past, harassed by a host of sparrows. Maybe O'Reilly had been delayed on urgent police business. Still, he could have called.

The sun climbed higher in the sky. She sweated in her blazer, but was determined to leave it on until O'Reilly arrived. She wiped her face. So much for looking nice.

She checked her watch again — 8:25 a.m. Where the hell was O'Reilly? She yanked out her cell phone and punched in his office number. She heard it ring in the room behind her. An answering machine clicked on and a pleasant female voice lilted, "Ontario Provincial Police, Conroy office. Please leave a message after the beep. For emergencies call 911."

"Crap." She cut the call. Surely O'Reilly had a cell phone? Why hadn't she checked that number before she left Orillia? If he didn't arrive soon, she'd call the office and get it from the admin staff, although she really didn't want them to know that O'Reilly had stood her up.

She got to her feet and strode to Main Street. Not a soul in sight. It was just like the movie, *The Day the Earth Stood Still*. She returned to the office, sat on the step and patted her neck. The tissues were wet through instantly with sweat. She could sure use a glass of cold water right now. And where in God's name was O'Reilly?

At 8:40 a.m., just as she was stabbing at her cell phone to call Orillia, an aging Chevy Impala with mud-covered OPP markings careened off Main and charged into the lot. It skidded to a stop in front of her, blowing dust into her face. A car door opened and closed. A mid-fifties man in a tight-fitting uniform emerged through the swirling cloud. He swaggered over and peered down at her, smirking, his feet planted like goal posts. "Let me guess." He raised a finger to his cheek. "The rookie detective from Orillia. Here to solve the McBride case."

12

She coughed out a lungful of dust, struggled to her feet and thrust out her hand. "Constable Jack O'Reilly, I presume."

He snorted. "Sure as hell ain't Livingstone." He seized the hand and gripped it tightly. "Just so you know up front, people in this town call me 'chief.' You can call me Senior Constable O'Reilly." He grinned.

Rebecca shot him a frosty look. She was good at those. "Detective Constable Bradley." She extracted her hand and felt her face flush. "You're late. Not got a cell phone?"

His reply was gruff. "Important matters. Anyway, nothing in Conroy happens on time. You'll get used to it. And, yes, I do have a cell phone. They call them mobiles in England, did you know that? It's with Sally, my assistant. She knows where to find me." He edged closer.

Rebecca held her ground. There were plenty of alpha male types in Orillia, but O'Reilly was overdoing it. "Maybe in future we can meet on time, if that's not asking too much." She matched his combative gaze with a hard stare.

"All business, eh? *Officially*, work here begins at nine." He made a show of studying his watch. "Half an hour to kill. First thing I do is Duffy's. Coffee and doughnuts, like all self-respecting police officers. Care to join me?"

She sighed. "I wouldn't want to disrupt your daily routine. I take it Duffy's is the hot spot for local gossip." There was no point in trying to hide her sarcasm. O'Reilly was an irritating son of a bitch, and he knew it. Things were going to be lively between them.

He didn't disappoint. His watery blue eyes opened wide. "Amazing. Detective skills are rare in these parts. You'll have the case licked by noon. I'm just a small-town cop. I didn't go to no fancy police college." He pushed his double chin out.

Rebecca held her tongue with difficulty. She wasn't impressed with O'Reilly's lack of professionalism so far.

Maybe Cartwright had a point after all. O'Reilly cast her an amused look and strutted towards his Chevy. "Hop in. Ride's on me. Don't say thanks. It's just one of the many services I provide."

Rebecca counted to three and followed him to the car. She tugged on the passenger door handle. Nothing happened. She sucked in a breath and pulled harder. A slight movement. Through the dusty window, she saw O'Reilly jiggle his hand. She got it — shake the handle and jerk on it at the same time. The door screeched horribly and opened just enough for her to slide in. In a puff of dust she sat down and began slapping grime off her skirt.

O'Reilly cleared his throat and eyeballed her Mercedes. "My Rolls is at the garage. Although your little number looks like it could use a good wash." He laughed heartily and gunned the Chevy. The car lurched forward, and Rebecca's head thumped back against the seat. She scrabbled to fasten her seat belt.

They motored sixty yards along Main and swerved into an uneven tarmac lot. Rebecca seized the door handle and hung on as the Chevy suddenly braked, catapulting her into the safety belt. She fired an incredulous look at O'Reilly. "You drove half a block just to get here?"

He placed a chubby hand over his heart. "Can't get your new shoes dirty now, can we?"

Chapter 3

Thaddeus Hounsley, known to folks in Conroy as 'Hound' for his hobby of tracking wild animals, lowered his gargantuan frame into a chipped plastic chair. He tossed a comic book onto the table and waved at Daisy, who reached for an ice cream scoop to make his usual chocolate milkshake.

Duffy's was filling up. Across the aisle, Shorty Davis and Lukas Walker, Hound's friends and former schoolmates, were engaged in a verbal sparring match, their heads almost colliding over the table. Four years after graduation they still behaved like schoolboys.

Shorty leaned back in his chair and glanced sideways at Hound. "Hound," he whispered, "When are we going fishing again? I need to get away from this town and the jerks that live here — one of them anyway." He nodded at Lukas.

Hound blinked rapidly and swivelled to face Shorty. His chair cracked like a rifle shot, briefly quelling all conversation in the room. "We can go tomorrow morning, Shorty. Meet you out front of Herman's. Six sharp."

Shorty turned to Lukas and raised a stubby middle finger.

The chatter bubbled up again. All the local wags and gossips were there, most of them retired or middle-aged and exhausted from scratching out a living in a dying town. The last decent jobs had disappeared twenty-five years ago when Conroy's sawmill had closed. Young people fled town as soon as they could break free of their weary families. Hound felt sorry for the survivors – if they could be called that.

Daisy brought Hound's milkshake to him and cast a rueful look at his busted chair. He hung his head, until the squealing of tires made him look up.

O'Reilly's Chevy slid to a stop. The chief flung open his door and wriggled free. He stretched out his arms and turned his face to the sun, a beatific smile on his ruddy face. Nothing unusual about that, but the smartly dressed young woman he was with was a revelation. She squeezed through the half-open passenger door, then reached into the car and dragged out a shiny leather briefcase. She slammed the door shut, glared across the hood at O'Reilly, and smoothed her skirt and jacket with her free hand.

"Morning, Daisy." O'Reilly strutted into the shop, nodding and smiling at the patrons as though he'd won an Olympic medal. "Got a special visitor, all the way from Orillia — DC Rebecca Bradley. We've come to take a look at Conroy's finest dining establishment."

Every face in the room turned towards Rebecca. Hound thought she seemed uneasy, angry even. Whatever, she was a total stunner. She was a couple of inches over medium height, with shoulder-length auburn hair, slender and athletic-looking. He rolled her name around in his head. Rebecca. He'd never met anyone with that name before. He liked it.

"What'll it be, chief?" Daisy winked at Rebecca.

O'Reilly continued to survey the room. "A large coffee — you know how I take it. And one of your famous jelly doughnuts." He turned to the woman. "How 'bout you, Officer Bradley? It's on me."

Rebecca fired him a glacial look. "Thanks." She didn't sound grateful. "I'll have a coffee, black. And a glass of water, please." She made for the nearest table.

O'Reilly harrumphed.

Rebecca stopped and turned, one eyebrow raised.

He pointed to a corner booth. "That one will do nicely."

She ignored him and continued to her table, while a buzz of voices broke out around her.

Hound's eyes widened. Spunky. Challenging O'Reilly? Hound liked that. Fascinated, he watched her open the briefcase and extract a folder. Instead of reading it, she fanned her face nonchalantly.

O'Reilly narrowed his eyes. "Have it your way." He straightened his shirt and marched like a parade soldier to her table, shoulders squared. Daisy fell in behind, mimicking him, loaded tray balanced on one hand.

O'Reilly settled into the chair opposite Rebecca and held out a hand for his doughnut. Daisy placed it on his upturned palm, and set two coffee mugs and a glass of water on the table. With a friendly nod at Rebecca, followed by a quick roll of her eyes at O'Reilly's imperious behaviour, she retreated to the front counter.

Hound inched lower in his chair and dragged his milkshake towards him, studying Rebecca's distorted figure through the half-empty glass.

"Great weather for this time of year, but hot as Hades, eh?" O'Reilly bit into his doughnut, oblivious to the blob of red jelly that plopped onto his shirt. Rebecca seemed to focus on a wisp of steam that curled up from her coffee mug.

Hound listened attentively, eager to hear her voice again.

"You'll want to interview the townsfolk, right? Well, some key people are here now. Like Daisy Plum. She knows just about everything that goes on in this town. And the guy sitting alone over there is Herman Vogel. He saw Abigail McBride pass by his gas station on the day she went missing. Then there's Charlie Taylor, the mayor, at the packed table along the far wall. Great friend of mine. Lots more people I could name. You could say I know everyone in this town."

Hound watched Rebecca flip open her folder and scribble something down. She had delicate hands and wore an elegant watch on her slender wrist. He wondered why she was here. The last time a detective came to Conroy was after Abigail's murder. He swallowed hard, the memory of his former best friend always made him sad.

"When we're finished," O'Reilly was saying, "I'll take you to my office. Show you how real detective work's done." He finally spied the blob of jelly and dabbed at it, leaving a purple smear.

The coffee shop patrons continued their low-pitched chatter, sneaking glances at Rebecca from time to time. She sipped her coffee while O'Reilly demolished the rest of his doughnut. That done, he wiped his hand across his mouth and peered into her mug. "Ready to go?" He looked happy again, pleased with himself. Hound knew what he was like — his mood changed from moment to moment.

Rebecca snapped her briefcase shut and got to her feet.

Hound jerked upright in his seat. She was looking directly at him. His thick legs smashed into the table and he toppled back, shattering the weakened plastic chair. One flailing arm knocked over his milkshake as he crashed to the floor, the frothy liquid running over the table edge and pouring over him.

The rest of the locals burst out laughing, pointing and mimicking Hound's fall. Tears streamed down Shorty's cheeks. Only Lukas sat calmly, watching Hound, the faintest hint of a smile lifting one corner of his mouth.

Daisy rushed forward, waving a dishtowel.

Hound's shoes slipped on the greasy floor as he scrambled to his feet. Blushing furiously, he took Daisy's towel and wiped his neck, but his eyes never left Rebecca as she left the shop. The Chevy rumbled to life. She peered through the car window at him, and a soft smile touched her face.

Mortified, Hound wrenched his head away. All his life, people had laughed at him. He'd just discovered that sympathy was even worse.

* * *

"Who was that?" asked Rebecca.

"The big guy's called Hound," said O'Reilly, still guffawing. "Like the dog. Helps me out when I ask. Routine patrols, petty crimes. Useful lad. Did some training to become an auxiliary officer. An unusual character, even for this cockeyed town. Not someone to tangle with when he's riled, though. No siree, Bob."

Chapter 4

I had a massive fight with Dad today. He wants me to go to uni and get a business degree, then come back and help him run his stupid gold mines. But I've got other ideas. I told him I'd be applying for a job as a police cadet. Then I'll train at the college in Aylmer to become a constable, and then a detective. He wouldn't listen to me, he just stormed out of the room.

— The diary of Rebecca Sarah Bradley (2000)

O'Reilly zipped his Chevy into the OPP lot and stomped on the brakes. Rebecca pitched into her seat belt again. She cursed silently, trying to ignore his grin of triumph. She knew she shouldn't let O'Reilly's childish stunts bother her. They did, though, didn't they? He knew exactly which levers to pull. She recalled Cartwright's parting shot. *"Watch out for O'Reilly."* He couldn't have treated Cartwright this way, surely?

O'Reilly went to the station door, unlocked it, and bowed low. Rebecca brushed past and found herself in a clean and orderly room.

"My assistant, Sally Partridge, does the filing, in case you're wondering why everything's so spiffy. Sweeps up doughnut crumbs and gets rid of coffee cups. Wouldn't want you to get the impression it's me. But the good ol' days are about to end, thanks to the new superintendent. First thing he did was cut my budget. Sally's job's kaput, officially, but I'll keep her on part-time anyway. Go over budget and see what the bastard says."

"I see you've heard about DI Cartwright's promotion," Rebecca said casually.

"Huh?"

"Last month. He's now the central region superintendent."

"Sonofabitch. Just skimmed the circular. Didn't pay attention to the name." O'Reilly wasn't smiling now.

"He went for a year of senior management training, right after he led the McBride investigation. The youngest superintendent on the force. A good friend of mine too." Oh, why had she said that?

O'Reilly hoisted a shaggy brow. "Friends in high places. How nice for you." He raised his nose in the air. "A stuffed shirt, that's what he is. Did a lousy job on the McBride investigation. Marched about like he owned the town. Should've stayed in Orillia." He headed for his private office.

Rebecca couldn't let him get away with this. "What did you expect him to do? One month and not a shred of worthwhile evidence found. Was that his fault?" She stood at the door and glowered at him. "Well, was it?"

He flopped down onto a worn leather chair. "Who are you, anyhow?" He leaned forward and shoved his face at her. "How can you afford those expensive clothes and a fancy car on your pathetic salary? Why do you even do this work, Constable Bradley?"

Through clenched teeth, she said, "Take it easy, Senior Constable O'Reilly. Your job is to help me on this case. What I wear and what I drive is none of your business. As you already know, I've been appointed Detective Constable for this assignment. Temporary, but official. It's 'DC' Bradley to you. Now show me anything Cartwright hasn't already provided. I'm sure you've seen his files."

He gave her a dull stare. So Cartwright hadn't shared anything with him. "Okay, *DC* Bradley." He pointed at a wooden chair opposite his desk. "Make yourself comfy. New shoes hurt if you stand in them too long."

She sat down. "Please, just show me."

"Sally pulled my files. Cartwright said he didn't want them, although he copied the interview notes I made. Probably burned them later." O'Reilly swept an arm towards a side table. "You're welcome to go through the whole lot. I'm sure you won't find much you haven't already seen."

Rebecca glanced at the files and gave him a weary look. "Tell me in your own words."

"Don't need to. Wrote my own summary, with a little help from Sally. You can read my other stuff too, if you want. Thoughts on the murder. Ideas Cartwright said he had no use for. Called me an amateur, but *his* investigation was a total bust." He rose to his feet and strutted out of the room.

Rebecca gazed at the imposing heap of files. More than she had anticipated. He'd antagonized Cartwright big time — a fatal mistake, especially now that Cartwright was the regional superintendent. She didn't feel comfortable assessing the office, as well as O'Reilly's competence, but Cartwright had insisted on it. Not that her opinion would hold any weight. She was too junior for that kind of task. He just wanted someone else to agree with him. Anyway, if assessing O'Reilly's performance was the price of getting the case, so be it. Cartwright obviously expected her to advise office closure and instant retirement for the chief. And based on O'Reilly's behaviour so far, Cartwright had a point. O'Reilly certainly hadn't endeared himself with his boorish antics, but she'd met people like him in Prospect.

He wasn't as tough as he pretended. She would give him a chance.

She kicked off her shoes, settled into O'Reilly's chair, and grabbed the top file. His case summary had been written formally, as if he'd expected Cartwright to use it as an official document. She suddenly felt sorry for the 'chief.' He really had tried to play a useful role in the investigation.

She read it slowly.

On the morning of 12 May, 2006, Abigail McBride went out on what appeared to be her daily stroll along Hagger's Creek in Conroy, Ontario. She left her house at 8:15 a.m., according to Agnes Jackson, an elderly neighbour across the street. She passed two townsfolk on her way to the creek, and two more when she crossed the south bridge to follow the east side path. She kept her head down and didn't acknowledge any of their greetings.

She should have reached the north bridge at about 8:28 a.m., but no one saw her there, and she wasn't seen again until she entered Robbie's Diner at approximately 8:45 a.m. Although she ordered a coffee and was seen by more townsfolk at the diner, she didn't speak to anyone, including Robbie Johnson, the proprietor. Mr. Johnson said she acted distant, but that wasn't unusual. She left Robbie's at 9:05 a.m. One minute later, she entered Parker's Grocery and shopped at a leisurely pace. She left the store at 9:16 a.m., according to staff. That was the last time anyone interviewed saw her alive.

At 6:00 p.m., her husband, Kingsley McBride, came home from work. She wasn't there, which surprised him, because she always had dinner ready. Mr. McBride became worried. He checked with the neighbours, and with her only close friends in town — Hound and Herman Vogel. All of them, except Mrs. Jackson, said they hadn't seen Abigail all day. He went to find Constable O'Reilly. They went through the town and found no evidence of Mrs. McBride's whereabouts. That evening, Constable O'Reilly filed a Missing Person Report. The following morning, local volunteers searched the town and nearby lands.

On 14 May, police from Orillia arrived and interviewed the townsfolk. They scoured the surrounding area, using canine support, but found no trace of Mrs. McBride. CIB detectives, led by DI Cartwright, came to Conroy on 15 May. They searched for several days and came up with nothing. On 28 May, sixteen days after Mrs. McBride went missing, Mr. McBride came home from work and found his wife's body propped upright on a kitchen chair. The autopsy said she'd been dead for two days. Rope burns and soft tissue injury to her neck were evident. Death was by asphyxiation, but there were no signs of a struggle. The coroner's report said it was a homicide. The investigation lasted one month, then was put on hold due to lack of evidence and the need to deal with other cases.

Rebecca closed the file and leaned back in O'Reilly's chair. The case had stumped Cartwright, who had told her he'd found no motive for Abigail's murder. Her husband, Kingsley, was the first suspect, but Cartwright said he seemed shaken by her death. He had no criminal record, not even a speeding ticket. And he was at his office in Conroy the day that Abigail was returned to their house, according to his private secretary. A search of his house by Constable O'Reilly soon after Abigail's disappearance, and another, more thorough, forensics search after Cartwright and his detectives arrived, turned up nothing to suggest Kingsley had been involved with the homicide. Moreover, there was no life insurance coverage on Abigail, and no known disputes within the marriage, so Cartwright had ruled Kingsley out as the prime suspect.

As far as anyone knew, there had been no strangers in Conroy on the day Abigail disappeared, leaving the investigation with no discernible motive for the murder, and no clear suspects. Rebecca returned to the mysterious question at the heart of the case: how had Abigail been strangled without showing any evidence of resistance?

Cartwright had been sent away on senior management training soon after the initial investigation, so he didn't have a lot of time to devote to the murder. He evidently had no good ideas on what to do next, but he had still kept the lead on the case, with DI Sykes's encouragement.

A year had passed and no progress was made.

Now *she* was here and she was determined to solve this case. That would force Sykes into giving her a job in the CIB. Once there, she would track down her mother's killer. There was also a chance that the McBride investigation might help her achieve her life's mission sooner: there were disquieting parallels between the murders. Her mother and Abigail were both thirty-two years old when they disappeared, and they were both found later in their kitchens, strangled. It was conceivable, although a long shot, that the same killer was involved. If so, Rebecca had to know. Her main goal had always been to catch her mother's murderer and bring him to justice, and solving Abigail's case would boost her confidence. Joining the CIB was only a step along the way.

Rebecca returned her thoughts to the task at hand. She found it hard to believe that nobody in Conroy had seen Abigail after she left Parker's Grocery. Where could she have gone? Was she kidnapped? If so, why wasn't there a ransom note? Why was she murdered? Why would someone keep her alive for two weeks, then kill her and cart her body to her own house during the day, when someone might see it? Why not bury her in the woods, where she might never be discovered?

She sighed and focused again on O'Reilly's files. The investigation had been thorough. Dozens of townsfolk had been interviewed, to no avail. The town and surrounding area had been searched thoroughly, and nothing was found. Kingsley McBride had been questioned several times, and his story never varied. The neighbours had been asked about their relationship, but there was no domestic strife that anyone knew about — or would admit to. Everyone in Conroy had claimed that the McBrides got along well.

DI Cartwright had conducted a conventional investigation. But Rebecca planned to take a different approach, one that would mesh with her assignment to assess the Conroy office. She would get to know the townsfolk. Having grown up in northern Ontario, she knew how small towns worked — at least, she thought she did. Cartwright was a big city boy, Toronto born and raised. He had never hung out with small-town locals, and never would. He wouldn't fit in. But she could. Small towns were much the same everywhere. It wasn't easy to break into the social circles of any town, and Conroy had a particularly close feel to it. But if she got to know the people here, she was convinced she would turn up evidence that had been missed last year.

Chapter 5

Hound lumbered out of Duffy's, his eyes fixed on the ground in front of him.

The incident brought back memories of his unhappy childhood, how it felt to be taunted by his schoolfellows and shunned by his cold family. He told himself it was all behind him now. He'd found a quiet haven in Canada, far from the devils that had plagued his youth. But he couldn't help remembering that incident at Baysford Academy back in London, when he was ten years old . . .

"Get lost, fat boy, you'll never be on my team," Albert Thatcher shrieked. His hulking protector, Harley Bronson, hovered next to him, flexing his muscles.

A horde of schoolboys gathered round, gabbling to each other in excitement.

Hound swallowed, his eyes watering. He stared about the yard, seeking help, but no teachers were in sight. He didn't belong at Baysford. He would never fit in. Life wasn't fair. No one cared what happened to him. His rage began to build and his meaty hands curled into fists.

The world sped up and Albert's snotty face came into focus. He was finished with being taunted and pushed around. Today, he would not retreat.

Hound drew himself to his full height and glowered down into Harley Bronson's small, mean eyes. A hush descended on the schoolyard.

Harley's snarl melted and his stance faltered. His feet braced as though preparing to run. He lowered his gaze . . .

* * *

Hound headed for home, just outside the town. Shorty trailed after him. "Boy oh boy, did you ever treat this town to a show."

Hound picked up the pace. Wisecracks were the last thing he wanted to hear right now.

Shorty hustled to keep up. "Slow down, I'm getting tired. Hey, I'll bet that doll with O'Reilly thinks you're a class act."

Hound stopped abruptly, causing Shorty to run up against him and lose his balance. "What the—?"

"Forget the fishing." Hound stalked off.

He crunched up the gravel driveway to his front door. Inside, he descended the creaky wooden steps to his library, where he slumped into his massive leather armchair. He settled back and stared at the ceiling.

He thought about his meaningless life. Twenty-two years old and, until today, all he'd wanted was to forget the past. He still mourned Abigail. In the year since her death, he'd felt lost and unloved, just as he had in England. Abigail had been his rock. Now he was floating, without an anchor. Seeing Rebecca had made him want to move on again. He wondered briefly what it would be like to be with someone like her. But she would never pay any attention to him. He was a loser, going nowhere. What did he have to offer her, or anyone else for that matter?

He sat on for a while, until he grew tired of wallowing in self-pity. What he needed was to bring some purpose to his life.

Chapter 6

Amazing news today!! I've been accepted for training at the police college, makes those months in Toronto as a cadet totally worth it. I'll be a constable, and then a homicide detective. And after that, I'll catch Mom's murderer. Dad almost disowned me when I told him, but I know he won't do that. I'm his only child, after all.
— The diary of Rebecca Sarah Bradley (2002)

It took Rebecca until the early afternoon to read through O'Reilly's stack of files. She went to the outer office and sat at Sally Partridge's cheap metal desk. O'Reilly offered to take her on Abigail's route the day she disappeared, but Rebecca wanted to take her first look alone.

"If you don't mind, Constable O'Reilly, I would rather do it by myself. Perhaps we can go over it tomorrow in more detail."

His back stiffened. He retreated to his office and closed the door, very gently. Rebecca cursed under her breath. She should have been more diplomatic. He probably thought she was just like Cartwright. Well, maybe she was. She gathered up her papers and left the station.

The McBride house was two blocks away, in the direction of Hagger's Creek. Rebecca planned to interview Kingsley McBride today. According to the chief, Kingsley was the only chartered accountant in Conroy and handled the financial affairs of all the prominent townsfolk, including the mayor.

When she went to Kingsley's office, his secretary told her that he'd left town and she didn't know when he would be back. Rebecca was certain she'd lied, but anyhow, she wasn't overly concerned about Kingsley. DI Cartwright had checked him out thoroughly last year and he came up clean. She couldn't waste time retracing Cartwright's steps.

She headed alongside Hagger's Creek, as Abigail had done last May. Abigail seemed to have been following her daily routine — a pleasant walk, visits to Robbie's Diner and Parker's Grocery, then back home. Her neighbour, Mrs. Jackson, had seen her setting out, but the old lady's eyesight was poor. Rebecca went over to sit on a vacant bench to think. If Abigail had been on her usual morning excursion, why did she ignore the people who had greeted her along the way? People that she would normally have acknowledged, even if she didn't socialize with them. Her behaviour suggested to Rebecca that she was distressed, but what about?

Last year, in Orillia, the McBride case had been a topic of intense debate. What was the motive? Love, hate, jealousy, revenge, money? None of these seemed to apply. What interested Rebecca most of all was that Abigail's body had been found propped carefully upright, rather than slumped forward or sideways. Why had she been put on a chair at all? Why was she positioned so carefully? There had to be an explanation.

Rebecca believed that the key to solving the murder was to be found in Conroy. Someone there knew what had happened, and why. Sitting Abigail on a chair wasn't something a stranger would do. Cartwright called it sick, but it struck Rebecca as intimate, suggesting that someone who knew her had brought Abigail home.

Rebecca fanned her face and continued along the creek. Sweat trickled down her neck and soaked her blouse. And now the deer flies swarmed out. She flailed her hands about, swatting at the winged monsters attacking her arms and legs. Added to that, a painful blister was forming on her heel.

She wondered about the possibility that the same person had killed both Abigail and her mother. It was remote, but at least it was something she could cling to. As a cop, she wanted justice for Abigail's death. But for her mother she wanted something else — vengeance. She wanted to look the killer in the eye and let him know that Sarah Bradley's daughter had put him behind bars. And if she was forced to shoot the bastard in the process, so much the better. Ever since she found her mother's body lying on the kitchen floor, Rebecca had suffered from nightmares. By her early teens, she'd convinced herself that what she needed to get rid of that horrifying image was revenge against the killer. Until that mission was fulfilled, there would be no lasting relationships for her, no children, and no close friends. Nothing to distract her.

She got to her feet and continued on her scouting trip. Hagger's Creek tumbled and splashed over glistening stones. The footpath was well used, with tall grass crowding the edges. It ended at the north bridge, beneath majestic weeping willows. At the bridge, Rebecca heard a gentle rustling of leaves and she stopped short, sensing someone following her. She whirled around and scanned the path, but nothing caught her attention. She watched for a few more seconds, then dismissed the eerie sensation as an overactive imagination.

Tomorrow morning she would retrace Abigail's entire route with O'Reilly. They would begin at the same time as Abigail had done, and she would write notes along the way. O'Reilly's presence was essential. He'd boasted that he knew the entire town, and Rebecca needed to talk to anyone who might be implicated in Abigail's murder. She headed back into Conroy, passing two people. She lifted a hand to wave, but they rushed on. Getting to know the locals might be tougher than she had expected.

Two minutes later, she reached Main Street and headed south. She passed an ancient gas station with a rusty sign proclaiming Herman's Fuel Emporium. Herman's bland face stared at her through the spotless office window. She recognized him from Duffy's, recalling that O'Reilly had told her that Herman saw Abigail pass by his station on the day she disappeared.

Guessing he wouldn't respond, Rebecca didn't bother waving at him. Then she paused. She was certain that neither Cartwright's files nor O'Reilly's personal notes had mentioned Herman seeing Abigail that day. Why not? Had Cartwright known and forgotten to write it down? It was hard to believe. He was meticulous to a fault, and Herman was known to be one of Abigail's close friends – a sighting like that should have been recorded. Could O'Reilly have withheld information from him, as Cartwright suspected? Maybe the 'chief' had slipped up when he told her. An uneasy feeling grew in the pit of her stomach.

She made a mental note to query O'Reilly about the omission. She was beginning to understand why it was useful to look at cold cases again. People could only hide things for so long before they forgot what they had or hadn't said. She decided to interview Herman tomorrow, when O'Reilly was with her.

She arrived at Robbie's Diner one minute later. It took her three minutes to get there from Hagger's Creek. Eyewitnesses last year had placed Abigail in Robbie's after seventeen minutes. Tomorrow she would check how far Abigail could have travelled if she'd made a fourteen-minute detour. Her uneasy feeling intensified. Something was definitely wrong.

A man she assumed to be Robbie gave her a curt nod. She chose not to ask him any questions. She would interview him tomorrow when she returned with O'Reilly.

To her surprise, the diner was empty. Was everyone avoiding her? That would be awful. How could she carry out her plan? She sighed inwardly, ordered coffee, and settled into a corner booth. She tried to imagine herself in Abigail's shoes. Had she planned to leave town that day, or was she merely following her usual routine? According to O'Reilly's case summary, nobody at Robbie's had spoken to her, which wasn't atypical with a woman who generally kept herself to herself. But still, it was all very perplexing to Rebecca.

After nursing her coffee for twenty minutes, she put some coins on the table and slid out of the booth. Robbie didn't look up when she left, but the cold treatment no longer surprised her.

It took her one minute to walk to Parker's Grocery, the blister burning all the way.

She thought about O'Reilly. He did seem anxious to solve the murder, so why didn't he want her around? He should be pleased that someone was looking at the case with fresh eyes. Was he hiding something? She had better watch him closely.

The shoppers in Parker's Grocery glanced at her furtively. If she met anyone's gaze, they turned away. She began to panic. If she couldn't get to know the locals, her investigation would fail. Surely they must want this murder to be solved?

"Hello, miss. Can I help you?"

At last, a friendly voice. "Yes, please. I need disinfectant, gauze, and some bandages for my blister." She stepped back and pointed at the reddened skin on her heel.

"Yes, ma'am, right away." The clerk hurried off, returning moments later with the items. She caught him looking her up and down.

"You're not from around here, are you?"

"I'm from Orillia. DC Rebecca Bradley. With the OPP."

He blenched and stared at the floor. "Well, y'all have a nice day."

"You too." Rebecca left the store smiling.

She headed south along Main, past Duffy's Doughnuts. Townsfolk stared and a rusted Buick LeSabre slowed to a crawl beside her, the driver leering and gesturing from within. She realized it was the car that had almost hit her this morning on her way in. Rebecca bridled, and briefly pictured herself holding a flamethrower to Conway.

It took her two minutes at a casual pace to get to Abigail's house, where Kingsley still lived. By her reckoning, the total time needed for Abigail to walk the entire route and return home should have been forty-nine minutes. But Abigail had taken fourteen extra minutes to get from Hagger's Creek to Robbie's Diner, and no one had seen her return to her home.

So what happened to her? How could she have vanished in broad daylight without anyone in this close-knit town seeing anything? Those added minutes puzzled Rebecca. Did Abigail meet someone on the way to Robbie's, or go somewhere? But she had shown up later on at Parker's Grocery. The crucial question was what happened after she left the store. Rebecca could only conclude that Abigail was abducted, or had been picked up by someone, right after she left Parker's. But that was just what Cartwright had thought a year ago. She'd made no progress at all.

Then an image of the wild-eyed jerk in the Buick flashed into her mind, causing the hairs on the back of her neck to stand up. He wasn't just a jerk. There was something menacing, something threatening about him.

Chapter 7

Rebecca had been right about someone following her at Hagger's Creek. At Duffy's that morning, a woman had been watching her closely. She studied Rebecca's features, noting the slender build, high cheekbones and auburn hair. Then O'Reilly called her DC Rebecca Bradley, and she knew who this must be. Steven Bradley's granddaughter, or maybe a grandniece. Steven Bradley, the rotten crook who had ruined her life.

She had long dreamed about getting revenge for what Steven Bradley did to her and her family. Then someone murdered him, along with her dreams of retribution. The filthy con had peddled hundreds of worthless goldmining shares to the gullible folk of Conroy. His rough charm and handsome, deceitful face still haunted her.

When Rebecca left Duffy's, the woman trailed her to O'Reilly's office. She hid in a clump of bushes and waited until Rebecca emerged. She followed her to Kingsley McBride's house, and to the south bridge of Hagger's Creek. At the north bridge, Rebecca whirled round to look behind her, and the woman hid behind the long branches of a weeping willow. Then she trailed Rebecca again and saw her pause at Herman's Fuel Emporium before continuing south along Main to Robbie's Diner and on to Parker's Grocery.

The woman's pupils shrank to tiny black dots. *I know what you're up to.* O'Reilly had called her DC. That meant Detective Constable. She was here about Abigail. That was why she'd gone to Kingsley's house, and then returned to it. But he was in Toronto, at his mother's funeral. He would be away for days. Anyway, the bitch would get no satisfaction from Kingsley. He was far too clever for her, and too clever for Constable Jack O'Reilly and those stupid detectives who'd stumbled about Conroy last year. They didn't figure out what really happened to Abigail, and neither would DC Bradley. She wouldn't live long enough.

* * *

Kingsley McBride sat glumly in the Toronto funeral home, his right foot tapping to the rhythm of some half-remembered rock song. He was bored. When would this service end? He put a hand over his ear to muffle the droning of the funeral dirge. The priest noticed and glowered down at Kingsley while he continued to prattle on about his mother's virtues. As far as Kingsley was concerned, she had none. He had never been close to her, even when he was a child. A childhood in Conroy. Such a boring town. Kingsley was sorry he'd ever gone back there. He would have left his childhood home forever if there wasn't so much profit to be made. The abandoned gold mine north of Conroy, along with his linked subdivision scheme, would soon net him millions. Who could have guessed that old Steven Bradley had been right, although his timing was way off base. The mine had turned out to be viable after all, now that rapidly rising gold prices made it worth developing. The gold assays Kingsley had seen were promising and his new partner, George, Steven Bradley's son, had made a convincing case for reopening it. It would cost Kingsley a bundle, especially with the heavy front-end payments to George for his mining expertise.

Kingsley's thoughts returned to his mother. As a young woman she had run around with all the local men. She'd even made money at it from time to time, so Kingsley had been told. Then she got tired of the fast life and tried marriage. She couldn't be bothered with a child, and paid scant attention to Kingsley when he came along. She soon wearied of marriage too, and made life miserable for his father, who put up with her abuse for fifteen years before abandoning both of them. Walter was another pathetic parent Kingsley had no use for. The fool hadn't turned up for the funeral, so maybe he was dead. Kingsley didn't give a damn.

Two years before she met Walter, Kingsley's mother had borne an illegitimate child. She had never told Kingsley about his half-brother, but Tony Albertini was sitting next to him now. Kingsley admired Tony. He was a big shot in the Ontario crime scene, tough, dynamic, rich — and now a silent partner in his subdivision deal.

Kingsley had discovered him a year ago. He visited his mother's shabby flat in Toronto, in order to rummage through her belongings and cart away anything of value before she died. She had owned nothing worth keeping, except for a scribbled note stapled to a faded yellow certificate that stated where the baby had been placed.

Kingsley checked around and found out that Tony hadn't been adopted. He'd spent his childhood and early teens in various children's homes — when he wasn't in juvenile detention centres. At fifteen, he ran away for good. Kingsley eventually tracked him down in Hamilton, Ontario, where they met, and got along famously. Tony became the brother Kingsley had always wanted, and Tony had family for the first time in his life. He'd never been told who his mother was, and didn't care, until he met his half-brother. Although Kingsley professed not to know who Tony's father was, he had his suspicions. These he kept to himself. No point in sharing information that might be useful further down the line.

Kingsley's lifelong fascination with criminals meshed perfectly with Tony's. *The Godfather* was their favourite movie, and Kingsley often imagined himself as Don Michael Corleone.

* * *

When the funeral service finally ended, Tony got up to stretch his legs. Kingsley greeted the few mourners and suffered through several minutes of insincere condolences. Finally the last of them shuffled away.

Tony strutted over to him. "Well, Kingsley, you're free of her now. She didn't have many friends, did she?"

Kingsley snorted. "No close ones that I know of. Nobody from Conroy bothered to come. Maybe they didn't know about the funeral. I sure didn't tell anyone, except for my secretary and one very discreet friend." He glanced at the coffin and chuckled. "Anyway, good riddance. I'd better take one last look before I close the casket — the priest didn't seem pleased with me. At least all this gave us the chance to get together again, that's the only good part of the whole thing. And thanks for the great time last night."

Tony slapped him on the shoulder. "Don't mention it, bro. Guess I'll be going now. Try not to cry too much. And remember, there's a job waiting for you in Hamilton. I need a good accountant, and the sooner the better. Your future's bright with me. And I owe you for bringing me into your scheme. You wouldn't believe the profits we make in my kind of business, I'm always looking for places to invest the money, if you get what I mean. But know this, pal. Making dough's the easy part. It's cleaning it up that's hard work, and risky. That's where you come in." Tony strode away.

Kingsley looked around, and then made his way to the coffin. He stared down upon his mother. "Thanks for nothing, you penniless old hag." He reached out to close the lid, and saw something glitter. Her wedding ring. She had insisted that it be buried with her. Well, she wouldn't need it anymore. That stone might even be a diamond.

Kingsley glanced over his shoulder, the priest was nowhere in sight. He lifted her ring finger and intoned, "Farewell, dear Mother. Thank you for what I am about to receive." He wrenched it from her finger, tearing the skin, and slipped it into his jacket pocket. He placed her hands so that they covered the damaged joint. Then he closed the coffin lid, and, whistling a happy tune, left the building.

Chapter 8

Sorry I haven't written for a while, diary. I've been busy at police college – it's so exciting I can hardly believe it! I met a real homicide detective today, DI Cartwright. He caught my eye while he was lecturing and there was definitely a spark there when we talked after. He went off to Orillia, but I've heard he's coming back next year for a longer stay. His lectures are very popular with the new students.
— The diary of Rebecca Sarah Bradley (2002)

By 4:30 p.m., Rebecca still hadn't looked for a place to stay. The Royal Oak, a fleabag hotel on Main, didn't appeal to her. Then she recalled a note on a bulletin board at Parker's, advertising *Maggie's Home Away From Home — best and only room and board in town.* She pulled out her cell phone and called, arranging to visit there and then.

She strolled through Conroy, looking around. There wasn't much to see. Stan's Hardware, Duffy's Doughnuts, the Royal Oak Hotel, a bank, once elegant, now converted to a library, Parker's Grocery, Robbie's Diner, Herman's Fuel Emporium, and a disreputable-looking pub named Georgie's, all interspersed with backyard repair shops and houses advertising local hairdressers and various other services. A few tired-looking houses were mingled with small businesses along Main. The residential streets branching off it ended in stands of hardwood and softwood trees surrounded by lots of scrubby bush. The only attractive building was an elegant mansion at the north edge of town, which happily turned out to be Maggie's.

The mansion was delightful, with lime-green shutters, whitewashed siding and a freshly mowed lawn. Neatly trimmed shrubs surrounded the front yard, and a lush flower garden hugged one side of the house.

Maggie was waiting for her on the doorstep, straw broom in one hand, dustpan in the other. Rebecca got the impression of a friendly, but no nonsense, landlady. Maggie had shaggy grey hair, cropped short, and looked to be in her late fifties. As soon as Rebecca got out of her car, she set down the brush and pan and bustled forward.

"Welcome!"

"Hello, Maggie. My name's Rebecca Bradley. Sorry, I don't know your last name."

"Not to worry, just Maggie to you and most folk around here. Mrs. Delaney to those I've got no time for, although the 'Mrs.' is a front. I never married. But Delaney's a fine Irish name, don't you think?"

"Yes, indeed. I've met many of them. I had Delaneys as neighbours when I was a kid."

A shadow seemed to cross Maggie's face. Then she ushered Rebecca inside.

"It's a beautiful place." Rebecca peered down a hallway that led to a parlour and, farther on, to a large dining room. The high ceiling gave the foyer a stately air, but the interior was homely. She stepped through a carved wooden archway leading into a living room that stretched the length of the house. Massive bay windows at either end let in the light. The back window opened out onto beds of colourful blooms.

Maggie beamed at the admiring look on her face. "Gardening's my passion. Now, should I call you Rebecca, or Ms. Bradley? Surely not Mrs. Bradley?"

"Rebecca, please. And definitely not 'Mrs.' I'm not sure when that will happen, if ever."

"Well the pickings in this town are rather slim, I have to say."

Rebecca laughed.

"Staying long?" Maggie asked.

"One week for sure, maybe longer."

"Best news I've heard all summer. You're a welcome addition to my other two boarders. I take it you're here on business, although I can't say there's much of that going on these days."

"Yes. I'll tell you about it later. Right now, I'd like to unpack and make a call."

"Certainly. Let me show you to your room. It's on the second floor. It has an en suite washroom, a large window, and a private balcony where you can relax in peace. It's quiet, especially at night. Apart from the crickets, that is."

"Sounds lovely."

The bedroom was magnificent, with a four-poster oak bed, and matching chest of drawers and side tables. Antique lamps, faded paintings, and a Persian rug resting on a shiny hardwood floor complemented the tapestry drapes. There was no air conditioning, but the large ceiling fan would suffice, Rebecca was sure. Mature sugar maples in the backyard cast a welcome shade.

"This is better than I could ever have imagined." Rebecca ran her fingertips over the highly polished chest of drawers. The waxy smell reminded her of her home in northern Ontario. She thought of her mother, and her throat tightened.

"Dinner's at six." Maggie backed out of the room and headed downstairs.

Rebecca unpacked, deciding to leave her call until later. There was just enough time to take a bath and tend to her blister before dinner. Judging by the wonderful smells seeping into the room, it would be a treat.

* * *

Two men were seated at the dining room table when she arrived, and rose to their feet.

She smiled brightly. "Hi, I'm Rebecca."

The first to reply was an eager-looking man, fresh-faced and she guessed in his early thirties. "Fred Stafford. Pleased to meet you. Call me Freddie."

"A pleasure, Freddie." She turned to the older man standing at the head of the table. He was somewhere in his sixties, lean and darkly tanned, with a sour expression and a shrewd, calculating air about him.

"Archie MacDougall, an ye please." He sat down. His accent was hard to follow. A dour Scot. She'd met others like him in Prospect.

A rich meaty aroma filled the room, and Maggie appeared, bearing a platter of roast beef. Rebecca's mouth watered.

"Dig in. There's no formalities here." Maggie hurried back to the kitchen and the room filled with the sound of scraping cutlery.

Freddie ate with gusto. He gave the impression of being a happy-go-lucky guy, and he wasn't bad looking either. Rebecca looked up and found Archie staring at her. He lowered his eyes.

Rebecca ate her fill and leaned back in her chair. She planned on wringing as much useful information from her fellow guests as she could, as well as from Maggie. Both Freddie and Archie must be outsiders to Conroy, but that could be useful. They might notice things the locals took for granted.

"Okay, Freddie, tell me about yourself."

He wiped his mouth with a napkin. "Let's see. Oh, yes. I was born in Windsor in 1972 — makes me thirty-five next month. My father worked at the Chrysler plant, assembling cars and trucks. He got me summer jobs when I was in high school. I started university there, did civil engineering, but dropped out and went to work in Toronto. Served tables and did low-paying jobs. My goal was to have fun, and I did." He closed his eyes for a moment. "But time passed and my crowd moved on, so I applied for a job with a construction firm. Slaved on roads for a while and got laid off. I moved to Conroy seven years ago. I work at Stan's Hardware now. Life's pretty quiet and I spend too much time at Georgie's Pub. You're welcome to join me there for a drink or six." He laughed. "So what's your story?"

Rebecca knew she would have to tell them sooner or later, and it might as well be now. But just then, Maggie barged into the dining room carrying a pot of coffee and a huge apple pie. Freddie licked his lips theatrically, but Archie stared straight ahead. Rebecca had a feeling something was bothering him.

Maggie sat down. "I'll join you now, I ate dinner while I was cooking." She cut the pie into four huge pieces.

Rebecca thought wistfully of her waistline. A week of this and her clothes wouldn't fit.

"What've you kids been talking about?" Maggie passed the plates around the table. "Not me, I hope. There's nothing to tell there anyhow. Flowers, cooking, scrubbing, gossip, that's my life. Hear any gossip, you bring it straight to me. Understood?"

Freddie cut in. "Rebecca was about to tell us about herself. My story's done, and you've heard it before anyhow. Shall I tell it again?"

"Not on your life," Maggie shot back. "I'm waiting for the movie."

Rebecca laughed, noticing that Archie still sat stony-faced. Before she could speak, he stood up, plate in hand, and thanked Maggie for the meal. He nodded at Rebecca and went upstairs, apparently to finish his pie in solitude.

"Barrel of laughs, that one." Maggie waved her fork in the air. "You'll get used to him. Has two words in his vocabulary — hello and goodbye. Added a new one tonight — thanks. First time I've heard it, though I've known him for years. Flowed like honey off his lips, it did." She turned to Rebecca. "Well? Care to tell your story?"

"Okay. But first I want to tell you why I'm here. Maybe you can help."

"We'll get the whole story later, over some fine Irish whiskey," Maggie declared. "What say you to that?"

"It's a deal. Suit you, Freddie?" Rebecca looked at him.

"Sure. Long as Maggie's pouring."

Maggie smiled.

Rebecca cleared her throat. "Well, actually, I'm a police officer. I work at the OPP Central Region office."

Maggie interrupted her. "Wait a minute. What's a classy young lady like you doing on the beat? Expensive clothes, a posh car, and I can tell you're educated. Why waste your life on the police? Begging your pardon and no insult intended."

"I've got my reasons. I'll tell you another time. Anyway, my goal is to become a detective and maybe someday open my own private investigation agency. I finished basic training four years ago and got a job in Orillia. So far, all I've done is routine police work. But I'm in Conroy to investigate the death of Abigail McBride."

"Well I'll be stuffed," Maggie exclaimed. "A real detective in my house. Won't that be the talk of the town? Freddie, better watch yerself. Keep the drugs out of sight. And Archie'll have to move the stiff from the basement. Please, Rebecca, go easy on us. We's just simple folk tryin' to get by." Her eyes darted around the room.

Freddie burst out laughing and choked on his pie.

Rebecca waited for him to recover. "I got this assignment because all the homicide detectives are tied up on other cases." She crossed her fingers. "But I'm having trouble coming up with new ideas. Constable O'Reilly's helping me, but he thinks the case might never be solved." She sighed, and turned to Maggie. "Do *you* know anything about what happened last year?"

"Of course, dear girl. Oops! Guess I should be calling you Detective. Anyway, Conroy's a small town. Never had a murder before poor Abigail, as I recall. You were here, Freddie. You remember."

Freddie nodded. "Sure do. Never knew the lady, though I'd seen her around. And I've, uh . . . chatted with her husband a couple of times at Stan's — but I don't know him well. Nobody talked about anything else for months. But I'm surprised the police never caught the killer, because this is a close town. It's hard to hide a secret here. Must've been a stranger, someone passing through. Has anything new been found?"

"I think I've said enough for now," Rebecca replied. "But perhaps we can talk about the case tomorrow, after dinner? I'll buy the whiskey."

Maggie rubbed her palms together. "Done!"

Rebecca thanked her for dinner and bade them goodnight. She had some thinking to do.

She lay in bed, mulling over the evening, and three things in particular. Firstly, Maggie's frown when she said she'd grown up next door to some Delaneys. Secondly, Archie's abrupt departure from the dinner table, just as she was about to talk about herself – after which it would have been his turn to tell his story. Finally, Freddie's hesitation when he mentioned Abigail's husband.

Rebecca made a note of these observations, and settled back. But her brain still raced, and sleep would not come.

The hours of the night wore on. Suddenly, she heard the sound of rustling outside her window. Heart pounding, she told herself it was probably just an animal moving about. Then she heard the backyard screen door squeak.

Someone was trying to break into the house!

She jumped out of bed and rushed to the window. Opening the curtains, she pressed her nose to the glass. It was pitch black outside, but she was sure she detected movement below. She unlatched the window and thrust her head out, but the backyard was deserted. She watched intently for a few seconds, looking again for movement, then closed the window again.

Rebecca felt compelled to go and see. Her gun was in Maggie's safe, and there wasn't time to retrieve it. Trying to control her fear, she went downstairs and checked the windows and doors. They were all locked. She peered through the windows but nothing moved. Whether or not a burglar had been trying to break in, all was quiet now and the house was secure. She was probably just spooked from thinking about what had happened to Abigail.

She decided not to wake Maggie. She would tell her in the morning. Rebecca returned to her room and went back to bed, where she listened for another hour, but heard nothing. Eventually she fell into an uneasy sleep.

Chapter 9

So tired. This term has been crazy with studying. I'm ready to go home for the holidays, but I'm worried about how me and Dad will get along. We haven't talked for two whole months. I feel us drifting apart. My fault as much as his.
— The diary of Rebecca Sarah Bradley (2002)

Rebecca rose early on Wednesday morning, anxious to get on with her investigation. Outside, dark clouds threatened rain. Maggie was bustling about in the kitchen getting breakfast ready, so Rebecca headed out back to see if she could find signs of the intruder.

Gusts of wind whooshed through the towering treetops. She meandered about the yard, checking for footprints. On either side of the house fields of swaying grass stretched into the distance. Dense woods crowded against the back fence.

Rebecca's thoughts drifted back to her childhood. Her wealthy family traced its roots to poor English farmers who came to Canada in search of a better life. Their wealth originated with her paternal grandfather, Steven Bradley. He became a prospector and got lucky digging in the right place at the right time. But along with the riches came bodies buried in the cold Ontario earth, mysterious deaths, including her mother's, and the grandfather she had never met. Their murders hung like curses over her family.

The wind gusted and whipped her hair about her face. She turned to face the house, and saw curtains move in an upstairs room. Archie. Why had he stared at her yesterday?

Thunder rumbled, and droplets of rain began to fall. Rebecca scurried into the house. She found Freddie seated at the dining room table. Archie joined them moments later. He sat down and studied his placemat. The smell of frying bacon drifted in from the kitchen, accompanied by Maggie's happy humming. Again, Rebecca thought of her early childhood. Staying at Maggie's was like being at home with her mother. Tears came to her eyes.

Quickly, she went into the kitchen and told Maggie about the intruder, acknowledging she may have imagined the whole thing.

"Not to worry, dear," Maggie said. "There's a pile of petty theft going on around Conroy. My house has been burgled before, and someone stole a few antiques. The prime targets, though, are my home-baked pies. I once caught a little girl with her hand in my cookie jar. She got a stern lecture and was sent packing with a bag full of the evidence." They both laughed.

"Thanks, Maggie. I was worried so I checked all the windows and doors and it's pretty secure." She gave Maggie a big smile. "I've stolen some cookies in my time too. Please don't tell my boss."

Maggie nodded solemnly.

Rebecca went back into the dining room. "So tell me, Freddie, what's the second best way to start the day in Conroy?"

"Best being Maggie's breakfast, you mean?"

"Of course, what else?" Rebecca sensed Archie's eyes fixed on her.

"Well, you've already done it. Duffy's. But you should know — rumours about the new woman in town are spreading fast. Everyone's talking about it. Should've warned you last night, but I didn't want to spook you on your first day."

"And here I was thinking I'd been so discreet. Why didn't I think of Duffy's?"

Maggie came through the kitchen door carrying plates loaded with fried eggs and bacon. "Coffee's on the way."

Rebecca turned towards Archie, but he looked away.

"Heard you had some excitement at Duffy's." Maggie bustled back into the dining room, a carafe of coffee in hand.

Rebecca looked at her. "Does nothing escape you?"

"Not much." Maggie beamed.

"Good. You can be my master spy. Find out everything about everything. Freddie, you're my Baker Street Irregular, if you're willing to help me." She looked at him.

"Certainly, detective Bradley. Anything to catch Abigail's murderer. It was such a horrible shock to the town. But what's an Irregular? I'm not sure I like the sound of that."

"Sherlock Holmes," Archie growled. "Don't know yer Conan Doyle, do ye, lad?"

"Why, Archie, you can talk." Maggie blew him a kiss. He grunted, and stared down at his plate.

Rebecca nodded. "Yes, Archie's right. The Baker Street Irregulars were street urchins who helped Holmes with his cases."

"Fine, you can count on me." Freddie saluted. "I've always been a bit irregular, and now it's official. I'm Freddie the Irregular from here on in. But who's this Sherlock Holmes fellow?"

Maggie's mouth dropped open.

"Kidding!" Freddie dodged an imaginary blow.

"Thank goodness for that," Maggie said. "I was preparing to have you thrown out of the house."

"Sorry, Mom." Freddie took his seat again. "Does that make Rebecca Inspector Lestrade?"

Maggie snickered.

Rebecca turned to Maggie. She wanted to know more about the young giant at Duffy's who had stared so openly at her. "Maggie, who is Hound?"

Maggie took some time to answer. "I guess you'd say he's a man of mystery. He's a likable fellow, though a mite eccentric. He won't tell anyone where he comes from. He's been in town for seven years or so, moved here as a teen. He boarded with me for three years, then bought his own place four years ago, just up the road. No one has any idea where he got the money for it, but I'm bettin' he has a stash somewhere. He even imported an expensive old car from England, and he has a tiny roadster that he seldom uses. It's way too small for him." She chuckled.

"He was reading a comic book at Duffy's. Has he got some sort of problem?"

"You mean challenged, something like that? No way. Give him a crossword puzzle, a Sudoku, a brain bender of any kind, and he'll do it in minutes. He's a quick mind, although he hides it. He never went beyond high school. Didn't care much, I reckon."

Rebecca finished eating and rose to her feet. "Thanks, Maggie. Wonderful breakfast. I'll have another cup of coffee at Duffy's, then kick around town for a while, get a feel for it. Bye, y'all."

"Georgie's Pub at five," Freddie hollered at her retreating back. "First drink is on me."

Rebecca smiled over her shoulder. "Can't promise. And don't forget we have to be back here by six."

"Darn right," Maggie muttered. "Late ones get leftovers."

Rebecca peered out the front door. The rain had stopped, but the overcast sky promised more. She grabbed a guest umbrella and set off. She would leave her shiny new convertible at Maggie's. It could stop people talking.

Why had she brought her fancy car and smart clothes? Today she was wearing light brown cords and a cream cotton blouse, although blue jeans and a red-checkered shirt would have been better. And she should have rented a wreck like O'Reilly's Chevy.

The townspeople were already out and about. Most of them ignored her, but a couple did nod. One even mumbled a "hi." Well, it was something, she supposed.

She peeked through the window before entering Duffy's, hoping to see Hound. He intrigued her. She wondered what had made her look back at him after she'd left the coffee shop yesterday. She had a feeling that she'd met him before — which was impossible. No one could forget the sheer size of him.

She was lucky. He was sitting alone at a table, reading a large hardcover book. Rebecca squinted at the title — *War and Peace.*

She went up to the front counter.

"Hi, Daisy. A small coffee, please, black."

Daisy filled a mug. "Fresh perked, and served in my finest china. I save the regular cups for the chief. My best ones go to Hound over there, poor lad, although he likes milkshakes better." Daisy looked at him and smiled warmly. "He's my favourite, but don't tell him I said so. Too bad about what happened yesterday. And I haven't seen you-know-who today, in case you're looking for him."

"Thanks, Daisy."

Rebecca took her coffee to a booth across the aisle from Hound. She was about to sit down when he looked up from his book. "Uh, hi. Nice day."

"Sort of." Rebecca glanced out the window towards the heavy clouds that darkened the sky.

"I mean, if you want a good soaking." He looked timid, almost frightened.

"Care to join me?"

"Me? Sure." He laid down his book, grabbed his brimming coffee mug and wriggled free of his chair, which creaked ominously. The coffee shot out of his mug, and Rebecca jumped back, spilling her own drink which sprinkled her pant legs.

Hound jerked his mug back, slopping more coffee onto his white shirt. He looked horrified. "Oh, God! I'm sorry."

"No problem." Rebecca dabbed at her pants. "But you'll need a refill."

He peered into his empty mug and winced. "I guess the coffee's on me."

Rebecca smiled. A hush descended on the room as Duffy's regulars openly strained to overhear their conversation.

"I guess it's better than a milkshake bath," Hound said, and his face flushed crimson. He waved at Daisy and pointed at his coffee mug.

Rebecca slid into the booth, and Hound wedged himself in across from her.

"My name's Rebecca." She spoke gently, to ease his discomfort. "And yours?"

"My friends call me Hound." He patted his shirt with a napkin.

"Good book?" She pointed at *War and Peace*.

"Pretty good, I think. Not really my style, but better than comic books." His eyes shone.

Rebecca could tell he was attracted to her. Plenty of men had told her how beautiful she was, but it only made her suspicious. Her mother had been beautiful, and look what happened to her.

"I never got into comics. My father tore them up whenever he caught me with one. Made me read classics like that." Rebecca pointed at his book. "I'm a mystery junkie, myself."

"No kidding? Me too." Hound positively bounced. "I read everything I can get my hands on. Got most of the

53

movies on DVD too. I've even helped Chief O'Reilly a few times. Petty theft, things like that. You're a detective, aren't you? I heard O'Reilly call you 'DC' yesterday. Are you here on an investigation?"

Rebecca bent towards him and lowered her voice. "I see I've met the right person."

Hound inhaled sharply, and blew the air back out. "How can I help?"

She spoke casually. "I'm investigating the death of Abigail McBride."

At the mention of that name, Hound's shoulders slumped. His voice was flat. "That was a year ago. Even Chief O'Reilly couldn't figure it out."

"You're right. The police investigation didn't turn up any leads. But before I came to Conroy, I found one new piece of information. Abigail McBride wasn't her birth name. She was born in the Netherlands as Marijke van Rijn. She moved to Canada thirteen years ago and changed her name to Abigail Smith, before she married Kingsley McBride and took his name. Everything seemed to be fine. Until someone killed her." Rebecca decided to reveal this information now to see if Hound knew about Abigail's past – they were apparently close friends. She wanted to do it before she quizzed O'Reilly on it, because it was a detail he should have known about and told to Cartwright during the original investigation. In any event, Abigail's birth and childhood records were among the first things that Cartwright should have checked. She was beginning to understand Commissioner Hardy's decision to move him out of the CIB, although it puzzled her why he'd been promoted, rather than demoted.

Hound broke into her thoughts. "I knew Abigail well." He spoke more urgently now. "I talked to her a lot at Robbie's Diner. She never came to Duffy's. Sometimes we hiked along Hagger's Creek together. I used to help carry her groceries home from Parker's. I was devastated when she died."

"Didn't anybody interview you?"

"The chief and I talked about it, but I couldn't help him, so he left it at that, I guess. The investigators didn't ask me anything."

"Very interesting. Would you mind if I interviewed you formally? Not now. Later this morning, say, at eleven o'clock in O'Reilly's office?"

Hound twisted his hands together.

"What's wrong?"

He hesitated. "All right, but could you come to my place instead? People around here notice things, you see. I live a short distance outside of town, at the north end along Main. I could show you my mystery collection." He looked up with an eager smile.

She nodded. "That's okay with me. Write your address and phone number on this napkin." She would have to tell O'Reilly about the interview. Hound didn't look dangerous, but you never knew.

He scribbled on the napkin, stood up and tucked *War and Peace* under his arm. Rebecca reached for her purse, but he touched her shoulder gently. "Remember, it's my treat."

"Thank you, I forgot." She watched him lumber to the front of the shop.

On reaching the counter, he shoved a hand into his pants, and stopped. He pulled out an empty pocket and stared at it, a horrified look on his face.

Someone sniggered.

Chapter 10

My worst Christmas since Mom died. Dad and I argued for days. He's still angry at me. I have to leave here – I'll just stay in Toronto for a while before college starts again. We can't be around each other, that's for sure.

— The diary of Rebecca Sarah Bradley (2002)

The storm clouds had cleared. Rebecca left Duffy's and strolled along Main to O'Reilly's office, shaking her head. Hound was awkward, but no fool. She sensed he was holding back a tremendous amount of energy, like a pressure vessel about to blow.

When she entered the office, O'Reilly was ensconced in his private room, with his face hidden behind the *Orillia Packet and Times*. She went in and planted herself in front of him.

"Good morning, Constable O'Reilly."

He lowered the paper. "Top of the morning to you too, DC Bradley." His words were uttered through clenched teeth. Rebecca sensed that something bad was about to happen.

"I hear you're planning to close up my shop."

Rebecca's heart sank. This wasn't just bad, it was awful. How had he found out? Her review of his office, and him, was supposed to be a secret.

She could think of nothing to say, except, "Let's just get on with retracing Abigail's route."

He leaned back and glared at her. Then he shrugged. "Okay, let's boogie. Snappy outfit, by the way. Shall we take your shiny new convertible or my old Chevy?"

"Yours will do."

"Well then, everything's just fine." He tossed the newspaper on the floor and stormed past her.

She followed him out to his car and they drove in strained silence to Abigail's house. Rebecca noticed Mrs. Jackson peering at her from across the road as O'Reilly wandered about the yard, his hands jammed deep in his pockets, until it was time to set off.

Rebecca started towards Hagger's Creek, with O'Reilly trailing behind her, whistling tunelessly. She could tell he was hurt. How had he found out about her assignment? He must know someone close to Cartwright.

They reached the creek and crossed the south bridge, where the tension became too much for Rebecca. She turned back to face him. "Look, Constable O'Reilly, we have to work together on this case."

He raised his eyebrows. "Of course. Why would you think otherwise?"

She didn't know what to say.

"Just because I'm angry doesn't mean I won't help," he continued.

Rebecca apologized. "Could you describe what you did, how you carried out your search after Abigail disappeared?"

To her relief, he quit sulking. "At first I wasn't concerned. People often go missing for hours, even days, and then they show up. But Kingsley persisted. He told me he was really worried, it was uncharacteristic of her. I hiked Abigail's path along Hagger's Creek, looking for signs that someone had strayed off it, but didn't find anything. The next morning, I asked Hound, the milkshake guy at Duffy's, to go over the path. He's a gifted tracker and spends hours in the countryside hiking off into the bush to follow animals, or whatever. He confirmed that nobody had moved off the path for at least a day."

"Why didn't you record it in your case notes?" Was this another slip by the chief? They were starting to pile up.

He gave Rebecca a sharp look. "No need. My observations were accurate. If Hound had said otherwise, I would've noted it."

She decided not to press the point. "All right. Anyway, I've arranged to interview Hound later this morning, at his house."

O'Reilly shrugged.

They were now nearly halfway to the north bridge. The day was heating up fast. Deer flies once again swarmed about Rebecca's head, apparently preferring her to O'Reilly. She quickened her pace to shake them off.

"You have the names of the people Abigail met on her walk," O'Reilly said. "I'll set up interviews."

"Not yet, please. I don't intend to cover all the same ground that you did. I'm trying to approach the case from a different angle. But please continue with your account."

"After leaving the path, Abigail went straight to Robbie's Diner."

"How long did it take Abigail to get from the north bridge to Robbie's?" She slowed to match O'Reilly's pace.

"About fifteen minutes, more or less." He sounded hesitant.

"I walked it yesterday, Constable O'Reilly. It took me three minutes. Eyewitnesses at Robbie's said she arrived at around 8:45 a.m. That would mean she took seventeen minutes to get from the north bridge to Robbie's. If she took that long, what happened during those extra fourteen minutes? Where could she have gone? Not far on foot, obviously. She might have stopped to talk to someone. But if so, who was it, and why didn't they come forward? Perhaps someone picked her up in a car. But who, and why, and where would she go?"

He shrugged. "The car explanation's possible. But, I repeat, nobody saw her, except like I told you earlier, Herman Vogel. He saw Abigail pass by his station at 8:30. I checked out the entire area after that. I walked five minutes at a brisk pace either side of the route between Herman's and Robbie's, and found nothing. After Herman's, Abigail must've headed to Robbie's, just a whole lot slower than usual. Then she went to Parker's, and that's when she disappeared."

Rebecca was certain he was hiding something.

"I want to interview Mr. Vogel. Let's go see him."

O'Reilly spoke curtly. "Suit yourself. You won't get much out of him. He's a tight-lipped sort." He lengthened his stride and marched towards the gas station.

Herman was standing inside, watching them through the window. "Good day, Herman. Detective Constable Rebecca Bradley of the Ontario Provincial Police is with me. We're doing a follow-up investigation on Abigail."

Herman's office surprised her. Everything in it was neatly stacked and labelled.

"Mr. Vogel, I hope you don't mind answering a few questions. It won't take long."

Herman's eyes were moist and red, his eyelids puffy. His face was pallid and grey, and his shoulders and back were stooped like an old man, but on closer examination, Rebecca estimated his age at about sixty. He must be sick, or perhaps he was suffering from heavy stress of some sort. She wondered if it was linked to Abigail's death.

Herman slowly replied. "No, Miss, I will help you, if I can." He seemed hesitant to talk, and his lips were quivering.

"Thank you. Now, I understand that Abigail McBride passed by your station on the morning she went missing. Can you tell me what time that was?"

"I told Chief O'Reilly. It was 8:30."

"Exactly 8:30? Did you look at a clock, or your watch?"

Herman spoke with a pronounced Dutch accent. "Ja. I saw the clock on the wall. I always keep the time fine. It is my way."

"Yes, thank you, I can see that. So if Mrs. McBride passed here at 8:30, she should have arrived at Robbie's Diner a minute later, two at most. Witnesses say she arrived at 8:45. Do you have any idea why that might be?" Rebecca gave him an encouraging smile.

O'Reilly stepped in front of Herman. "You know, DC Bradley, we're not sure about Abigail's exact arrival time at Robbie's. Like I said, she must have slowed up after passing the station and arrived later than usual. There's only ten minutes or so that need accounting for. Maybe she just sat somewhere and had a rest." O'Reilly pursed his lips. He looked uncomfortable.

Rebecca glared at him. "And like I told *you*, Constable O'Reilly, fourteen minutes. That's a lot of missing time, no matter how you cut it. Where could she have gone?" She looked around him at Herman. "Have you any idea, Mr. Vogel?"

He stared through the office window and spoke in a distant voice. "No, I could not say. I am sorry, Miss."

O'Reilly intervened again. "I think we should move on, DC Bradley."

This made Rebecca angry, but she gave in. "Thank you, Mr. Vogel. Perhaps we can talk another day."

Herman didn't respond.

Outside, she turned and glowered at O'Reilly.

He spoke quickly. "Constable Bradley, you should know that Herman and Abigail were very close. Both of them came from the Netherlands. They talked a lot about what they called the 'old country.' Other than Kingsley, I don't know anyone in town who's been there, except now that I think about it, perhaps Hound. Otherwise, why would he spend so much time with Abigail? I've often wondered about that."

"Why Hound?" And she thought: *So you did know about Abigail's past, and Hound's long-term friendship with her.*

O'Reilly sighed. "I don't know. But he and Abigail used to chat for hours on end. I have no idea what they talked about. Hound's never told me much about himself, and I've never tried to find out. Abigail told me he'd had a difficult childhood and wanted to forget things. Her death was hard on him. But now I wish I'd spent more time with him on the investigation last year. Like most people, Abigail had depths to her that didn't show on the surface, but if anyone knew about them, it would be Hound."

"You seem to have a great regard for Hound, Constable O'Reilly. Why? Because he helps you?"

"Yes, when I call on him. But he's different. Some call him strange, but I think special is a better word. You'd understand that if you got to know him."

"What do you mean? Why is he special?" Rebecca instinctively put a hand on O'Reilly's arm.

He looked down, and she pulled it away. "I can't pin it down, really. He's like a child of nature. He's really competent when he sets his mind to something, like tracking animals. He's deeper than you might think. Certainly not the goofball you saw at Duffy's."

"Tell me more."

This was a mistake, Rebecca realized when O'Reilly said, "You're interviewing him later. Find out for yourself." Then he clammed up.

Rebecca shrugged. "Have it your way. But why did you interfere with my interview? Herman was really tense. I want to find out why, and I will. He knows something, I'm sure of it."

O'Reilly grunted. "If you say so."

"And why didn't you record in your case summary that Herman saw Abigail pass by his station?"

He studied the ground. "No reason, DC Bradley. An oversight. You can tell Cartwright I'm a negligent note-taker."

"Constable O'Reilly, I'm not going to get anywhere if I go over the same ground as the original investigation team. I need to follow new leads."

"Fine, then. Just be careful not to hurt innocent people along the way."

Rebecca bristled. "Okay, if that's how you feel about it." She moved off, with O'Reilly trailing along behind. The people they interviewed at Robbie's told them nothing new, and no one at Parker's had anything to say.

This seemed to please O'Reilly, and he bustled back to his office. Rebecca was fuming. He'd stopped her questioning Herman. Why? She would try again when O'Reilly wasn't with her.

She set off to find Hound's house, frowning. Something had happened last year that linked Abigail, Herman, and O'Reilly, and Hound might also figure into it. Rebecca's suspicious mind started to work overtime.

Chapter 11

I'm on tenterhooks. DI Cartwright's coming back to give a series of lectures at the college and he'll be staying here all next week. I hope he remembers me!!
— The diary of Rebecca Sarah Bradley (2003)

Hound's secluded home was not far from Maggie's. Rebecca followed a tree-lined driveway to a two-story Victorian-style house, nestled in a grove of poplar trees and surrounded by fields of tall grass.

Hound was waiting for her, a huge figure on the front porch, like a grizzly defending its den. He was over six feet ten inches tall and must have weighed at least three hundred and fifty pounds. Rebecca felt like David looking up at Goliath.

"Good morning, once more." He greeted her with a shy smile. "Now it really is a nice day."

"Yes, the sun's come out." She gazed around her. "What a lovely house and yard. Before we do the interview, though, I believe you offered to show me your mystery collection?"

"Of course. Come in."

The house was astonishing. The foyer and living room were furnished with exquisite English antiques, all highly polished. Rebecca gazed at the ornately carved wood on the wainscoting and doors. A gorgeous spiral staircase wound up to the second floor.

"What a stunning place! Where did you get the wood? It's black oak, isn't it?"

Hound blushed. "Yes. I carved it."

"Extraordinary. Where did you learn to do that?"

"I taught myself. It took a long time before I figured out how to get it right. I like working with my hands. It helps me focus my thoughts."

He had real talent. Rebecca was impressed. "What about your books? I truly want to see them."

His eyes sparkled. He pointed at the steps leading to the basement. "You're the first visitor to my private rooms. Not even Shorty and Lukas have been down there."

Rebecca was suddenly nervous. What did she really know about him? She considered postponing the interview until O'Reilly could be with her. But then she decided to risk it. O'Reilly would only interfere again, especially if he was somehow linked to Abigail's murder. This increasingly complicated case was putting her on edge – she could take no one at face value. She began to sympathize with Cartwright and his detective team.

She cleared her throat and said, "I'm flattered."

Hound didn't seem to notice her discomfort. "You're a detective, so you'll understand what draws me to mysteries. My friends wouldn't get it." He led the way down and opened a heavy wooden door to reveal a black velvet curtain. By now, Rebecca was almost shaking.

"Ready?"

"Any time." She ran a hand through her hair and fought down the impulse to flee. Maybe she should have brought her gun along.

Hound reached out and drew back the curtain. The first thing she saw was a large-scale model of Sherlock Holmes's living room in Baker Street, displayed on a massive table. Standing about were lifelike miniatures of Holmes, Watson, and Mrs. Hudson. A light shone on the figure of Inspector Lestrade in a corner, trench coat open and gun in hand. In another darkened corner lurked Moriarty with two thugs.

Rebecca forgot all about her misgivings and stepped forward, amazed. "Hound, this is terrific. It's a work of art."

He rocked on his heels, blushing.

"You didn't do this yourself?" She looked up into his beaming face.

"Took me two years to complete. Do you like it?"

"I'm speechless." She moved closer to the table, awed at the detail.

"Wait till you see my mystery collection. When you're ready, open the far door."

The next room contained row upon row of hardcover books, arranged on shelves that reached to the ceiling.

He coughed. "Lots of first editions."

"Incredible. Must be a thousand, at least. It's like a bookstore." Rebecca moved from shelf to shelf, reading the titles. Where had he got the money for all this? The furniture upstairs must be worth a fortune. She sat down in a leather armchair and heard the gentle hum of a dehumidifier.

Hound came and stood next to the chair, and Rebecca realized she no longer felt uneasy. She looked up at him. "I've heard you don't often speak about your past, but I'd really like to know where you come from, if you don't mind talking about it."

Hound seemed to struggle with himself. After some time, he shrugged his massive shoulders. "Okay, but only where I grew up and why I'm in Conroy."

"Thank you. I don't want to pry too much, though I did come here to find out more about your relationship with Abigail."

His forehead creased. "I thought you were only checking into my part in the investigation last year."

"To be honest, there's more to it than that. But if my questions are too intrusive, you can refuse to answer them."

"Okay," he replied warily.

"I appreciate that, Hound. Perhaps we could chat about your past another time, say at dinner tomorrow. I don't want you to think it's part of my formal interview."

He found a chair and sat down facing her.

"As you know," she began, "I'm investigating the Abigail McBride murder. I'm trying not to cover the same ground as the detectives last year. They did their work thoroughly, as far as it went. But I'm interested in learning more about the relationships between Abigail and Herman Vogel, and you too. That's a line the investigators didn't pursue."

He stared at the floor and pushed out his lower lip.

"What's bothering you, Hound?" Was she breaking new ground? Her heart rate increased.

Hound sighed. "I don't know Herman well, but Abigail and I were best friends. She was a private person, like me, and didn't want to dwell on the past. But you can't shut out who you are or where you come from, no matter how hard you try, can you?" He looked at Rebecca, as if she had an answer. "We talked about England and the Netherlands, but never about our families."

"I don't understand. Were you born in England?"

"Yes."

"When did you come to Canada? Where's your family? What happened to your accent?"

He raised his hands. "Aren't you supposed to be asking about Abigail?"

"Sorry. I got carried away." She silently cursed herself for the volley of questions. Rookie mistake.

"You said we could talk about that other stuff later, over dinner."

She smiled, eager to get him back on side. "Okay, I'll stick to script. How about we meet at seven tomorrow evening, at the Royal Oak?"

Hound nodded.

"Now, back to business. Tell me about Abigail."

He seemed to relax a little. "I guess you should at least know how Abigail and I became friends."

"Please tell me." She opened her notebook.

It was a while before he began, the whirr of the humidifier fan the only sound. "I was born in London, to a rich family. The Hounsleys are well known in the upper ranks of British society, mostly because my father spreads lots of money about. I met Abigail on a family trip to Amsterdam. As you already know, her name then was Marijke van Rijn. The Hounsleys and van Rijns have been doing business together for generations. My father and Nicholas van Rijn are friends, or rather business associates."

"What do you mean exactly?"

"Just that they've been partners in many deals around the world. They're ruthless when it comes to their interests, which are money, money, and more money." Hound was breathing hard.

Even the mention of his father seemed to distress him. Rebecca moved on. "One thing that interests me is why Abigail changed her name, and why she chose Abigail and Smith?"

Hound grunted. "She chose Smith because it's a common name. Marijke wanted to be inconspicuous. She chose Abigail to get back at her family for rejecting her. Abigail means 'my father rejoices.' You'll soon see the irony."

"Go on, please."

He sighed and massaged his temples for a few seconds. "Like I said, I met Marijke in Amsterdam. I was only eight years old and she was nineteen, but we hit it off immediately. Marijke showed me around the city, and we had a great time together. We wrote to each other after the trip, up until she left home for Canada. Anyway, despite my young age, my eyes were opened to both of our fathers' dubious activities. I had never been close to any of my family, my father, my mother, or my younger brother, who was my father's favourite. Marijke understood all this. She was in a similar situation. Her parents ignored her, and she had a monster of a younger sister. Both our families expected the eldest children to take up positions in the family empires, but Marijke and I were disappointments, especially me. We asked too many awkward questions, we knew what it was like to be given the cold shoulder by your own flesh and blood."

"So that's the bond." Rebecca welcomed Hound opening up about his own life.

"In part," he said. "But there's more to it than that. I came to Canada two years after my trip to Amsterdam, when I was ten. Back in England, there was an incident at my public school that gave my father a perfect excuse to get rid of me. He told me I was an embarrassment to the family and packed me off to Lakefield, Ontario."

Hound clenched his fists. He must really hate his father, Rebecca thought. She wondered what Richard Hounsley was like. Her father was tough, but he had never actually rejected her. She changed the subject.

"What happened to Marijke?"

"She came here a year before I did. When I arrived at Lakefield, she was waiting for me. She'd come to Canada to be with Kingsley McBride. She told me the details when I was older. He'd struck a business deal of some sort with her father in Amsterdam and she was introduced to him there. Three weeks after she met Kingsley, he asked her to marry him. She refused. She'd just turned twenty, and she told me later that she was in love with another man. After Kingsley returned to Canada, her parents told her it would be better if she didn't stay in the Netherlands. Then her lover broke things off with her. Maybe marrying Kingsley offered her a way to leave the country with her pride intact. Anyway, she accepted his proposal, with one condition. She wanted to live in Toronto for two years before coming to Conroy. Even then, she didn't marry him for another four years after she got here." He paused and took a deep breath.

"But why was she waiting for you at Lakefield?" Rebecca could see him withdrawing, and she wanted to hear the rest.

He looked at her. "Because we were good friends, and she wanted to look after me like a younger brother, but there was no way that my father would allow it. Marijke wrote to him, and he refused outright."

Hound's face was turning red and blotchy, and Rebecca began to worry about him.

"I know this is hard for you, Hound, but please don't stop. Just a little more, please." She felt bad about pushing him, but she was sure he had important things he could tell her. She was building up more and more of a picture of Abigail's complicated past.

He swallowed audibly and continued. "At Lakefield, Marijke told me she'd agreed to marry Kingsley. I had never met him, so I couldn't say much about it. I was just happy to see my only true friend again. She tried to persuade me to move closer to her, but I decided not to. Years later, I met an old Jesuit priest in Lakefield. I talked to him about it and he convinced me to change my mind. I came here a year after Abigail married Kingsley." Hound's shoulders sagged.

"Hound, is there anything you can tell me that might shed light on her death?" Rebecca didn't want him to stop, but his expression was so utterly forlorn that her heart melted. She knew how it felt to lose someone close. This would be her last question.

"I can't tell you anything. Abigail was my dearest friend, the only one I could share things with. I miss hearing her voice and helping comfort her. She never had a chance to be happy." Hound got to his feet and wandered about the room.

Was that it? She had gained some new information about Abigail, but nothing that advanced her investigation, as far as she could tell. Hound could have told her more, she was convinced, but she didn't want to press him any harder. Had he been in love with Abigail? And what might that mean? A motive for murder? Unlikely, perhaps, but something else to ponder.

"Thank you, Hound. Let's leave it there for now."

He slumped back onto his chair. "Thanks. I've had enough. I'll walk to town with you. I visit Abigail's grave every day to put flowers on it." Tears pooled in his eyes and he blinked rapidly.

"I'd like that, Hound." She put away her notebook. When she stood to leave, her eyes, too, were moist.

Hound rose to his feet, and they walked to town in silence.

"Tomorrow evening at seven," Rebecca said when they arrived.

Hound nodded and trudged slowly away as Rebecca thought about the complex webs of relationships that stretched over Conroy, and beyond. Surely somewhere within it was an answer.

Chapter 12

It's two in the morning and I just can't sleep — I'm on a total high! DI Cartwright gave a great presentation today on a murder case he solved. He knows so much I can hardly believe it, he's amazing. I stayed after class and talked to him and told him about how I want to become a homicide detective. He seemed really interested!
— The diary of Rebecca Sarah Bradley (2003)

Rebecca headed to the Royal Oak Hotel to reserve a table for the following day. Maggie had told her it was the second-best dining place in town. Duffy's only served breakfast and lunch, and Maggie hadn't even mentioned Robbie's. Rebecca suspected that she and Robbie had fallen out.

The people on Main avoided eye contact, except for a guy who ogled her from across the street. It was the jerk from the Buick again. She observed him more closely now. A bulky thug with a buzz cut, a mean-looking mouth and cold eyes. She tried to ignore him but it was hard to dismiss the malice in that look and the fear he struck into her.

The hotel lobby was gloomy and dingy. A cheap paisley carpet covered a creaky wooden floor. The walls were pasted with filthy red velvet paper, and a stale and musty odour pervaded the place. But the perky young blonde standing behind the scratched front desk was quite a contrast. She flashed a smile that lit up the hotel and suddenly it felt like a wonderful place.

"Hi, miss. What can I do for you today?" The smile grew even brighter.

Rebecca smiled back. "I'm here to reserve a dinner table for tomorrow. Should I go to the dining room?" She felt like hugging this warm and friendly creature, especially after the cold reception she'd been getting in the rest of Conroy.

"No need for that, I can do it. Is it in the name of Rebecca Bradley?"

She raised her eyebrows. "News travels fast."

"I'm Sally Partridge, Chief O'Reilly's assistant."

"Oh, that explains it." The thought of O'Reilly wiped the smile from Rebecca's face.

"Not entirely. You're the talk of the town. We don't get much excitement around here so a new face is always a big event, especially when it's a detective from Orillia." Sally looked impressed.

"I'll bet you already know I'm just an acting detective." Rebecca raised her eyebrows, smiling again.

"As far as I'm concerned, you're the real thing. Chief O'Reilly spoke well of you — kind of." Sally giggled. Rebecca burst out laughing.

"It's true. He said you're *almost* like a breath of fresh air. For him that's quite a compliment. He did take a few cheap shots at you, but nothing like Cartwright. He sure didn't take to him."

"I'll say. Cartwright *is* a stuffed shirt, but he's a good cop. You know he's the regional superintendent now?" Rebecca was forced to stick up for him — she needed his support.

"Oh, yes. The chief nearly exploded when he told me. I've never seen him so angry. He's a volatile guy, but he's never held a grudge like that before."

"As far as I can see, both of them did a decent job last year. It must be a personal thing."

Sally lowered her voice and glanced around the lobby. "Has anything new come up in the case?"

"Perhaps. But I don't have time to talk about it now. Can you meet me later?" Sally might know more about O'Reilly than anyone else in Conroy. She might also know lots about the strange cast of characters who inhabited this forgotten town.

"I'm off for lunch in half an hour. We could talk then, if you're not busy."

"Perfect. Here?" Rebecca nodded towards the dining room.

"Better not. The walls have ears. The best place is Duffy's. There's a corner booth where nobody will overhear us. And Daisy makes great soup."

"Done. See you there. Meanwhile, can you book a table for two at seven p.m. tomorrow? Try for one where the walls are sound-proofed."

"I have just the spot. It's the mayor's favourite nook. All the secret deals are done there. They turn the microphones off at night."

"By the way, who *is* the mayor of Conroy? Constable O'Reilly told me, but his name didn't stick."

"Charlie Taylor. He's the father of a miserable brute named Butch." Sally curled her lip.

Rebecca inhaled sharply. "What does he look like?"

"Mean. Buzz cut. Brawny. Stay away from him."

Rebecca sighed. "It might be a bit late for that. He's got to be the nasty-looking guy outside. He stared at me when I was coming in here, and yesterday he made a disgusting gesture."

Sally moved from behind the desk and peered through the hotel entrance. "That's Butch all right." She yelled through the door, "Get lost," and then turned back to Rebecca with a grimace on her face. "He's a real pig, and a sleaze too. Doesn't work at all, at least nothing honest. Hangs out at Georgie's Pub when he's in town. He spends the rest of his time intimidating people on Main Street. He steers clear of O'Reilly though. He's wary of the chief, so he leaves me alone, but the looks he gives me freeze my bones. He frightens almost everyone in town. Even his father gets nervous around him. The only person Butch is afraid of is a guy called Hound. You've met him, I believe."

"That's interesting. Why Hound?"

The phone rang and Sally moved to answer it. "I'll tell you over lunch."

"Okay. Thanks, Sally. See you at Duffy's."

Rebecca left the hotel. Across the street, Butch leaned against a building, and watched her like a hungry dog. She hurried on towards Duffy's, avoiding eye contact.

Intrigued by what Sally had just told her, Rebecca wondered about Hound. So many things in the McBride case seemed to revolve around that young giant. Perhaps too many. Maggie was right, he was a mysterious figure. O'Reilly called him special, and he certainly had artistic talent. She wondered what other secrets lay beneath that massive exterior.

At Duffy's, Daisy beamed at Rebecca from behind the counter. "Welcome, Officer Bradley. You're becoming a regular. You take your coffee black, right? But I'm guessing you're here for something else now — my famous soup. Even Maggie comes in for a bowl from time to time and that's a real compliment."

"Actually, the receptionist at the Royal Oak recommended it."

"Sally Partridge, my best referral agent. She's addicted to my soup. Let me guess. She's joining you for lunch?" Daisy looked pleased. "Now sit down and I'll bring you a cup of freshly brewed coffee." She reached for a mug.

"You're a mind reader. Is everyone here as gifted as you?"

"You bet. Well, maybe not Shorty and Lukas over there. Good thing they've got Hound to look out for them. I don't know how they'd cope otherwise. Probably kill each other arguing about something important, like who ate more doughnuts yesterday."

They were huddled over a small table, spitting words at each other. Shorty swished his arms about, and she wondered why Hound was so attached to them, given their apparent simplicity and his obvious talents. But then she recalled Abigail's layers of complexity and started to wonder if Shorty and Lukas had their own surprises to unveil.

Rebecca shook her head and went to the corner booth that she guessed Sally had in mind. Daisy arrived right behind her, coffee in hand. Rebecca smiled. "Thanks, Daisy." She continued to study Shorty and Lukas. They caught her looking, forgot their battle and stared back at her. Feeling silly, she gave a little wave, which Shorty returned.

She turned away and glanced out the window. Butch was slouching against a building across the street, glaring at her again. She looked down, her heart beating fast. When she raised her eyes, he had gone, and she saw Hound tramping past. Interesting that Butch had scarpered out of his way.

Sally entered Duffy's, and headed for the booth. She called out, "Soup for two!"

Rebecca smiled at her. "Ready for the interrogation?"

Sally took in a breath. "Yup."

Rebecca drew out her notebook. "First, tell me about Butch and Hound. What happened between them?"

Sally looked thoughtful. "I didn't see what happened, but people told me about it. About nine months ago, Hound was taking a walk along Hagger's Creek. Butch came out of the bushes and blocked his path. He taunted

Hound and tried to pick a fight. Instead of cowering like most people here, Hound stared him down. Then he grabbed hold of him and threw him into the creek. Butch crawled out and slunk away. Since then, Hound's been our hero, and Butch has been a bit quieter. I don't think it'll put him off for good though. He loves looking for trouble. My advice is to avoid him, although it's not easy in this little town. Fortunately, he goes off somewhere for weeks at a time. I don't know where."

"Thanks, Sally. He gives me the creeps. He followed me here after I left the hotel, then Hound showed up and he disappeared."

Sally frowned. "Be careful. Don't let him get anywhere near you, especially if you're alone. Make sure he sees you speaking to Hound. And tell O'Reilly he's been stalking you."

"Good advice. Though I'm sure I can handle him if I need to. I'm trained for that sort of thing. Now let's talk about Hound. He's such an unusual guy, and he's got so many sides to him — tracker, landowner, bully fighter. Can you tell me anything about his life before he came to Conroy?"

"Nothing much, except that his family must be loaded. O'Reilly told me you went to his house."

"I did. It was really impressive. I'd like to know more about it, but that can wait. I also want to hear anything you can tell me about Abigail McBride."

Sally paused for a moment. "All I know is that she was a quiet woman, and Kingsley's wife."

"And Herman Vogel?"

Sally shook her head and shrugged. "Sorry, I'm not being much help. I don't really pay attention to what goes on in Conroy. Mom calls me flighty. Chief O'Reilly just laughs it off. Without him, I would never have held down a job, even in this town." Rebecca's heart went out to her. It must be pretty boring being stuck here.

She put her notebook aside. "Okay. One more question. Maggie Delaney. What about her? When did she move here?"

"Very little again. Not doing well, am I?" Sally sighed. "Anyway, Maggie came here about fifteen years ago and moved straight into that big house. Must've had piles of money to afford it, not to mention all the improvements she's made. I've been there a few times with Chief O'Reilly. He told me the house used to belong to a rich old man who moved to Conroy two or three decades ago. I can't remember his name, just that he peddled goldmining shares."

Rebecca's stomach lurched. "Where did Maggie come from?"

"Some mining town in northern Ontario, I think," Sally replied.

Rebecca stared at her. "You sure about that?"

"Yes, O'Reilly told me. Why? You've gone pale."

"Was it a town called Prospect?"

"That's it, I think."

Rebecca was silent.

"Penny for your thoughts." Sally looked puzzled.

Rebecca grimaced. "Do you believe in fate?"

"Haven't given it much thought. You okay? You look all shaken."

"It's really bizarre. I came here to investigate a homicide, and now I've run into a mystery that looks like it ties back to me, or at least to my family. I'm from Prospect." Rebecca stared into space.

Sally wriggled in her seat. "Wow! That's so strange! They do say fate works in mysterious ways."

Rebecca looked at her. "Please don't tell O'Reilly I'm investigating anything beyond the homicide. He's giving me a tough enough time as it is."

"Don't worry, I can be discreet. Working in a police office has taught me that, at least."

"Thank you, Sally."

Daisy arrived with soup and side salads. They ate their meal in a comfortable silence.

Sally had to leave but Rebecca stayed behind, deep in thought. She felt she'd made a friend in Sally. And she needed her help. The townsfolk would know and trust her - how could they not? That could be invaluable. Rebecca groaned inwardly. She still had nothing concrete to go on, and was beginning to understand the lack of clues the original investigation had turned up. Now she had learned about a goldmining scam linked to Prospect, and almost certainly to her family. She was eager to know more. But first she had a murder to solve.

Rebecca waved at Daisy and headed out to O'Reilly's office. On her way over, she passed Georgie's Pub. Hadn't she said she'd meet Freddie there at five? But there was an afternoon of work to get through first, including a call to Cartwright. She spotted O'Reilly's Chevy parked in the near-empty lot of the station. Good. She wanted to be alone when she spoke to Cartwright. O'Reilly had reluctantly given her an office key, so she was able to get in.

She hurried to his private room and dialled Cartwright's number.

"What's up, Rebecca? You're not due to report back until tomorrow. Is O'Reilly misbehaving?" Cartwright's mocking tone made her feel suddenly protective towards the chief.

"Sir, something bad has happened. O'Reilly found out I'm assessing him and his office. He knows his job's on the line. He confronted me with it this morning."

"What? How did he find out?"

"I don't know. Someone in Orillia must have told him."

"Impossible. Only four people know about it — you, me, Sykes, and the commissioner. I had to tell Hardy in case Sykes files a complaint. I got a right royal dressing down but at least I'm covered. Wait. The commissioner and O'Reilly go back a long way. I'll bet O'Reilly called him. Anyway, don't worry. Just continue with your assignment."

"Yes, sir."

There was a brief pause. "What about the McBride case? Any progress?"

"Not much yet, sir. I'm pursuing a new line of investigation. I'll brief you later, if you don't mind."

"Okay. Just let me know if anything important turns up. I'm busy this weekend but I'll come to Conroy on Monday and have it out with O'Reilly. You can give me an update then. Your week will be over, but I guess I can allow you three more days if you need it. I'll clear it with Sykes." He paused. "Actually, I'll just *tell* him." Rebecca heard a faint chuckle. Her heart sank at the prospect of Cartwright turning up.

"Do you have to come here? Can't you just call O'Reilly?"

He spoke gently. "I'm not checking up on you, Rebecca. It's just that I miss you. I want to see you again."

Rebecca shifted in her chair. "Jonathan, our relationship can't be anything other than professional. You know that."

"Okay then, we'll leave that subject for another time. And don't worry," his voice turned icy, "I'll deal with O'Reilly."

Rebecca put a hand to her head. "Yes, sir. See you on Monday. But the investigation's *my* responsibility. Don't interfere, unless I call on you." Yikes! What was she saying?

He laughed, softly. "Just remember that *I'm* the superintendent, Constable Bradley." The line went dead.

Now what should she do? Cartwright had to back off. She would never resume their affair. Sooner or later his obsession with her would create trouble for both of them. But he didn't seem to care.

Outside the office, a squeal of brakes heralded O'Reilly's return. Rebecca leapt from his chair and out of his room just as he came through the door.

"Well, DC Bradley, I hope you've had a productive day so far. Case solved?" His eyes twinkled. Was he teasing her?

"Getting close, Constable O'Reilly. Find out anything new at Georgie's?"

"Beer's fresh," he said. "Otherwise, nothing. People here don't like outsiders poking about in their town."

Rebecca ignored the barb. "How long have you been here, Constable O'Reilly? I get the feeling you're not a native yourself."

He glowered at her. "Am I a suspect now?"

Damn. She'd made another gaffe. "Just curious, that's all. And no, you're not a suspect." What a short fuse he had.

"Then leave it. You don't have to know anything about me or my past."

Rebecca shrugged. "I was just trying to make conversation. But I do have some questions to ask you about the investigation."

He seemed to relent. Slightly. "All right. Ask away, *Acting* Detective Constable Bradley."

Rebecca wondered if they would ever get along. "First, I'm pleased to inform you that Superintendent Cartwright will be visiting us on Monday morning. Should I pick up coffee and doughnuts on the way to the office, or will you take him to Duffy's?"

He snorted. "I'll buy some half-price doughnuts this evening and leave them out to get stale."

She gave him a cool look. "By the way, I met Sally this morning. We had lunch at Duffy's."

"Cream of broccoli soup." He smiled. She'd never met anyone who had such rapid mood swings — other than Cartwright, but he had medical issues. O'Reilly could shift from happy to angry and back again in seconds. She couldn't do that. Once she got angry, she stayed that way.

O'Reilly licked his lips. "I'm off, right after I make a couple of calls."

Rebecca laid a hand on his forearm. "One quick question, please. You must know Freddie Stafford and Archie MacDougall. They board at Maggie's. What can you tell me about them?"

He stared at her hand, and she took it away. She would have to stop doing that. "I told you before, I know everyone in this town. Freddie's a great guy. Been here for seven or eight years. And Archie, well, he's my only exception. Nobody knows him, other than Maggie. He's rather closed, if you get what I mean. He's been here off and on for nigh on two decades, but he goes away for months at a stretch. When he's in town he does odd jobs for the local businesses. Freddie lines up clients at the hardware store. I don't understand what Archie gets out of this place, but then I don't know where else he'd fit in, apart from a logging camp or a mine site."

"So far, all I've heard him say is hello, goodbye, and thank you," Rebecca said.

O'Reilly snorted. "You're doing well. Never heard him say thanks. But you'll have to quiz me another time. I have to get to Duffy's before the soup's gone." He dashed from the office without making his calls and, Rebecca noted, avoiding further questions.

She thought about the little he had told her. Logging camps and mines were the kinds of places she would expect to meet someone like Archie MacDougall, not Conroy. But this town seemed to have more than its fair share of people with hazy pasts — Archie, Maggie, Hound, Herman, and perhaps even O'Reilly himself.

Chapter 13

Bumped into DI Cartwright in the hallway. He winked and smiled at me. Now I know for sure he likes me. I'll be at his lecture later today. Thinking of asking him for coffee after. He could be a real help with my career plans.
— The diary of Rebecca Sarah Bradley (2003)

Rebecca sat at the small desk outside O'Reilly's office and sorted through her notes. Mid-afternoon, the chief came in, darted a furtive look at her and hurried into his office, closing the door behind him. She heard him talking on the phone. Her questions would have to wait.

She thought about her investigation. Abigail's death could be linked to her husband, Kingsley, and Herman Vogel, and possibly Hound, given his close relationship with her. O'Reilly might also be involved in some way, given his notetaking lapses and his reaction to her question about his past.

Something dodgy was going on in Conroy, Rebecca was sure of it. And she had a strong hunch that O'Reilly knew what it was. Kingsley McBride could be mixed up in it too. She'd been wrong to leave him off her list of suspects just because Cartwright had cleared him last year. She wondered what deep secrets Kingsley was hiding.

At half past four, she rapped on O'Reilly's door.

"What?"

"I'm leaving for the day." She hovered outside his office.

"Humph."

Miserable cuss. He needed a kick in the ass. Rebecca slammed the door behind her, and then headed along Main Street to Georgie's Pub. She looked around for any sign of Butch. He was high on her list of people of interest. If there was shady business going on in Conroy, he would be involved – she'd put money on it. But what could it be? All she had to go on were O'Reilly's curious notetaking oversights, and his evasiveness concerning Herman Vogel and himself. Then there was that disturbing connection to her family, no doubt through her grandfather, Steven Bradley, and his dubious goldmining shares. The puzzles were piling up.

Rebecca now saw that Conroy was very different from her hometown. Prospect had secrets, but everyone pretty much knew what was going on and who was doing it. It seemed that in Conroy few people knew about any activities at all, legal or illegal, not even Sally Partridge. And unveiling Conroy's secrets might be dangerous. Rebecca suspected that this seemingly simple place had a dark underbelly.

Georgie's was dank and sour-smelling, the perfect setting for shady deals. She spotted Freddie in a corner, drinking beer with a young girl who looked underage. Rebecca had done that very thing as a teenager, but she was a cop now.

Freddie looked in her direction and shot to his feet. "Rebecca! You actually came." He glanced at his companion, who sat staring at the table. "Uh, Rebecca, meet Bridget. Rebecca's the famous detective everyone's talking about."

Bridget turned an angelic face to Rebecca and gave her a shy smile. She looked at Freddie, and he cleared his throat. "Well, Bridget. Guess I'll see you later then."

"Okay, Freddie."

Bridget got up obediently and scuttled off.

"Giving extracurricular lessons, Freddie?" Rebecca pulled out a chair and sat facing him. "Please don't let me see that again."

"Yes, ma'am, but don't look at me that way. It's not what you think." He hunched over his drink.

Rebecca wasn't so sure, but changed the subject for now. "Well, weren't you going to buy me a beer?"

Freddie called out, "Harry! A pint of your finest ale, on the double." Then he sank into his seat.

"Thanks, Freddie. Now, let's talk. I went to the Royal Oak today, and a mean-faced punk ogled me from across the street. He followed me to Duffy's and kept staring through the window at me. Turns out it was Butch Taylor, the mayor's son. What do you know about him?"

Freddie grimaced. "Bad news. Stay clear of him. He scares the hell out of most people. Never bothered me, but I wouldn't want to meet him alone at night."

"Has he lived here his entire life?" Rebecca reminded herself to ask O'Reilly if Butch had a criminal record.

Freddie shrugged. "As far as I'm aware. Better to ask someone else though."

"Does he know Abigail McBride's husband, Kingsley?"

"I think so. Kingsley handles most of the town's financial affairs, including the mayor's. Butch must've met him, but I've never seen them talk. Never seen him talk to Mrs. McBride either." He ran a hand through his hair.

"You'll have to do better than that if you want to be my Baker Street Irregular. See what you can find out about Butch, but discreetly. I don't want him to know I'm checking up on him. And don't tell O'Reilly."

"I'll see what I can do, but I'm not a trained investigator, you know. Where should I start?"

"Good question. Just keep your ears open. You meet lots of people at the hardware store. When you can, ask questions about Butch. Get them to talk. I want to know what he does when he's out of town."

"Okay, I'll do my best."

Harry set down Rebecca's glass. He didn't look at her. He had a shaggy mane of hair, a straggly beard, and curly brown hair on his forearms. She stifled a smile. She turned to Freddie, hoisted her glass and saluted. "To your success in the detective business."

He drained his half-filled glass and yelled, "More beer! On the double, or I'll drink at someone else's joint."

"Yeah, go enjoy the Orillia saloons, asshole," Harry growled from behind the bar.

Freddie stiffened and turned to Rebecca. "You're a barrel of laughs, aren't you. Are you always this much fun to be with? What's next, fingernail inspection?" He rubbed his hands on his thighs.

She forced a smile. "Sorry, Freddie. I really am way too serious." Feeling suddenly sorry for herself, she thought of her mother's horrible death and the trauma she had suffered. Was it any wonder she wasn't much fun? She shook her head. "It's five o'clock now, and I'm off duty. What do you want to talk about? Sports? Fishing? Surely not politics?"

"I don't know. I was having a good day until a minute ago."

"All right, I'll be nice. Tell me about Conroy. How come you stay in this place?"

His eyes met hers. "Because life is simple here. Cities are complicated, they're impersonal. I know lots of people in Conroy. When I hang out on the street, folks stop to talk. No one's in a rush."

"I understand. Sometimes I miss that too, but I like the fast pace of big cities. I enjoy Toronto, or even better, New York."

"You can have them. Give me Conroy any day." His beer glass was still empty, and he shot a nasty look at Harry. "What do you want to know? There's not much to tell."

"Maybe there isn't, but I grew up in a small town. There was always something going on. Wasn't always nice, either." An image of her mother's strangled body flashed into her mind and she had to force it back.

"That's true here too." Freddie spoke slowly. He looked concerned. He must have seen the pain on her face. "But people keep their affairs to themselves, despite all the gossip that goes on at Duffy's. You might think nothing at all was happening, and then you might wish you didn't know."

"What do you mean?"

Freddie hesitated, tapping his fingers on the table. Was he afraid? "Okay," he said. "Take Bridget, for instance." He stopped and looked as though he wished he hadn't spoken.

Rebecca leaned across the table. "Go on."

"I know you thought I was flirting with Bridget when you came in. And maybe I was a bit, because she's a pretty girl. The thing is, I'm trying to help her. We were talking about her family situation. I won't go into it since it's something O'Reilly should deal with."

"Perhaps, Freddie, but try me."

He frowned. "All right. But don't let anyone know."

"Depends on what you say." Rebecca knew he'd tell her anyway.

He licked his lips. "All right, then. I think Bridget's being hit on by her father. She won't come straight out with it, but she trusts me. She's starting to hint at things. I don't know enough to tell O'Reilly yet, but I will soon. I

86

just hope you haven't scared her off." He glared at Rebecca.

"Sorry I came so early."

He smiled thinly. "It's not your fault. I know what it looked like. I'm not immune to a pretty face, but I would never take advantage of a kid."

"Maybe she's not such a kid."

"Yeah, she's growing up way too fast. Something has to be done. Chief O'Reilly can take care of it. He's a good cop, but I can get the story faster than him. One more meeting should do it."

"Tread carefully, Freddie. You aren't trained for this sort of thing. Just report your suspicions to O'Reilly. Let him handle it."

Freddie looked hurt for a moment. "I guess you're right." He paused. "Okay, I'll tell him."

"I'm serious about this, Freddie, because if you don't, I will."

"Just leave it to me, all right?" he snapped. She was losing him again.

"Good, then, that's settled. Let's get back to Conroy. What wouldn't I see here, coming from outside?" She patted his wrist. "Come on, Freddie. I need your help."

He grunted. "Well, there's Bridget, like I said, and drugs, same as any small town. Butch figures into that. The odd case of domestic violence, though not much that I know of. Oh yeah, and land speculation." He clapped a hand over his mouth. He really did have an incurable case of speak first, think later. Very useful. Rebecca smiled at him encouragingly.

He wriggled in his chair. "All right then, damn it. There were strangers came through Conroy last year, several times. Three men in a limousine. They stayed overnight at the Royal Oak. They met with Kingsley McBride, and sometimes Mayor Taylor. I also saw them with O'Reilly, just once. They were arguing."

"Hmm. Not such a quiet place then." Now she had new information on O'Reilly. Maybe Cartwright was justified in being suspicious of him. The man wasn't a fool, even if he behaved like one at times.

Freddie perked up. "Yeah, and now that I think of it, a few months ago I went to Orillia and I saw Butch talking to a couple of the limo guys. The same ones that came here."

"Can you describe them?" Rebecca took out her notebook.

He shrugged. "I'm not good at that sort of thing. Except one of them. He stood out from the rest. A monstrous man with curly dark hair and the face of a boxer who's had his mug punched too often. Has a jagged scar on his neck, a knife attack I'd guess, something like that."

Rebecca froze. This had to be Guido Daglioni, the bodyguard of Marco Perez, a southern Ontario crime boss who occasionally visited Orillia. Both men were involved in drugs, gambling, prostitution, and money laundering. Dangerous men, well known within the police force.

"Why would thugs like that be interested in Conroy?"

"Beats me." Freddie fidgeted with his shirt buttons. "O'Reilly probably knows what they were up to." He glanced at his watch.

"Perhaps, but keep this to yourself. Officially, I'm not here to investigate anything other than Abigail's death. Anyway, I think we should go now or we'll be late for dinner."

Freddie grimaced. "You're right. Drink up, and let's boot it out of here." He blew out a huge breath.

Rebecca raised a finger. "One more thing."

Freddie looked worried.

"I didn't see a liquor store in town. Where can I get my hands on a bottle of Irish whiskey?"

His face brightened. He gave her a conspiratorial wink. "Hand me sixty bucks. I'll meet you in the lot."

"Mum's the word." She slipped a few bills under the table, and left the pub.

Freddie joined her a minute later carrying a paper bag and they set off at a brisk pace.

Rebecca smiled despite herself. Small towns. Some things were the same everywhere.

Chapter 14

No coffee with DI Cartwright today, but something even better. Dinner tomorrow, in another town, where no one will see us. He said people would frown upon our relationship and he didn't want to cause me any trouble. He touched my hand when he said it. I was surprised at this intimacy, but I'm excited. Now to decide what to wear . . .
— The diary of Rebecca Sarah Bradley (2003)

Dinner at Maggie's was a treat. Roast chicken, scalloped potatoes, boiled carrots, freshly baked bread. And blueberry pie for dessert. Once more, Rebecca feared for her waistline.

Maggie watched them attack their food and beamed. Even Archie was in a good mood. He said little, but agreed to join them later for whiskey.

Maggie wouldn't accept her help cleaning up, so Rebecca went to her room to write notes on her investigation.

At eight o'clock sharp, Maggie bellowed from the foot of the stairs, "Whiskey and gossip, in that order. Five-minute warning starting now."

Downstairs in the parlour, Rebecca sank into a comfortable chair and gazed out the window. It was still light outside and birds were chirping. Before long they would settle into the trees and go quiet for the night. It was a beautiful evening, and everyone seemed relaxed, including Archie, who lounged in an armchair, cradling his whiskey.

Maggie broke the silence. "Rebecca, you're up. Your entire life story."

"Good heavens, no. You'll all be asleep before the sun goes down. I'll give you the highlights."

"We'll see," Maggie said. "Go on, please."

Freddie shimmied forward to the edge of his chair. He seemed to have recovered from their chat at Georgie's. Archie's face was still dour, but possibly a touch softer than usual.

Rebecca sipped her whiskey. It burned a satisfying trail down her throat. She hadn't intended to say much, but then she changed her mind. Sally had told her that Maggie came from her home town, and Rebecca wanted to find out more. And the only way to do that was to change the habit of a lifetime and open up.

"I was born in a small town in northern Ontario called Prospect." She looked at her companions. Maggie had averted her gaze. "Prospect was, and remains, a mining town. My grandfather, Steven Bradley, arrived in Canada as a dirt-poor immigrant from England. He tried his hand at prospecting, and got lucky. He struck a rich vein of gold and became the owner of a lucrative mine. In the space of a decade he became one of the wealthiest men in northern Ontario. Everything was going well, and then he was murdered." Rebecca watched them again. She recalled Sally saying that Maggie's mansion once belonged to Steven Bradley.

Freddie's mouth hung open. Archie looked at her from beneath his craggy brows. The glass of whiskey in his hand trembled ever so slightly. Maggie was staring at her now. Nobody spoke.

"The murderer was never found. My grandmother, who'd been married to Steven for three years, fell ill and died. She was just forty years old. She had one child, my father, George. A month before she died her sister moved to Prospect from England, in order to care for George. He grew up wild, with money to burn. He never finished high school, but he was bright and strong willed. Nobody fooled with him. They still don't. He's been a decent, if largely absent father to me." Rebecca let out a short laugh. "But he did make sure I got a quality education. Like him, I was independent by nature, and I had my share of adventures, but I never got into serious trouble. I didn't get to know my mother though." Rebecca swallowed. "She was murdered when I was eight years old. As with my grandfather, the murderer was never caught." She slumped back in her chair, tears in her eyes.

"Poor dear," Maggie murmured. Freddie and Archie sipped their whiskeys in silence.

Rebecca sniffed. "Because of the murders, I developed an interest in police work. I studied at the police college in Aylmer and got a job with the OPP in Orillia. My goal is to become a detective and eventually run my own private investigation agency."

Nobody spoke. Even the birds had stopped chirping.

"I'm sorry it's such a tale of woe." Her voice broke.

To everyone's amazement, Archie spoke. "Life can be hard, lassie."

Maggie rose to her feet. "Here's to life, death, intrigue, and mystery." She raised her glass and drained it. Freddie and Archie followed suit.

Rebecca was the last to stand. "May I find the bastard who killed my mother and send him to a special place in hell." She tossed back her whiskey. "Refill, please."

That evening was the most bizarre Rebecca had ever experienced. It was filled with wild tales of tragedy and revenge, laughter and shouting. All thought of Abigail's murder vanished from her head, but she hadn't forgotten

Maggie's connection to Prospect, and Steven Bradley. She needed to have a private chat with Archie too. The tremor in his hand intimated that he, too, was linked to her father in some way.

* * *

The following morning Rebecca awoke with her head pounding. She'd forgotten to set the alarm and Maggie had let her sleep in. She showered quickly and hurried downstairs. Freddie had finished breakfast and left for the day. Archie was sitting in his usual spot, with his gnarly hands wrapped around a mug of coffee. He nodded at Rebecca. She glanced towards the kitchen and heard the clatter of plates and running water.

After a moment, Archie said, "Not to worry, lassie. She's in a right good mood this mornin'. Said she'd be makin' a special breakfast when ye gat up."

"Thanks, Archie. I don't want to offend her. To be honest, I don't feel too good. My stomach's queasy."

He poured a cup of coffee and handed it to her. She sipped it slowly.

"Archie, have you ever been to Prospect?"

"Aye. Ye have a sharp mind, jes' like yer father."

Rebecca was stunned. This was all too much. What was going on in this town? Was she part of it, even central to it in some bizarre way? She put down her cup and stared at Archie, who held her gaze.

Rebecca heard Maggie come into the room. "Sorry I'm late. I drank too much last night."

Maggie grinned. "Not at all. You slept soundly 'cause you let out all the stress that should've been set free long ago. You'll sleep well tonight too, but set the alarm or it'll be stale coffee and cold toast for breakfast tomorrow. It comes from your English heritage, you know. Stiff upper lip, and all that. Am I right?"

"Afraid so." Rebecca smiled weakly.

"Ye should ha' been born a Scot," Archie declared.

Maggie looked at him, started to speak, then shook her head. She ambled back to the kitchen, muttering under her breath.

Rebecca turned her attention back to Archie. "Please tell me. I need to know why you're in Conroy, and how you know my father. My grandfather too, right?"

He spoke gently. "Not now. Some things to tend to first."

"Soon, Archie."

And then it happened. Archie smiled.

Chapter 15

Dinner tonight was a dream. DI Cartwright — Jonathan from now on — was charming and attentive. I find him so attractive, even if he is a few years older than me. I guess it's time I tried to trust men; ever since Mom's death, suspicion has been my default. I've never had a close relationship with a guy. But Jonathan's different. We're going to see each other again.

— The diary of Rebecca Sarah Bradley (2003)

Rebecca lounged in Maggie's backyard under the shade of a maple tree, reviewing her case notes. It was a glorious day, and the summer flowers were in full bloom.

Maggie had invited her to Duffy's for a late lunch. No soup today, Maggie said, but Daisy made a great macaroni and cheese. Rebecca asked if she could talk to her later in the morning, and Maggie agreed.

Kingsley McBride had returned sooner than expected and Rebecca was going to interview him today. She had called his secretary again and leaned on her until she caved in. Then she wondered why Kingsley seemed to be making it hard for her to meet him. Surely he wanted to see his wife's murderer caught. Or did he?

* * *

At half past ten, Maggie brought tea and biscuits and settled into a lawn chair next to Rebecca.

"Maggie, how long have you been in this town?"

"About fifteen years, I reckon. Seems like forever." She laughed softly and began to fuss with the tea.

"Why did you come here in particular?"

Maggie put down the teapot. "I've been dreading this conversation ever since you told me you knew the Delaneys in Prospect." She hesitated. "I'm one of them."

"I know the Delaneys well, but I don't remember you." Rebecca frowned.

"That's because you were a young child when I moved away." Maggie sounded sad. "I've never gone back there. I had a nervous breakdown and eventually moved to Conroy. Before that, I was in various rehab centres. I visited your house a lot when I lived in Prospect. I knew your parents, and even held you in my arms when you were a baby. But I was gone by the time you were four, so you wouldn't remember me. When you came here two days ago, I knew at once who you were. Your name of course, but you also have your father's eyes, though yours are gentler than his were. You've got your mother's cheekbones too." Maggie gazed into the distance and sniffed.

Rebecca was puzzled by her response, and she wondered why Maggie had spoken of her father in the past tense. He was still very much alive. Surely Maggie knew that?

Rebecca's voice quivered. "Maggie, if I don't leave this town soon, I'm going to go nuts."

Maggie laid a hand on her arm. "Prepare yourself, dear. It gets worse. Archie came to Prospect quite often, although he didn't live in the town."

Rebecca nodded. "I know that he's been there."

"What?"

"He told me this morning. I don't remember him, either."

"Well I'll be skewered. What's getting into that man? He's turning into a right chatterbox. He never talks to anyone except me."

"Maggie, what the hell is going on in this crazy town? Everything is so entangled with my own life."

Maggie stared into the distance. "For sure there are magical lines of force running through Conroy. There's no other explanation. This little town has lots of secrets, mostly to do with Kingsley McBride, and possibly Jack O'Reilly, much as I hate to say it. Butch Taylor's involved in something illegal, like drugs. He's in partnership with Harry, the bartender at Georgie's, and he has links to a biker gang that passes through town every few months." Maggie's gaze settled back on Rebecca. "I guess you might be wondering why I came here. The honest answer is, I don't know. I lost my short-term memory when I had the breakdown. I moved here about fifteen years ago. Archie brought me. He and I go back a long way. It's Archie who chose Conroy, but I've never asked him why. When I got here, I was in a terrible state and just wanted to be in some place where nobody knew me. One thing I *have* discovered during my time here, though, is that this is a shadowy and dangerous town. And there's some very strange people live here. Have you met a woman named Jackie Caldwell yet? She works part-time at the Royal Oak Hotel. I mention it because she seems to be spending more time with Kingsley McBride than I would have expected."

Rebecca blew out a breath. "No. I'll do it, now that you've mentioned her, and I'd love to know about anyone else you believe I should talk to. I've been here almost a week, and all I have is scattered bits of information and loads of questions. You've given me a lot to think about. But can't you help me more? There must be a pattern to this confusion."

Maggie was silent for a while. Then she sighed. "I guess it's time to tell you everything I know — well, most of it anyway. But there's a lot I don't know, not yet." And Maggie began.

When she had finished, Rebecca sat on, trying to digest this pile of information. It still bothered her that she hadn't heard of Maggie before, or Archie. Her father had never mentioned either of them, nor had anyone else in Prospect.

Thanks to Maggie, she now had more information than Cartwright and O'Reilly had recorded in their case notes. Maggie had just hinted at a relationship between Herman Vogel and Abigail McBride, along with a secret land deal involving Mayor Taylor and Kingsley McBride. And Rebecca now knew that Conroy's shady deals were all conducted in the dingy shadows of Georgie's Pub.

Things were getting interesting.

Chapter 16

Valentine's Day. I'm going out with Jonathan again tonight. Two nights in a row! There was a glint in his eye when he asked me this morning. He touched my hand again and left it there for a few seconds. I need another new dress. Something sexy this time.
— The diary of Rebecca Sarah Bradley (2003)

Rebecca and Maggie strolled along to Duffy's. The macaroni and cheese lived up to its reputation, and Maggie was great company. It felt like they were becoming friends, although Rebecca was convinced Maggie was keeping something important from her. She'd hoped she would open up during lunch, but Maggie kept the conversation light.

Shorty and Lukas were there, as always, and Rebecca decided to stay behind and question them. She watched the two of them finishing up lunch. They were like a pair of comic book characters. Shorty lived up to his name, and with his curly red hair he looked like a cherub descended from some old painting. Lukas was tall and lanky, pale, with a thin face and stringy blond hair. Shorty was ebullient, whereas Lukas was taciturn.

Maggie got up to leave. "Good luck with those two. They're a funny pair."

Rebecca nodded absently. On her way out, Maggie passed O'Reilly. He gave her a nod and sauntered over to his usual booth, pretending not to see Rebecca.

Was he a crooked cop? She hadn't thought so, until she'd talked to Freddie and Maggie and they'd mentioned his involvement in secret deals. And there were also the omissions from the case notes to consider. She stood up and went over to Shorty and Lukas's table. Arguing again. She had never seen them do anything else.

"Hi, guys. Mind if I ask a few questions?"

Lukas looked up at her and slid lower in his chair. His grey eyes were blank. Rebecca wondered what was going on in his head.

Shorty smiled. "Sure. My name's Shorty, at least that's what they call me around here. The dumb-looking guy across from me is Lukas. We're friends of Hound's."

"I know. Since high school, I believe. Can I join you?"

"Sure, sit down. Take a load off your . . . uh, take a seat." Shorty slid over to make room for her.

"Thank you." Rebecca sat next to him. Opposite, Lukas stared back at her.

"Don't bother about him," Shorty said. "He can talk a bit when he wants to, but nothing intelligent of course."

Lukas appeared to rouse himself. "I would be pleased to converse with you, Detective Constable Bradley. If I appear to be uncommunicative, it's just that I've had to listen to this moron for the past half hour."

"You're a social worker, then, or a psychiatrist?" Rebecca tried to hide the sarcasm in her voice.

He didn't notice or maybe he didn't care. "No, I'm a philosopher. The first one this town has ever produced, and probably the last. Shorty's a study in primitive man. It's rather tedious to listen to his incessant chatter, but one can learn much about the evolution of primates by studying him."

"He's just a dumb alien," said Shorty, "from a backward planet in some remote corner of the galaxy. Hound brought him here on a spaceship he built out of spare parts from the local junkyard."

Rebecca didn't know what to say. These guys acted like children. She wouldn't get any useful information if they kept this up. She smiled weakly. "Would it be okay if I talked to you separately?"

Shorty jumped in. "Not at all. It'd be great if Lukas got lost, but since he can't take a hint, let's move to where we can trade secrets in private."

Apparently indifferent, Lukas turned to gaze out the window. Rebecca moved to another booth, followed by Shorty.

"What can I tell you?" he asked.

She opened her notebook. "You know I'm investigating the death of Abigail McBride?"

He nodded.

"You may also know there are no good leads in the case. Nobody has any idea what happened."

Shorty replied slowly, "I wouldn't be so sure of that."

"What do you mean?" Rebecca leaned forward.

"I mean, Hound probably knows what happened."

She raised her eyebrows. "Why would he know?"

"Because he sees everything and knows everything. Well, maybe not everything, but he figures out things nobody else can. Like the time he helped Chief O'Reilly catch the thief who stole Maggie Delaney's home-baked pies." He giggled.

"I see, but why do you think he knows who killed Abigail McBride?" She was ready to give up on Shorty.

"I didn't say that. I said he *probably* knows what happened."

"Okay, sorry. Why do you think he probably knows?" She sat back, gritting her teeth in frustration.

"Because he never offered to help the chief solve the case."

"But he did check along Hagger's Creek the morning she was killed."

"The chief asked him to. Hound never offered to help."

"Shorty, are you saying you believe Hound knows what happened to Abigail, and he hasn't told O'Reilly?"

"Maybe."

"I don't understand."

"Ask him."

"I will."

"That's all I've got to say. Hound's never told me anything, but Abigail was his best friend. Believe me, he knows. If he didn't, he'd have turned this town upside down until he found the answer." Shorty nodded resolutely.

"Shorty, I don't know what to think. Why would you tell me this now, when Hound's your friend?"

"Because Hound wants to help you, I can see that. He just doesn't know how to do it. With Hound, things are never simple. His mind works differently from other people's. Even that cretin Lukas sees it. That's why we're his friends. It's a lonely world if you're Hound. It's hard to make friends, and even harder to trust anyone."

"Thank you. You've given me a lot to think about. I'll talk to Lukas now." She closed her notebook.

"Forget it. He left while we were yakking. Wait before you talk to him. He won't tell you anything until he's checked it out with Hound. He's strange, but loyal."

Rebecca shook her head.

She left Duffy's and headed along Main to Kingsley McBride's office. There, his secretary told her that he had appointments all day today, and tomorrow, and couldn't be disturbed. Moreover, he would be away all weekend. After a lengthy struggle, Rebecca arranged a meeting for Monday afternoon.

She left his office building. A weird feeling made her glance over her shoulder and she shivered. Once again,

Butch was watching her, this time through the window of his Buick. She hurried off along Main. Butch gunned the motor and followed. She looked around. The street was deserted.

Where the hell *was* everybody?

O'Reilly's office was a block away. She should go straight there and report the jerk, but he was right behind her now. Panicked, she turned into a gap between two buildings, eventually finishing up in the town cemetery.

Then the squeal of brakes sounded. A car door opened and slammed shut. Butch was coming after her. Too late, Rebecca realized that she should have stayed on Main.

She broke into a run.

She darted between the gravestones, hearing his footsteps thud behind her. Her mind raced and her heart thumped. She was getting farther and farther from Main. Then she slowed to a walk. What was she doing, running like this? How could she let this jerk frighten her? She turned around to confront him, and saw Hound rise up from behind a tombstone.

Butch skidded to a halt. All the colour drained from his face. He spun about and made to run, but Hound lunged forward and grabbed him by the scruff of his neck. He picked him up and shook him like a rag doll, then threw him to the ground. Butch lay there, stunned.

Hound stood over him and his hand balled into an immense fist.

"Stop!" Rebecca cried out.

Hound froze. He whirled round to face her. He looked savage.

"Leave him, Hound," she gasped. "Please."

He looked back at the figure on the ground and grunted. Butch scrambled shakily to his feet and stumbled out of the graveyard.

Rebecca and Hound were both breathless. "Thank you," she said. "That man is crazy. He followed me around town yesterday and tried to intimidate me."

Hound nodded grimly. "He won't come near you again. If he does, I'll kill him."

"Please don't talk like that, Hound. I'll be careful from now on, and I'll tell O'Reilly about him."

"Do that, and watch out. This town's dangerous."

"What do you mean?" Rebecca frowned, recalling what Maggie had said.

"Just take care."

"All right, I will. Don't worry. I can take care of myself. I'm going back to Maggie's now to rest before dinner."

"I'll go with you."

"Thank you. I'd like that." Her legs were shaking. So much for taking care of herself.

When they arrived at Maggie's, Hound asked, "Are you still okay for dinner this evening? We could do it another time."

"I'll be fine. I'm pretty resilient, you know." More bravado.

He nodded slowly, turned, and walked away.

O'Reilly had said Hound wasn't someone to mess with when his blood was up. Now she knew what he meant.

Chapter 17

It's official, sort of. But still secret. Jonathan and I are a couple. We'll be discreet, even after I finish constable training. We can find ways to get together on weekends and holidays. I trust him, and that's an amazing feeling. Other than my father, he's the first man I've trusted since I was eight years old.
— The diary of Rebecca Sarah Bradley (2003)

Rebecca climbed upstairs to her room. She collapsed onto the bed and fell asleep immediately, exhausted by the adrenaline. The sound of dinner chatter downstairs woke her at half past six. She showered and put on a clean shirt.

When she arrived at the Royal Oak, Hound was sitting at a corner table, looking smart in a brown suede jacket with a black silk tie. The other diners too were well turned out, and Rebecca realized she should have worn her skirt and blazer.

Hound saw her and rose to his feet, Gulliver surrounded by Lilliputians.

She waved, headed straight towards him, and tripped, crashing into a table of elderly diners. Loaded plates slid to the floor and a carafe tipped over, sending red wine everywhere. People watched in horrified silence while the serving staff fussed around the angry, wine-splattered diners.

Rebecca followed helplessly, offering profuse apologies, but staff and diners brushed her aside. She cast a mortified look at Hound, noticed that red wine had stained the front of her shirt, and hurried off to find a washroom. Just outside the dining room a woman barred her way. The hotel manager gave Rebecca a glare that could have melted steel.

"I'm so sorry . . ." Rebecca began. The hostess's dark eyes had narrowed to slits. Rebecca saw the venom there and felt a chill hand grasp her heart.

"Tell those poor people I'll pay for their dinner and dry cleaning."

"I most certainly shall." The woman swivelled about and disappeared behind a door.

Hound materialized beside Rebecca. "That lovely creature is Mrs. Jackie Caldwell. I've been told she shot her husband in a hunting accident some ten years back. I saw the look she gave you. You'd better watch out." This last was said with a smile.

Rebecca tried to laugh. It withered quickly. What a town. So that was Jackie Caldwell. How many more bizarre characters would she meet?

Hound was waiting for her when she came out of the washroom. She peered down at her stained clothes and sighed.

"Perhaps you'd like to go to Maggie's and change into something fresh," Hound said. "I've told them to hold dinner until eight."

"Thank you. I hope Mrs. Caldwell will let me back in. I think she's digging my grave out back."

Hound chuckled. "I can't guarantee it. She wasn't happy when I told her, but this is the only place in town where you can get an evening meal. We'll risk it."

"You're right. I'll dash back to Maggie's. See you at eight."

"Hold on, my car's out back. I was planning to give you a ride home later."

Rebecca smiled up at him. "You think of everything."

They went out to the parking lot, and Rebecca gaped when she saw a vintage Bentley, like something out of a classic film.

They rode to Maggie's house in silence, and Rebecca felt as if she were in a dream. When they arrived, she turned to thank Hound, but he was gazing through the car window, seemingly lost in his own reverie. She caught his attention and thanked him, then left the car to enter the house.

* * *

In the end, they had a wonderful dinner. When they had finished laughing at Rebecca's earlier dramatic entrance, Hound told her about his unhappy childhood and how he came to be in Conroy.

Rebecca told him her own story, about her family, and life in Prospect growing up as the spoiled only daughter of George Bradley.

As they finished their wine, Rebecca said, "Hound, don't you find it strange that years can pass without anything much happening to you, then in a few days, events seem to change your life forever?"

"It can happen quicker than that." He looked through the restaurant window at the night sky. "What will you do when you finish your work here?"

Rebecca shrugged. "Return to Orillia, I guess, and carry on with my career. And you?"

He shook his head. "If you had asked me two days ago, I'd have said my life will just keep going, day after unchanging day. Now I'm not so sure."

"But you can do anything you set your mind to, Hound. Conroy's just a place you came to for peace of mind, isn't it? You can always move on."

"Where would I go? I've got more than enough money, and I have friends here, good ones. Life in Conroy is pleasant, in a quiet sort of way — at least it was until Abigail died. It could be again, I suppose." He didn't seem convinced.

"How about police work? Have you thought about that? You're interested in mysteries."

"I can't see myself as a policeman on the force. I wouldn't fit in. Perhaps I could become a private investigator. I've thought about it, but not seriously. I enjoy helping O'Reilly when he asks, although I've only been involved in petty stuff. But perhaps you're right, maybe it *is* time for me to consider moving on. I just don't know where."

Rebecca recalled what Shorty had told her earlier. "Hound, Shorty said something strange this afternoon."

He gave her a wary look. "He does that sometimes."

"He said you might know what happened to Abigail. Actually, he said you *do* know. What did he mean by that?"

Hound grunted. "He's a clever fellow. At least, he is when he's not having a go at Lukas."

"You mean he's right?"

Hound huffed out a long, slow breath. Rebecca's heart began to race.

"Hound, I'm here to solve her murder, and you wait until now to tell me?"

"Sorry, but I've been trying to figure out what to say. It's difficult, and I can't even be sure I'm right." He shifted his enormous bulk, and his chair creaked.

"I don't understand. Why? And why didn't you tell Cartwright or O'Reilly last year?"

Hound was silent for a moment. "Because I'm protecting someone."

"Who?"

He sighed. "Herman Vogel."

"Please. Just tell me everything." Rebecca gripped the table edge.

"Not tonight. I need to talk to Herman first and let him know. I'll do that tomorrow morning. He won't like it."

"You're kidding. You really won't tell me now? Hound, Abigail was murdered." Rebecca's hand tightened on the table, but he remained silent. She sat back. "Okay, then. Just show up at the station tomorrow at nine. Tell O'Reilly and me you have new information about Abigail's murder."

"I can't," Hound said simply.

"Why not?"

"Because she wasn't murdered."

"What!"

"Like I said before. I'll tell you about it tomorrow." And Hound leaned back in his chair and folded his arms.

Chapter 18

Hound stayed up most of the night, worrying about Herman. He wanted to help Rebecca, but he also wanted to spare Herman. He couldn't avoid telling Rebecca now that he'd begun, but Herman had bound him to silence. He didn't know what to do. He kept picturing Herman driving Abigail's body to her home while Kingsley was at work.

Kingsley's secret deals were distressing enough for Abigail, but when she learned that Herman was in charge of the finances her father had invested, she felt so betrayed that she hanged herself. She did it in Herman's basement. He'd told Hound that he had to take her back to her home. Herman was a deeply religious man, and burying Abigail without a church funeral was unthinkable.

Abigail had told Hound in confidence that she was planning to leave town with Herman, so he wasn't worried when she disappeared. He was glad she was leaving Kingsley; such a secretive and cynical man didn't deserve her. And she had become more and more quiet and reserved every year that she was married to him. She was still his best friend, though, and they would meet again. But when O'Reilly gave him the news of her horrific death, it shook him to the core. He went to Herman's house, and was told everything. Since then, he couldn't get the image of Abigail hanging in the basement out of his mind.

* * *

The morning after his dinner with Rebecca, Hound rose early and headed into the town. As he approached Herman's Fuel Emporium, he saw blue flashing lights. A police van and an ambulance stood outside, and a small group of townspeople had gathered, whispering among themselves.

O'Reilly was leaning against his dust-covered Chevy. He waved to Hound.

"What happened, chief?"

"Herman was murdered last night, sometime after closing." O'Reilly pointed at a man standing beside a blue Honda Civic. "That guy over there came in early and found no one on duty, so he went behind the station to look. He found Herman lying in a pool of blood, stabbed in the back." O'Reilly shook his head, his voice weary. "Jesus, Hound, another of my people murdered."

Hound's stomach lurched. How could this be?

"Was he robbed?"

"No," said O'Reilly, "that's the puzzling part. Herman didn't have much money on site. People mostly use credit or debit cards these days. Gas station robberies don't happen often, especially around here."

They watched the police photographers going about their work.

Hound looked at O'Reilly. "Why aren't you helping with the investigation, chief?"

"Because that asshole Cartwright ordered me to stay clear." O'Reilly struck the door of the Chevy with his fist. "This is *my* town. The bastard has no right cutting me out." He paused. "Uh oh, here comes Miss Fancy Pants in her fancy car."

With a squeal of brakes, Rebecca's convertible came to a sudden halt. She leapt from her car and stood still, peering around the lot.

"Oh no," mumbled Hound.

O'Reilly looked at him. "What is it, Hound? Get it out, fast, before she comes over."

Hound swallowed hard. "I came here this morning to tell Herman I was going to reveal what happened to Abigail."

"What! You know who murdered Abigail?"

"Except it wasn't murder. I wish I'd told you last year when I first found out."

"Out with it. Quick."

"Abigail . . . Abigail committed suicide. Herman told me she hanged herself." Hound looked down.

"Go on. Bradley's heading towards us like an express train."

Hound sighed. "Abigail and Herman were lovers. They were planning to run off together. Abigail had had enough of Kingsley and his shady deals. So instead of coming home from Parker's that day, she came here, and Herman drove her to his house. She hid out there for two weeks, until she found out Herman was involved in Kingsley's schemes. It was too much for her to bear, and she killed herself. Herman waited two days, and then took her home. It was Herman who put her on the kitchen chair. Nobody saw him do it. I asked him what had happened, and he told me everything."

"Hound, you're an idiot. How could you keep that from me?"

"I'm sorry, chief. It's just that I promised Herman I wouldn't tell anyone. I didn't want the whole town to know about their affair, I wanted to protect him from the stares and the gossip."

Rebecca hurried up to them and the men fell silent. She glared at Hound. "You let the investigation proceed although you had crucial evidence. You should have told me everything last night."

She was right, of course. Hound suddenly understood the enormity of his mistake. And O'Reilly was right too — he truly was an idiot. "I don't know what to say, other than I'm sorry. I made Herman a promise, and I wanted to respect Abigail's reputation, and her privacy. I know that's no excuse." He wrung his hands.

"We're going to O'Reilly's office now to take down your statement." Rebecca sounded weary.

O'Reilly frowned.

"Cartwright will want a firsthand account of this," Rebecca said. "Sykes's detectives are already here and he told them he'll come to Conroy as soon as he can. Dammit — Sykes — that's all I need right now." She shook her head. "Hound, go over and wait by my car. I need to talk to Constable O'Reilly, and then I have to call Superintendent Cartwright. But don't you dare leave on me."

Hound nodded and trudged off.

"O'Reilly, this is really bad," Rebecca said. "Cartwright will be furious. We don't know who stabbed Herman. But if it turns out that whatever information Hound withheld could have prevented it, we're all in trouble. Come to the station with me. Cartwright won't let you in on Herman's case, but you can still help with Abigail, as long as he doesn't cut you out of her case too."

O'Reilly nodded.

Rebecca called Cartwright. He had heard the news about Herman, and he was in a foul mood. After wishing the entire town of Conroy would go to hell, he ended the call before she could tell him about Hound's suicide claim.

* * *

Rebecca was numb with shock. O'Reilly sat next to her, with Hound hunched over on the opposite side of the table.

"Let's begin." Rebecca switched on the tape recorder. "Friday, 6 July, 2007. DC Rebecca Bradley, Orillia OPP, Central Region, joined by Senior Constable Jack O'Reilly, Conroy office, questioning Mr. Thaddeus Hounsley about the death of Abigail McBride on or around 26 May, 2006. The interviewee is asked to state his name, address and telephone number, for the record."

Hound began to talk.

Chapter 19

I can barely concentrate in class. All I can think about is Jonathan. He's finished lecturing, but he invited me to spend next weekend in Toronto with him. I'm excited, but really nervous too.
— The diary of Rebecca Sarah Bradley (2003)

Rebecca left the station, still angry that Hound hadn't talked to her last night, and stunned by his claim about Abigail's death. The whole investigation was a mess. She headed to Duffy's to think.

When she arrived, Daisy was nowhere to be seen, and a new woman was staring at her from behind the counter. Rebecca ordered a coffee and went to a window booth. Butch drove past and glanced at the shop. He didn't seem to notice her. Well, thanks to Hound, Butch no longer worried her.

Cartwright was in meltdown. Herman's murder had rekindled talk of his failure to solve the McBride case. Sykes had taken over Herman's investigation, and he would take over Abigail's case as well. He'd solve both of them and make her and Cartwright look like fools. She would never get into the CIB now, leaving her mother's murder less and less likely to be solved. And, if it was true that Abigail had taken her own life, her longshot hope that these cases were linked was over. She was further away from catching her mother's killer than ever.

The door to Duffy's squeaked open and the young girl she'd seen with Freddie came in. Bridget bought two large coffees to go and hurried out to join Butch, who was parked nearby. Rebecca watched her hand him the coffee and climb in beside him.

Butch gave Rebecca a hostile glare, and the Buick sped away.

Seeing Bridget with this unsavoury character made Rebecca even more dejected. She tossed a few coins on the table and left Duffy's. She decided to visit the library and find out more about Conroy's history before Sykes turned up. He would demand to know everything she had discovered so far, and she'd better give a good account of herself. She still led the McBride investigation until told otherwise.

The library was near the centre of town, housed in an imposing limestone building that had been a bank in more prosperous times. She entered between two weather-beaten Doric columns to find Jackie Caldwell behind the checkout counter. Typical small town, people often had more than one job in Prospect too. And of course, Jackie was bound to recognize her, given their encounter at the Royal Oak.

She took a breath and straightened up. "Hello."

Jackie raised her head and Rebecca saw her jaw muscles tighten.

"What can I do for you?" Her tone was caustic. 'I hope you manage not to trip up on anything this time.'

Rebecca decided to let that one slide. "I'm interested in articles and media clippings on the murder last year, and any books that cover the history of this area. Can you help?" Rebecca smiled sweetly and steeled herself. Jackie's head swayed slightly. It made her think of a cobra preparing to strike.

Jackie looked her up and down. "There may be *some* information here, but not much. The Orillia library would have more. You can check that yourself."

"I'll start here, thank you." Rebecca bristled under the woman's hard stare.

Jackie got up, disappeared into a back room, and closed the door behind her. Rebecca scanned the bookshelves while she waited. Nothing but romances, detective novels and aging reference texts. The musty smell of old books was soothing. Her father had a large library at home and Rebecca had read most of the books in it. She'd grown up with few friends and lots of free time. The other kids were afraid of her, and their parents didn't socialize with her father. After her mother's death, books had been her most comforting companions.

Jackie emerged from the back door a few minutes later carrying a folder of clippings and a book coated with dust. She laid the book on the desk and stacked the clippings beside it. She smiled malevolently.

Rebecca looked at the dusty book. *Horrible Hoax: The Promise of Gold Near Conroy, Ontario.* Curious, she looked at the publication date. 1984, two years after her grandfather was murdered. She suddenly remembered where it happened. He'd died on the Trans-Canada Highway, just north of Conroy. Her stomach turned over.

"Can I take this with me?"

Jackie snatched up a sheet of paper and thrust it across the counter. "Fill this out, and show me two pieces of ID."

Rebecca completed the form and handed over her driver's license and credit card. Jackie studied them like a customs official looking at a fake passport. Rebecca wondered why she was so hostile. Surely it wasn't that clumsy fiasco at the Royal Oak Hotel? It wasn't like she had done it on purpose. There had to be another reason.

Rebecca found nothing in the clippings that she hadn't already seen in the police files. She left the clippings on the desk, scooped up the book, and left the library.

Maggie's house was deserted when she arrived, which suited her just fine. She wasn't in the mood to talk. She tiptoed upstairs to her bedroom, shut the door and leaned against it, blinking back tears of defeat.

Hours later, she was awakened by a loud banging on her bedroom door.

"Dinner's in five!"

"Sorry, Maggie. I don't feel well. I'll pass on the meal tonight."

She could hear Maggie breathing outside the door. "Please, just leave me alone. And don't be concerned. I'm okay."

* * *

His head in a whirl, Hound hurried from O'Reilly's office. He suspected that Herman's death was linked to Abigail, and he was determined to find the killer. He didn't see Butch drive past, watching him with a wolf's predatory eyes.

He arrived home and went downstairs to his library, seeking inspiration from his murder mystery collection. Finding none, he emptied his mind of all thoughts and sank into a trance. He seldom did this as it took so much out of him, but sometimes it was the only way to think deeply about a problem.

He pictured Conroy and the people who lived there, bringing them up one by one, like a slideshow. Then he eliminated them, until only Kingsley McBride remained. But Kingsley wasn't right either. Why would he kill Herman? After all, he was the principal manager of van Rijn funding for those gold mine and subdivision deals.

Several hours later, Hound emerged from the trance and climbed slowly to his second-floor bedroom. He collapsed onto the bed, drained of energy, and fell asleep for over twenty-four hours. He finally got up on Sunday morning.

Chapter 20

Jonathan called this evening and talked for an hour. I had to cut him off in the end. I want to see him again, soon, but I have loads of homework to do, and I can't afford to fail.
— *The diary of Rebecca Sarah Bradley* (2003)

Superintendent Cartwright arrived at ten o'clock on Sunday morning, accompanied by DI Sykes. Detectives Chad and Hadi were huddled in a corner of O'Reilly's office, pointedly ignoring Rebecca. This must have been Sykes's doing, because Hadi usually treated her with respect. She admired his quiet and thoughtful manner, which masked a razor-sharp mind. In contrast, Chad was a loud football-player type who favoured fast cars and, by all accounts, fast women. He'd made a couple of half-hearted passes at her, but Rebecca knew she wasn't really his type. She'd paid no heed. She was well aware that the male officers in Orillia discussed her behind her back, but growing up in Prospect as George Bradley's daughter, she'd gotten used to that.

She was standing in the station's reception area, listening to the angry voices coming from behind

O'Reilly's closed door. Sally Partridge hovered next to her, wide-eyed.

Rebecca's nerves were on edge. She was prepared for tension between Cartwright and O'Reilly, and wondered how Sykes would fit in. She figured he had purposely left the McBride investigation to Cartwright so that he would botch it — which he had. And what was Sykes saying now?

The tempest in O'Reilly's office abated. The door flew open and smashed against the wall as Cartwright stormed out, followed by the diminutive Sykes, whose penetrating grey eyes took in the outer office as he passed by Rebecca, ignoring her. Despite his physical stature, Sykes commanded enormous respect. He was confident and intelligent, whereas Cartwright was pompous and petty. They both marched out of the office and towards Cartwright's car.

She went in to check on O'Reilly. He sat slumped in his worn leather chair, his head lowered, feebly pushing papers around on his scratched oak desk. He looked nothing like the man Rebecca had first met.

He raised his head. "Well, DC Bradley, what do I do now? Who will hire me after Cartwright's ruined my reputation?"

Rebecca felt badly for him. She suddenly remembered that her assignment from Cartwright included assessing O'Reilly's competence, and that his job was on the line. Cartwright would use any excuse to cut him loose. "I'm sorry things have come to this, Constable O'Reilly." She paused. "Can I call you Jack when we're alone? You can call me Rebecca if you'd like."

"Just O'Reilly, please. No one's called me Jack for decades. But I'll call you Rebecca. And I apologize for the rough ride I gave you. It wasn't fair." He mustered a wan smile.

"Apology accepted," Rebecca said. "Don't tell Cartwright, but I've grown to like you, although I've also considered giving you a kick in the ass from time to time." She gave him a lopsided grin.

"I'll try to be more civil, but don't look for perfection. I'm too old to change all my bad habits."

Rebecca smiled broadly. Actually, she didn't want him to change. She did like him, in spite of his rudeness — or maybe because of it. She just hoped he wasn't crooked "Okay then," she said to O'Reilly. "So what do we do now? At any moment, Sykes will be on my back. I bet you've never met anyone like him before."

"Heard about him, of course. Best homicide detective the force has ever had, so they say. He said nothing while Cartwright and I went at it. He didn't have to. He's not out to get me, isn't even interested. He looked at me like I was a bug."

"That's Sykes all right. He scares me. It might seem like he ignored you just now, but nothing escapes his notice. I'm not so lucky. He's determined to keep me out of the CIB. But please don't repeat that to anyone." Not that she cared all that much. It was too late now. She would tell him about Hound's claim, but Sykes wouldn't believe it either, and her own line with him was thinner than O'Reilly's with Cartwright. She might as well kiss her coveted CIB job goodbye.

O'Reilly said, "Completely. I wouldn't put you at risk. You might be my only friend. You're the only one who really knows what I'm going through. Can I call you my friend?"

Rebecca nodded. "But bear in mind that I'm still working on this case. I have to go wherever it takes me."

"Sure."

"That's settled then. Now, tell me what you know about Herman Vogel, Kingsley McBride, Butch Taylor, and Georgie's Pub. Do Butch first. He's been gnawing at me for days. Has he got a criminal record? Oh, and while you're at it, throw in Marco Perez."

O'Reilly looked surprised. "Okay, Rebecca, I'll tell you everything I can. But forget Butch. He doesn't have a record, though I've pulled him in a few times and threatened to arrest him. He's just a stupid thug who'll get himself in really big trouble someday. His father, Charlie Taylor, the mayor of Conroy, has vouched for his whereabouts at the times Abigail and Herman were killed. There's no evidence linking Butch to either murder. Charlie and I have been friends for fifteen years, and I have no reason to doubt him." O'Reilly cleared his throat. He suddenly looked uneasy. "As for Kingsley McBride, he's so secretive that I can't tell you anything useful. What else? Oh, yeah, Georgie's Pub. It's just what it appears to be, a sleazy bar run by a sleazy guy, Harry Adams. Harry is Butch's only friend in town. He too has alibis for the times of the murders. You'll have read his alibi for Abigail in my case notes." Rebecca nodded.

"As for Marco Perez," O'Reilly said, "you probably know more about him than I do." He got to his feet and began to wander about the room.

Rebecca was sure he was keeping something important from her. "Thank you, O'Reilly. You can understand why I want to stay a step or two ahead of Sykes. I need to know every detail you can give me."

O'Reilly turned to her. "I'm with you all the way, Rebecca, but we need more information. And I know who to ask."

Rebecca was doubtful. "You mean Hound? Why him?"

"Because he's got a sharp mind, and he probably knows more than he's told us. Anyway, Sykes will go after him when he learns about his friendship with Abigail, so we need to warn him and bring him on board. That shouldn't be hard to do." He grinned and tilted his head to the side.

Rebecca felt her cheeks grow hot. "Okay, let's go find him. I gave him a real grilling on Friday, though, and I don't know how he feels about me. I tried calling him this morning to see how he was doing, but no luck."

O'Reilly seemed filled with renewed vigour suddenly. "Then we'll try again. Nobody can stay hidden for long in this town — except Abigail."

Chapter 21

Hound was on his way to town. He felt light-headed, as if he were perched high above the lush, midsummer landscape. The world around him was sharp and clear, colours were vivid, and odours he wouldn't normally notice assailed him. He hadn't gone far when he saw Rebecca speeding his way, with O'Reilly beside her in the car. They skidded to a halt.

"Jump in!" Rebecca yelled over the engine noise. "There's no time to lose."

Hound wedged his massive body into the back seat and leaned forward. "What's up?"

"Cartwright and Sykes," O'Reilly shouted, as the car accelerated away from the town.

Hound looked puzzled. "Sykes?"

O'Reilly twisted around. "Ever watch *Star Wars*?"

"Yes . . ."

"Darth Vader."

Hound nodded. "Are we fleeing town?"

"Yup. We're smuggling you out to get you ready to meet Vader." O'Reilly grimaced.

Hound settled back into his seat. "Then head north on the Trans-Canada. I'll take you to a special place where we can talk in private."

Buffeted by the wind, they motored on in silence. Then Hound tapped Rebecca on the shoulder and pointed to County Road Thirty-Four. She turned and drove along it until Hound indicated a dirt road branching off to the right. "Turn here and drive to the end. The place we're headed for isn't far from there."

They pulled up at the edge of a large meadow enclosed by dense forest. Rebecca got out of the car and gazed about her. Tall grass swayed in a soft breeze. Bees moved amid the brightly coloured flowers. There was no other sound than their gentle buzzing.

Hound nodded in satisfaction. "We're safe now."

* * *

Hound crossed the meadow and went into the forest, threading his way along a narrow trail that petered out into dense bush, with Rebecca and O'Reilly crowding close behind. After a few minutes, they emerged into a clearing.

Hound turned to them. "Follow me. You are about to enter my secret abode." He crossed the clearing and plunged into a thicket that ran up against a granite cliff, and then led them into a small cleft in the rock face. It widened almost immediately to become a tunnel, which led into a dark cavern.

Hound struck a match and put it to a lantern secured to the wall, next to a crude wooden table and two chairs. Rebecca saw makeshift cupboards, a heavy oak stool, and a massive folding cot. She heard water trickling in a small opening in one corner.

Hound waved an arm. "Honoured guests, welcome to my home away from home."

"Well I'll be damned." O'Reilly circled slowly about. "Hound, you're amazing."

Rebecca put her hand on the wall and felt a tingle, like a tiny electric shock. "How did you find this place, Hound?"

"I followed the dirt road one day while I was roaming about the countryside. When I got to the rock face I took a closer look and found the cleft. I cleaned the place up, put in the furniture, and now I come here whenever I want to be alone. Really alone. There are some Indigenous people who hunt in this area, but except for one of them whom I've gotten to know a bit, they give the cave a wide berth."

"Now what? Why did you bring us here, Hound?" O'Reilly rubbed at the back of his neck.

"Now we talk. I led you to the cave because I've always felt safe here. You're both welcome to use it whenever you like."

There was something about the cave that unsettled Rebecca. She could tell that O'Reilly was nervous too.

Hound began to pace. The cave seemed to energize him. "Now, Rebecca. What did you want to ask me about?"

She folded her arms. "Well, it's all about DI Sykes. Superintendent Cartwright's a regular guy — kind of. All right, O'Reilly, I know, but he doesn't hide anything. What you see is what you get, at least when you know him. Sykes is another matter. Nobody seems to know anything about his life before he joined the OPP — where he was born and raised or what work he did, nothing. I got curious and tried to find out. He saw what I was doing and flew into a rage. He told me to back off, or else. It put me on my guard, and I became more determined than ever to suss him out. He's avoided me ever since, and done whatever he can to block me from joining the CIB. Now he's come to Conroy to take charge of Herman's case. He'll dig into my work on Abigail McBride and take over that case too."

O'Reilly lay sprawled on the cot. "What's your relationship to Cartwright? Boyfriend and girlfriend?"

Rebecca stiffened. So he knew. Probably everyone in the OPP did too. "It's over now," she stated flatly.

Hound spoke quickly. "Good. That means you're protected from Sykes."

She frowned. "I'm sure not counting on it. Sykes has some kind of hold on Cartwright."

"Why do you need to prepare me to meet Sykes?" asked Hound.

"Because he'll want to know about your connection to Abigail and Herman. Then he'll know you withheld information from Cartwright last year. You could get charged for doing that."

Hound nodded. "Well, I want to find Herman's murderer too. But there's more to it than that. The truth is I'm fed up with Conroy and its secrets. My friends Abigail and Herman are both dead. But what about you, chief? You know most of Conroy's secrets. What do you think?"

O'Reilly paused before answering, his face ashen. "I'm in big trouble," he muttered finally. "I need help more than either of you, and fast."

Rebecca spoke sharply. "I think it's time you spilled the beans, O'Reilly. The whole damned can."

Chapter 22

Cartwright decided to check the crime scene at Herman's Fuel Emporium. He and Sykes set off in his car.

"What do you make of all this, Sykes?"

"All what, sir?"

Cartwright waved a hand at the miserable streets. "This town. What else? Two homicides that even your crack team hasn't been able to solve. What's going on? There must be a link between these deaths."

"The second murder just happened, sir. And anyway, the first one was *your* investigation. But let's forget that and consider the motives. Money? Love? Hate? Revenge?" Sykes shook his head. "I should have taken on the McBride case last year. I was busy then, as you know, but I'm here now. Something in this town doesn't smell right. I think I'll stay awhile and see what I can dig up."

"Yes, yes, go ahead. I want both cases solved. That fool O'Reilly got in my way last year. I've kept him off the Vogel homicide. He'll be gone soon, so you won't have to put up with him."

Sykes held up his hand. "Actually, sir, I want him around. He might prove useful. I'll let you know when I'm done with him."

Cartwright bristled, but said nothing.

They arrived at the crime scene. Sykes hurried off to speak to his detectives while Cartwright stood beside his car. Absently, he stroked the scar on his cheekbone. He hoped Sykes would fail to solve Herman's murder. Better still would be if Rebecca cracked the McBride case and found a link with Herman's death. That would take the celebrated DI down a notch or two. He was sure Rebecca was right — Sykes had set him up last year.

But he could do nothing about it, not while Sykes had that damned Sword of Damocles hanging over him. He stroked his scar again. Only Sykes knew the truth — that the scar he so proudly bore was self-inflicted. During the shootout he'd run away to hide. Rather than confronting the criminals, Cartwright had in fact tripped up as he scuttled away, and only Sykes saw him shoot himself. It was all a clumsy accident. Afterwards, not only did the bastard keep quiet, he actually put Cartwright forward for a Medal for Police Bravery. Cartwright accepted, and still Sykes didn't say a word. The medal had done wonders for his career, but Cartwright lived in constant fear that someday Sykes would use his knowledge to ruin him.

Sykes returned to the car. "We should go back to O'Reilly's office, sir. I need to know what Constable Bradley has found out while she's been in town."

"DC Bradley, actually." Cartwright managed to look Sykes in the eye.

Sykes returned his gaze. "*Acting* DC. And not for much longer. After she gives her briefing, I'll take over the McBride case. I won't need her anymore."

Cartwright shuffled his feet. Rebecca would have a fit. He was beginning to regret the offer he'd made her. He looked at Sykes. "Can I ask a favour? Would you mind keeping her on the case? I went out of my way to give her this opportunity."

Sykes gave him a piercing look, then he shrugged. "Okay, but she'll be reporting to me."

Chapter 23

Jonathan called again, every day for the past week. It took me half an hour to get rid of him this time. I need to study for my exams and he seems totally insensitive to my needs. I think I made a mistake in getting involved with him.
— The diary of Rebecca Sarah Bradley (2003)

Hound and Rebecca stood side by side in the dim light of the cave, waiting to hear what O'Reilly had to say.

Rebecca gave an impatient sigh. "Out with it, chief."

O'Reilly ran his tongue over his lips. "Okay, here goes. I'm involved in a land development deal a few miles north of Conroy. Housing, shops, recreational facilities, a complete new community in fact. Kingsley McBride, Mayor Charlie Taylor, and Herman Vogel are part of the scheme — well, Herman *was*. But McBride's the main player. When I got caught up in it there wasn't anything illegal going on, as far as I could tell. Then the whole thing turned bad. A crime boss named Marco Perez got involved. McBride brought him in without consulting Herman or me, or even the mayor. I would've opposed it if I'd had the chance, believe me. I was horrified when I found out, but what could I do?" He shook his head. "Kingsley should never have gone near him. After Perez came on board, there was no backing out. At least, not without getting myself in really hot water."

Rebecca said, "Why would anybody want to start a development near Conroy? There aren't many jobs. Orillia and Midland are the closest cities of any size, and both of them are more than half an hour's drive away." So her suspicions about O'Reilly being involved in something nefarious were well founded. The thought saddened her.

"There'll be lots of jobs soon, good ones too. There's an abandoned gold mine a few miles north of Conroy. Kingsley has known about it for some time. He told me he could've developed it a decade ago, but the price of gold was too low to make it viable. Now the gold price has risen, so he got hold of a big shot in the mining industry and set up a partnership." O'Reilly glanced at Rebecca.

Rebecca's face went white, and she swayed on her feet. Hound grabbed the oak stool and helped her sit down.

O'Reilly spoke softly. "It's true, Rebecca. McBride's mining partner is your father. I didn't make the connection until I recalled your family tragedy. I read about your mother's murder many years ago. I should have guessed who you were when I heard your last name and saw your glitzy car and chic clothes. But I still don't understand why on earth George Bradley's daughter would become a policewoman?"

Rebecca shook her head. "Maggie lived in Prospect. Archie was there too, and I had no idea. Twenty-five years ago my grandfather launched a dodgy goldmining venture near Conroy. And now I learn that my father is Kingsley's partner on the very same mine! I don't know what's going on."

There was a long silence. Water trickled somewhere deep inside the rocks. She sighed. "Don't worry, I'm okay. Let's just get on with it."

Hound looked at O'Reilly. "Let me guess, chief. Kingsley McBride offered you a share in the land deal on condition you stay mum and help him keep it secret. Right?"

O'Reilly nodded. "Close enough. He recruited me a few months before Abigail died, and before Perez showed up. He didn't offer a share in the deal, just money — quite a lot too. That's what got me hooked."

"And Herman? Was he brought in at the same time?"

"No. He'd been involved for a considerable length of time."

Hound nodded. "He was a major source of funds."

"Yes. How did you know?" O'Reilly gave him a puzzled look.

"Despite appearances, Herman had access to big money. And I know where it came from."

"Six million dollars," said O'Reilly. "With a promise of more to come, so Charlie Taylor told me. And McBride put up his own money, a fair whack I believe. I still don't know where it came from. He's only a local accountant."

Hound looked from one to the other of them. "I have an idea of what's going on, and why."

Rebecca looked up. "Tell us."

Hound's forehead wrinkled. "There are some things I haven't told you yet." He gave Rebecca an apologetic shrug. "I believe Kingsley found out long ago that the gold mine had commercial potential. He already had the rights to it when he went to the Netherlands. While he was there, he set up a partnership with Nicholas van Rijn, Abigail's father, to help finance the mine and land deals. He also fell in love with Abigail, who was then named Marijke. Or maybe he just fell in love with her father's money.

"The man Marijke was having an affair with was Herman Vogel. When her parents found out, they tried to stop it. He was a second cousin, twenty years older than Marijke, and he owed them money. They coerced him into rejecting Marijke and sent him to Canada to look after their subdivision investment, and especially to keep an eye on Kingsley. He moved to Conroy and bought the old gas station with money the van Rijns gave him to make him look legitimate. Marijke, now Abigail, knew about the station, but not the mine or the subdivision deal, which were the real reason for his presence in Conroy. Until she ran away from Kingsley, that is. As for Herman, he wasn't a strong man, but he had a kind heart and he loved Abigail. He wanted to be near her, even if he couldn't have her for himself. That's why he agreed to work for the van Rijns and move to Conroy."

Hound looked at them. "Kingsley needed someone with mining expertise, so he went to George Bradley, the goldmining magnate. Hence, the Bradley connection. The mayor and Chief O'Reilly were brought into both deals because Kingsley knew they'd find out anyway. Better to have them on board."

O'Reilly stared at the ground. "That's what I used to think. Now I realize I've been a complete idiot. I never knew any of this."

Rebecca patted his arm. "Don't blame yourself, chief. How could you know? But I'd like to hear more about why Perez was brought aboard, and the nature of his involvement with Kingsley. You sure you can't help with that?" And if he could help, she thought, then he was in even bigger trouble than just taking a bribe.

"Sorry," O'Reilly said, and eyed her suspiciously. "I really don't know how Perez got brought in. I don't know what arrangements they made, but I do know Perez is involved in money laundering. By the time he showed up, it was too late to back out. At first I thought everything was legitimate. There's nothing wrong with opening a mine, or developing land. I just figured Kingsley was keeping everything under the radar to prevent other speculators moving in." O'Reilly lay back on the cot and put an arm across his face.

Hound took up his story. "Last year, Abigail found out what Kingsley was up to, and about Perez. She decided she'd had enough. She approached Herman for help and he took her in. Then she found out about his role in the deals and his business links to her family. Devastated by his betrayal, she hanged herself. At least, that's what Herman told me, and it makes sense." Hound blinked back tears.

Rebecca frowned. "It still sounds thin to me, Hound. The autopsy didn't find any evidence to suggest suicide. What's more, there's no way anyone could possibly find gold near Conroy. It's too far south of the rich veins embedded in the Canadian Shield. The geology around here isn't right, unless there's some sort of anomaly that I don't know about. I'll ask my father about it. Anyway, I shouldn't be interrupting you. Please go on."

Hound swallowed. "Then *you* came to town. When you spoke to Herman, it's my guess that all of his bad memories about Abigail resurfaced, along with his grief and shame. He might even have decided to go to the police and confess. If so, and if Perez found out, maybe he got one of his thugs to murder him. All just speculation, but I can't think of any other explanation."

"Even if that were true," Rebecca said, "I still believe an important piece of the puzzle around Abigail's death is missing." She stood up. "At least you've given me a clear direction for my investigation."

"*Our* investigation." O'Reilly's voice rang out. He was his old self again.

Chapter 24

Late on Sunday morning, Lukas sat across from Shorty in a corner booth at Duffy's.

"Where's Hound?" asked Lukas.

"Don't know."

"Oh very helpful."

Shorty ignored the dig. "I'm worried, Lukas. Hound's disappeared. I went to his house yesterday and knocked on all the doors, but there was no answer. I left messages and haven't got a response. Maybe he's on one of his retreats."

"Good point. You're making progress."

But Shorty wasn't listening. His thoughts had turned to Herman. He wondered who would want to kill him, and why. He knew it couldn't have been robbery.

"We need to find Hound," said Lukas.

Shorty nodded. "Where can he be?" He paused. "I know. At his cave, I'll bet."

"Maybe, but where is it? He's never taken me there."

"Me neither. But it's in the bush just north of here." Shorty waved his hand.

"Okay. So what should we do until he shows up again?"

"I don't know. What do you think?"

Lukas leaned forward. "I'm thinking we should find out what the police are up to and let Hound know. That head detective guy is a real shifty-looking character."

"Yeah? So?"

"His name is Sykes. I overheard his detectives yesterday, yakking about Rebecca. The big one said Sykes was going to stop her getting transferred into his branch. Maybe they're jealous. Anyway, we know Hound adores her, so it's up to us to protect her."

"OK," said Shorty. "Let's get to work. We'll split up and meet here every day at nine to compare notes. Be careful not to get caught. Call me if you see or hear anything important."

Lukas went out and Shorty settled back in the booth to mull things over. Lukas was right. They had to help Hound, but they should tell him what they were doing. He knew Hound better than Lukas did. No way would he sit still after Herman had been murdered. He was up to something, and Shorty wanted in on it.

Just then, Cartwright and Sykes walked in, ordered coffee and sat down. Shorty slid deeper into his booth and kept his head low. Maybe he'd learn something right now. That would show Lukas.

Luckily Sykes spoke loud enough for Shorty to hear. "Where's Constable Bradley? She's not answering her phone. And I can't find O'Reilly either. They must be together."

"I don't know where she's at, but she's due to brief me." Cartwright sounded vexed. "I'm worried. It's not like her to disappear like this. I told the boys to let me know when she turns up. I have to return to Orillia this afternoon."

"No problem," Sykes declared. "I'll take her briefing."

Cartwright cleared his throat. "I don't know about that. I'm having second thoughts about this case. I think I was hasty in passing it back to you. I've been handling it myself, and I gave Constable Bradley the lead, under my direction, of course. I think she should keep it."

"You assigned it to her without consulting me," Sykes said. "And if the second murder is linked to the McBride case that makes it active again. Bradley can't handle an active case. I'll send her back to Orillia to do research. Chad and Hadi can take care of things here."

Cartwright said nothing.

"Well?"

"All right, if you *must* have the case." Cartwright sounded angry. "But I insist that Rebecca stays here. She'll report to you. If she hasn't returned to Conroy by the time I leave, she can brief you. But the minute you find her, I want to be told. And I expect you to give me a full update tomorrow morning. Understood?"

"Yes, sir. Although I do it under protest," Sykes replied.

Sykes changed the subject. "Tell me about Hound."

Shorty's ears pricked up.

"Who?"

"There's a man in this town they call Hound. He was close to Abigail McBride and Herman Vogel. Chad told me this morning that Constable Bradley interviewed him on Friday. She sent Chad an email last night to let him know about it. You didn't mention him in your investigation notes from last year, and I'm wondering why."

Cartwright cleared his throat again. "Rebecca hasn't mentioned him to me. Who is he?"

"A local lad, that's all I know."

"Find out more about him and keep me posted."

Cartwright caught sight of Shorty leaning towards them. He slid out of the booth and stormed over. "Who the hell are you?"

The coffee shop fell silent.

Sykes came to stand beside Cartwright.

"I said, who *are* you?" Cartwright's face was flushed.

"Shorty Davis, sir. I come here all the time." He shrank back in his seat.

"Eavesdropping." Sykes yanked a notebook from his pocket. "Full name, address and phone number."

Shorty remained silent.

"Now!"

Shorty gave him the details in a quivering voice.

"I will speak to you later." Sykes snapped his notebook shut and marched off, Cartwright trailing after him.

Shorty watched until the door slammed shut behind them. Then he called Lukas.

Chapter 25

At four o'clock sharp, Cartwright climbed into his car and drove out of Conroy. Lukas peered through the library window and saw DI Sykes watching the car disappear. Then he turned to the library, and Lukas quickly backed into the bookshelves and remained hidden for a full minute, before leaving the library and proceeding with trepidation along Main. As he was passing one of the stores, he heard a familiar voice.

"Lukas Walker, I'll have a word wi' ye." Archie MacDougall was leaning against a wall, smoking a hand-rolled cigarette.

"Hi, Archie. Haven't seen you in a dog's age. Thought you'd left town."

"No, laddie, keepin' my head low, in a manner o' speakin'. But let's no' waste words. Step wi' me, where we can gab in peace." He nodded at the cemetery.

Lukas reluctantly agreed. The cemetery always set him on edge. He turned off his cell phone in case it disturbed the dead.

Archie halted by a gravestone and peered around. "I saw ye snoopin' on that detective, Sykes. Guard yerself, laddie. He's no' one to fool wi'."

"I'll say. He spotted me watching him from the library, I'm sure of it."

"Just guard yerself, and stay away from him."

"I can't. He's searching for Hound. He's got it in for that lady cop too. Rebecca."

"Then things ha' gone too far already."

Archie strode away.

Lukas stood where he was, confused and more than a little afraid. What was that all about? And where the hell was Hound? Something strange was going on in Conroy, and Hound and Rebecca were in the thick of it.

Lukas rubbed his arms and scurried away from the cemetery. He came out onto Main, and immediately caught sight of Sykes. He ducked into a used clothing store and hid behind a rack of women's dresses, then peeked out and watched Sykes trailing Archie, a block behind him. Lukas left the store and followed the detective, powering up his cell phone as he went. It rang at once, making him jump.

Shorty was on the line, out of breath. "Lukas, why wasn't your phone on? I've been trying to reach you. Sykes is a devil. I don't want to have anything do with him. Let's stop tailing him and just tell Hound he's here." He gave a garbled account of his run-in with Cartwright and Sykes at Duffy's.

Lukas cut him short. "Chicken out if you want to, but I'm in for the duration. So Sykes is scary, huh? All the more reason to watch him. I just met with Archie MacDougall for a 'wee chat' in the cemetery. He warned me to stay well away from Sykes."

"I told you. Take Archie's advice. I'm going to."

"Suit yourself, but I'm not going to let some two-bit detective from Orillia frighten me off. I'll keep you posted. I'm heading to Hound's house to wait for him. Meet you tomorrow at nine."

"Okay, but if I see Sykes anywhere near Duffy's, I'm out of there. Understood?"

Lukas ended the call. He would throw in his lot with Hound, his chosen leader, danger or no danger. He hurried to catch up with Sykes.

When he reached Maggie's house, Sykes stopped and stared at it for a long while. Lukas jumped behind a hedge and peered at him through the leaves. Sykes turned and ambled back with his head down, apparently deep in thought.

Once Sykes was a safe distance away, Lukas hurried to Hound's place. When he got there, he jumped onto the front porch and pounded on the front door. All was silent. He settled into a reclining chair to wait.

Chapter 26

Jonathan has called me every day since he went back to Orillia. I'm trying to be discreet, but I'm sure some of my classmates have figured it out. I need to cool things off for a while; he's so intense and I need to concentrate on my studies. I have my mission to fulfil.
— The diary of Rebecca Sarah Bradley (2003)

Rebecca, Hound and O'Reilly drove to the mine site. They saw no signs of development. All around them were abandoned buildings and rusted equipment. It didn't make sense.

They got back to Conroy late in the evening and went directly to Hound's house. Someone was lounging on the porch, appearing fast asleep.

Hound got out of the car. "Lukas! What are you doing here?"

Lukas rubbed his eyes. "Waiting for you, what else? Where've you been? Haven't seen you since Thursday."

"Never mind. Why are you waiting for me?"

"Because there's a whole lot of stuff happening in town. There's some detectives from Orillia here, one of them's a guy called Sykes. He's skulking about Conroy searching for Rebecca, and you."

Hound and Rebecca looked at each other. Hound sighed. "Lukas, I have some things to tell you. Can you stay the night? Then I'll want you to run an errand for me in the morning. There's something I need to have checked out in Orillia. Use my roadster, I know you've been itching to take the Midget for a spin."

Lukas broke into a happy smile. "You bet!"

* * *

Rebecca dropped O'Reilly off at his house and went on to Maggie's. The house was dark and silent. She tiptoed through the hallway and started up the stairs.

A voice boomed out from behind the dining room door, and the hall light came on.

"Gotcha!" yelled Freddie, making her jump.

"Come take your medicine, lassie," Archie hollered.

"Scheming rotters," Rebecca quickly retorted, and continued towards her bedroom, her heart pounding.

"Where's my broom?" Maggie bellowed from the kitchen, and a burst of raucous laughter brought Rebecca to a halt at the top of the stairs. Her tormentors were gathered down below.

"Get yourself cleaned up and down here in five minutes for leftovers, or you're washing the dishes," warned Maggie.

Rebecca pulled a contrite face. "Yes, Mum, but I've already had dinner."

"Dessert then, and no arguing," Maggie shot back.

Four and a half minutes later, Freddie and Archie sat watching Rebecca devour a generous slice of blueberry pie. Then Archie leaned under the table and came up with a bottle of scotch.

"Payback time." His leathery face creased in a grin.

Rebecca broke into a smile, then groaned inwardly as she recalled the morning after their previous whiskey night.

Settled in front of the fire, Freddie spoke first.

"Baker Street Irregular Freddie, reporting in. Not much to tell. Everyone's spooked by the second murder. The townsfolk are clamming up. The CIB detectives have them rattled. The head honcho — can't remember his name — seems to terrify everyone."

"Sykes," Rebecca said.

"What?"

"His name is Sykes. Detective Inspector Sykes."

"Right. Two detectives are helping him, going door to door. Looks like they plan to interrogate the entire town. Sykes spent the day with the superintendent — name's Cartwright. They parted company in late afternoon. The big cheese went back to Orillia, I think."

"Anything else?" Rebecca winced at the mention of Cartwright. She'd turned her cell phone off, and he would be having a fit by now.

"No, except . . . This might be important, I don't know," Freddie said.

"Go on." Rebecca edged forward.

"It may mean nothing, but I saw a black limo cruise through town at about five this afternoon. It passed by Stan's Hardware while I was stacking shelves. I only caught a glimpse, but I'm sure it was the car I saw in Orillia. Remember?"

"I do. Very interesting. Anyone else see it?" Rebecca glanced around.

Archie nodded. "Aye, t'was like Freddie told ye. The big car drove straight through town and out t'other end at five sharp. Three men in't. Didn't get a good look at 'em."

"That's all from me," Freddie added.

Rebecca turned to Archie. "What about you? Anything to report?"

"All I'll say is guard yerself against the chief detective, but ye'll already understand that, I reckon." He eased back in his seat.

Maggie sat up. "Conroy's a snake pit, and Rebecca knows it. You do too, Archie. And Freddie, you've lived here for seven years. Haven't you cottoned on to anything suspicious?"

Freddie broke into a fit of coughing.

Rebecca prompted him. "Maybe you should 'fess up, Freddie. Perhaps you know more about what's going on than Maggie thinks you do."

Freddie cringed. "I don't know what you're talking about."

Rebecca responded tersely. "Silence won't save anybody now."

"What's in this for you?" Freddie blurted out angrily.

Rebecca's eyes smouldered. "What's in it for me is finding the person who murdered Abigail and Herman before Sykes does. He wants to stop me joining the CIB but I'll get in, whether he likes it or not. How's that?"

Freddie scowled. She noticed he hadn't touched his drink.

"What's next, Rebecca?" Maggie said.

"You. But just things that might be linked to the murders, please, or we'll be here till Christmas."

"Right." Maggie straightened. "Now let's begin with some juicy bits, but don't y'all go round town telling tales. They're for Rebecca to use in her investigation, if she wants."

"Thank you." Rebecca gave her a grateful smile.

"First of all," began Maggie, "Jackie Caldwell, who I understand has taken a dislike to Rebecca, has been having a long-standing affair with Kingsley McBride. I'll bet none of you knew that. I guessed it, and then checked with Daisy Plum, the town's official grapevine. McBride's a careful bugger. It took me a while to figure it out, and I can't for the life of me understand what he sees in Jackie.

For sure she's no beauty. And why did he marry Abigail? She was as gentle as a lamb."

Rebecca nodded. "There's a story behind Abigail's murder, and I believe it might have roots that spread much further than Conroy."

"What do you mean?" Freddie shouted, startling her. "What are these so-called roots?"

Rebecca gave him a cool look. She stood up. "Okay, everyone, I think that's enough group talk for now."

But Freddie persisted. "What are you up to?"

Rebecca frowned. "Freddie, I'm conducting a homicide investigation. I'll be arranging separate interviews with each of you."

Archie nodded, his voice calmer. "Aye, Constable Bradley. I'll bide a while out back, if ye want to continue our talk, on or off the record."

"Thanks, Archie. Now would be great." Rebecca smiled at him.

Maggie added, "As for me, I'm always ready to chat."

"Thanks, Maggie." Rebecca turned to Freddie, who lowered his eyes. She gave him a hard stare. "And you?"

He hesitated. "I have things to do. Tuesday would be fine."

"I can't wait two days, Freddie. I'll talk to you tomorrow."

Freddie leapt from his chair and headed for the stairs. "We'll see about that!"

The remaining three exchanged puzzled looks. Then Archie cackled. "Aye, things are startin' to heat up in the old town." He threw back his head and drained his scotch.

"Okay, Archie," Rebecca said. "Meet you at the chair near the back fence. I'll just grab my notebook and join you in a couple of minutes."

He rose to his feet and headed outside. Rebecca went upstairs and crept along the hallway, stopping briefly to listen outside Freddie's door. He was talking quietly to someone. She lingered for a few seconds, but couldn't make out the words.

She went to her room and got out her notebook. Then she remembered that Cartwright had been in town today and she was supposed to brief him. He'd be furious. Cursing, she turned on her cell phone. Cartwright had left several messages.

She hurried out back and found Archie sitting on a deck chair, smoking. "Hi, Archie. Mind if I make a call? I'm overdue to brief Superintendent Cartwright, and I'll have to email him an update on my investigation. We could talk tomorrow, first thing, if you prefer."

"No need. Take yer time. Come back when yer ready. Not goin' anywhere. Be right here, enjoyin' the light o' the moon, as I do on fine summer nights."

"Thanks, Archie. I'll be as quick as I can."

Rebecca hurried to her room. Cartwright answered on the first ring.

"Rebecca! Where in the devil's name have you been all day? I waited in Conroy until four, and then I had to get back to Orillia."

"I'm sorry, Jonathan — I mean, sir. I was exploring the countryside, working on the McBride case. My phone didn't work out there, so I turned it off, and forgot to switch it back on until now. I apologize for not calling you. It slipped my mind, with all the frenzy around the new homicide."

"A feeble excuse," he grumbled. "Just what were you up to that took so long? And why did you leave town during the Vogel investigation?"

"I'm not on *that* team, sir. But I'd like to be. Could you talk to DI Sykes about it?"

His tone was frosty. "You should've been there, and you know it."

"I'm sorry, Jonathan. I was wrong."

"So it's Jonathan now, is it? What happened to 'sir'?"

"Sorry, sir, it won't happen again." Rebecca rolled her eyes. Boy, was he ever in a nasty mood.

"Now tell me what you were doing. Who was with you?"

She sighed inwardly. "How do you know anyone was with me?"

"Sykes said you've been spending time with a local man, someone named Hound. Who is he?"

"I was with Constable O'Reilly *and* Hound. His full name is Thaddeus Hounsley. We were checking out the site of a suspicious land speculation deal and an abandoned gold mine. Both might be linked to the McBride homicide." So that was it. He was jealous.

"And your joyride with this Hound character was more important than calling me?"

"I was pursuing a new lead, sir. I'm supposed to find out who killed Abigail McBride, remember?"

"And that, Constable Bradley, is because I did you a huge favour. Don't *you* remember? Oh, and by the way, Sykes is heading up both investigations from now on. You're reporting to him. And before you ask, you can remain in Conroy until Sykes tells you to return." Rebecca suddenly felt ill. This was bittersweet news, at best.

"Please, sir," she said shakily. "I still need your help on the McBride case. I'm making progress. I know I can solve both homicides, if you just give me a chance. Did you have to put me under Sykes?"

"He heads up the CIB, Constable Bradley. Who did you think you would report to?"

Rebecca paused. Time to cool things down. "Sorry, sir, you're right. I'll be pleased to work with him. Thanks for putting me on his team. Does that mean I can help investigate both cases?"

"Yes, of course — under his direction."

"I look forward to it, sir." She felt even worse. She dreaded having to work under Sykes.

Cartwight's voice became gentle. "Now, Rebecca, tell me what you did today."

She inhaled slowly. Crisis over. "I checked on O'Reilly. He was badly shaken by your threatened dismissal."

"Indeed." Rebecca pictured him smiling. The rat.

"I felt sorry for him, sir, so I offered to look at the land speculation area and the mine site with him. O'Reilly asked that Hound go with us."

"Hold it right there, Rebecca. What has land speculation and mining got to do with the McBride case? And why involve this Hound joker?"

She gave him Hound's ideas about the two deaths.

"So Herman was linked to Abigail McBride, and Hound knew both of them. Interesting. Tell me more."

About time too. She sighed. She told him the whole story, emphasizing Hound's belief that Abigail had committed suicide. She asked to have a forensics team sent to check out Herman's house, but a year had passed since her death, so vital evidence may have been lost.

Cartwright began to splutter. "Abigail did not kill herself, it's out of the question. You know that. You read the coroner's report. But if what you just told me is even halfway to the truth, we could be close to a breakthrough. You haven't told any of this to Sykes?"

"No, sir. I'll send my report to him tomorrow. I'll email it to you tonight."

"Do that. I'm sure he'll be pleased to know how far you've progressed on the case." Rebecca pictured him clapping his hands in glee.

"Actually, he'll be furious," she said.

Cartwright roared with laughter. Then he lowered his voice. "Rebecca, I miss you. We had such fun. Can't we get together again?"

"Time to sign off, Jonathan."

"Good night then, *Constable* Bradley." Cartwright hung up.

He rang again immediately. "But who exactly is this Hound character? Tell me more about him."

"Fill you in tomorrow, sir." She snapped her cell phone shut. He wouldn't call again. He was too proud for that, but she feared what he might do to Hound as a person of interest in the McBride case, and possibly Herman's death too. Cartwright might also view Hound as a rival for her affections, which wasn't true, but his jealous streak was coming through too strongly during the call.

Chapter 27

Freddie sat up in bed and tried to calm down. He was shaking uncontrollably. What if he went to prison? Terrible things happened to men like him in there.

He slid out of bed, opened a cupboard drawer and took out the cell phone Kingsley had given him for emergencies.

After two rings, he heard Kingsley's familiar drawl. "Yes?"

Freddie put a folded handkerchief over the phone to muffle the call. "Trouble."

"That you, Freddie? Speak up, I can barely hear you."

Freddie removed the cloth and spoke in a low voice. "I said, we're in trouble. That detective, Rebecca Bradley. She's wise to your scheme. She wants to interview me tomorrow, on the record. I don't know what to say."

Kingsley was silent for a few seconds. "Okay, Freddie, this is what you have to do. You must disappear for a while."

"Are you crazy? They'll think I murdered Herman. Let's just tell the police about Perez's involvement in the land deal. It was him that killed poor Herman, wasn't it?

Must have been. This whole thing has got way out of control."

"Slow down, Freddie. Take it easy. You've done nothing wrong, and neither have I. Nobody's going to find out anything they can use against us. The police will investigate, but I'll make sure they find nothing. By the time you get back, I'll have erased all traces of your involvement. You'll be clean. You're not a murder suspect so they can't stop you from leaving town."

"I don't like it, Kingsley. I don't like it at all. It won't work. That detective knows I'm involved. I told her there might be some kind of land speculation going on. Uh . . . I also told her Marco Perez was in Conroy."

"You did *what?*" Kingsley spluttered. He looked up. Perez was standing over him, listening.

Freddie tried to backpedal. "There's no need for you to get upset. I just said something *might* be going on."

Kingsley's voice turned steely. "Freddie, you have no choice. Perez has stated emphatically that he doesn't want to be exposed. And now there's more detectives in town. That's why you have to get lost for a spell. Don't panic. Perez knows how to deal with situations like this. Pack your things and leave now, before the others get up. Perez will pick you up at three a.m. on Main, near Maggie's house. He'll take care of everything."

Freddie's heart sank. What an awful mess. "I don't want anything to do with that bum," he whined. "Can't I just stay here and ride things out? I'll tell the police whatever you want, I just need to know what to say." He lowered his voice. "Archie MacDougall — the other guy who boards at Maggie's — he's sitting in the backyard now, waiting for Rebecca Bradley to interview him. I think he's wise to the deals. Maybe he's even spying on us, he'll tell her everything. Anyway, don't think I don't know what you're up to. I read your papers before I ran them to Hamilton." Oh shit, why had he said that?

Kingsley spoke slowly, emphasizing every word. "Pack your bags, Freddie. Go to bed. Set your alarm for three a.m. Leave the house and walk along Main, towards the Trans-Canada. Perez or one of his men will pick you up. That's it. No more discussion." The line went dead.

Freddie's gut churned. Who could he turn to? Archie? After all, they had boarded together for seven years.

He peered out the window at Archie, still sitting down below. He had to find out how much that crafty Scot knew. He left his room and crept past Rebecca's door. She was talking to someone — the police, probably. He tiptoed along the corridor, slunk downstairs, and slipped out the door.

Archie hailed him from his chair. "Freddie, poor laddie. Yer in a wee spot o' trouble, are ye not?"

* * *

Kingsley hung up the phone and swore.

"Well?" said Perez.

"You heard Freddie. He's caving in. We'll have to take care of him."

"I will talk to Guido."

"Don't kill him. Hide him somewhere safe until we decide on our next move. Guido can pick him up, but make sure he stays healthy. I don't want any unnecessary deaths."

"He is a threat. He will disappear, permanently." Perez gave Kingsley a hard stare.

"No! I want to hold on to him for a while. Another death here will draw too much attention from the police. He has to leave Conroy now, though. He's unstable."

"Consider it done." Perez settled into the armchair and drew on his cigar.

Kingsley took a breath. "Our next problem is someone called Sykes, who heads up the Criminal Investigation Branch. He's looking into Herman Vogel's murder. I don't know what to do about him."

Perez grunted. "That is another matter. I will talk to my associates. Killing this Sykes is not an option. We don't touch the police. They'd be down on us big time. I will look for another way to deal with him."

Kingsley thought he saw a shadow cross Perez's face. Fear? "Just take care of it, Perez, and soon. Sykes is a serious threat. We also have to do something about this woman detective. She's close to figuring everything out. How do we handle her?"

"I have never heard of any woman. Tell me more." Perez casually swept cigar ash from the mahogany table onto Kingsley's precious Aubusson carpet.

"She's been in town for the past week, conducting a follow-up investigation into my wife's murder. I've managed to avoid her so far, but I can't put her off any longer. And there's a complication. She's the daughter of George Bradley, my partner in the gold mine."

Perez shot upright. "Why did you not tell me this before, McBride?"

"I didn't know about it until yesterday."

Perez stubbed out his cigar on the table. "You know I want in on the mine deal too."

"Sorry, Perez, no can do. Bradley would never allow it. Anyway, I have all the money I need. He's only putting up the mining expertise."

"We will discuss this matter another time, McBride. I will get Guido to take Freddie somewhere safe. If he does not show his face tonight, Guido will do something permanent." Perez patted Kingsley on the knee.

Kingsley wasn't reassured. "Okay. Just let me know first thing tomorrow about Freddie. I'll sleep better when I know he's out of the way."

But there was worse to come. "The guy Freddie spoke about on the telephone, this Archie. I will take care of him too."

"Absolutely not," Kingsley snapped. "He's working for Bradley. Leave him alone." He reminded himself to call his half-brother, Tony, and ask him to please rein in Perez.

"It is your call, McBride, but do not leave loose ends. My associates would not like it."

Perez got up and left the room. Kingsley heard a car door slam and the limo backed out of the driveway.

Kingsley ground his teeth. By now the police would know about the land deal and the mine. He would tell them Perez was just another investor, like the van Rijns. Perez should be able to handle the money laundering. After Freddie, there would only be Mayor Taylor and O'Reilly to worry about, and they were too deeply implicated to talk. But Kingsley was puzzled. He'd been certain that Perez, or more likely his bodyguard Guido, had killed Abigail, and then Herman too, but Perez had denied it, and Kingsley believed him. He knew Perez better now. The moron would have bragged about it. Abigail must have committed suicide, despite the coroner's report. But then how did she get back to their house? Surely Perez wouldn't have done that. Kingsley thought about it for a moment, then shrugged it off. He had other things to think about.

He switched off the lamp. He always thought more clearly in the dark. Seconds later, though, the door creaked open and Jackie Caldwell slid into the living room. How long had she been there? Had she overheard?

He'd come to dread that husky voice. "Kingsley, I have to go now, but I need you tonight." She touched the nape of his neck, and his skin crawled.

"Good, dear," he mumbled. "You just go on ahead. I have a lot to think about."

"Come to my house at midnight, Kingsley. Don't be late." She gave a little wave and slipped away.

Kingsley put his head in his hands. How had he ever let himself get trapped by that harpy? More to the point, how would he ever get rid of her?

Chapter 28

Jonathan wants to be with me every weekend, but I can't do it. I have to study. And it's getting way too risky. Sooner or later someone will catch us. I can't afford that, it could cost me my career. His too, but he doesn't seem to care. I really shouldn't have got involved with him.
— The diary of Rebecca Sarah Bradley (2003)

Rebecca scooped up her notebook and hurried downstairs to meet Archie. She opened the back door and saw a dark figure leaning over Archie's chair, hunched like a vampire. She called out, "Hey! Who's that?"

The figure straightened. Rebecca saw something metallic glint in the moonlight, and then the shadow was gone, over the fence and into the murky forest beyond.

Rebecca ran across to Archie's chair and looked down in horror. Dark stains covered his shirt, and blood was dripping onto the ground beneath the chair. Archie's throat had been slashed.

He made a slight movement. Thank God, he was still alive.

Rebecca pulled out a handkerchief, pressed it tightly against the wound, and screamed for help. Maggie hurtled from the house, followed by Freddie.

Rebecca looked up at them. "Quick! Call an ambulance."

Freddie dashed back, while Maggie remained behind, staring down and frozen in shock.

Archie was fading fast. "Don't try to move," Rebecca urged. "We're getting help." She pressed harder. The wound didn't feel deep, but there was also a nasty gash at the back of his head. She didn't dare think what would have happened had she not interrupted.

When the ambulance arrived, Rebecca went with Archie and called Sykes along the way. She told him what had happened, and then asked him to meet her at the hospital.

When she got there, Sykes was waiting at the hospital entrance, with a concerned look on his face.

"What happened, Rebecca?"

"It's Archie MacDougall. Someone tried to kill him. He lives at Maggie Delaney's — the place I'm boarding at. He was sitting outside near the back fence, waiting for me to interview him. I came out of the house and saw someone standing by his chair. I yelled, and the attacker jumped the fence and escaped into the woods."

"Would you recognize him again?"

"Too dark. I couldn't see clearly. And his, or perhaps her, face was covered."

"How tall?"

"Five foot eight, more or less."

Sykes nodded. "Okay. I'll take a look at the scene and post an officer there overnight. We'll come back in the morning and make a full examination in daylight."

"Does that mean I can help?" Rebecca crossed her fingers behind her back.

"Yes. You're on the McBride and Vogel cases now, under my direction."

"Thank you, sir." Rebecca looked at him, searching for signs of annoyance, but his expression was neutral.

"How's Archie doing?" A note of stress crept into Sykes' voice.

"He's still unconscious. I'll wait at the hospital and let you know how it goes."

Sykes waggled his head. "You look shaken, Constable Bradley. And you're covered in blood. Where's O'Reilly? He can guard Archie."

"I dropped him at his house a couple of hours ago."

"Strange. I called his office and his home. I left messages at both places, but there was no reply."

"Leave it to me, sir. I'll have someone find him."

"Okay. When you do, tell him to show up at the office tomorrow morning at six. We'll need his help. The team will meet then. That includes you."

"Will do, sir."

Sykes stared after the fast-disappearing stretcher that nurses and doctors were rushing off to surgery, holding tubes and a drip stand. He turned and trudged away. Rebecca watched him go, intrigued by his noticeable concern for Archie.

She found a washroom and attempted to wipe off the blood. Then she checked on Archie's condition, but there was no news yet. She called O'Reilly at his home number, and then Sally, who still had his cell phone. Sally didn't know where he was at.

Rebecca called the OPP office in Orillia and arranged for extra police support to be sent to the hospital. She wouldn't tell Sykes about it until she found out where O'Reilly was at. Then she laughed to herself. She was becoming O'Reilly's protector again. It was turning into a habit.

Then she called Hound and told him what had happened. He agreed to watch over Archie until the police got there.

* * *

Hound arrived at the hospital, looking anxious. His voice was strained. "Rebecca, you okay?"

"Fine, Hound, just a little rattled."

"How's Archie?"

"He's in a coma. They're consulting a trauma specialist in Toronto. The doctors don't want to move him until they get an expert opinion."

"It's lucky you got to him when you did."

"I just wish I'd got there earlier and prevented the attack." Why the heck had she called Cartwright first? She should have interviewed Archie straight away.

"If you hadn't stopped the attacker tonight, he might have tried again when you weren't around to help," said Hound. "You're a hero, Rebecca."

"I sure don't feel like one, and there's something that's worrying me. The assault happened less than an hour after I was telling Maggie, Freddie and Archie about the McBride case. As soon as we finished, I heard Freddie on the phone with someone. Do you think he could be involved? I'll ask DI Sykes to trace that call. And I'm wondering whether the assault on Archie could be linked to Abigail's murder." All the possible ramifications were making her mind spin.

Hound shook his head. "I don't think so. I still believe that Abigail killed herself. Who would want to murder her? I've thought hard about it, and I can't come up with a single person."

"I'm sorry, Hound, but the coroner's report is clear. It wasn't suicide. I have to accept that, unless I find evidence to the contrary. By the way, Sykes is leading both investigations, and I'm on his team. At least they haven't sent me back to Orillia."

Chapter 29

Freddie sat on the edge of his bed. He'd tried, and failed, to get to sleep. The shock of the attack on Archie had begun to wear off, and now he was angry. Damn Kingsley for enticing him into his shady deals. Now he was setting him up as a murderer. Freddie had no idea what to do about it.

What did he really know about Kingsley anyway? They had never even spoken to each other, and then Kingsley began asking him to do odd jobs for him, mostly courier work, taking packages to Orillia and sometimes all the way to Toronto. Easy money, straight up, or so he thought. A short while later Kingsley told him about the subdivision deal and said he could make real money if he agreed to run secret errands to Hamilton. Kingsley was a respected local accountant, so Freddie thought everything must be above-board. Then that lousy criminal Perez appeared on the scene and Freddie started to worry. And now he was supposed to run away with the slime-ball!

Freddie got up and packed a bag. Just before three a.m. he snuck past Rebecca's room and tiptoed downstairs.

A crescent moon threw a dim light across Main. Freddie trudged along until he saw Perez's shiny black limo parked ahead of him. The headlights flashed on and off. Freddie drew in a deep breath and approached the car.

His feeble greeting evaporated when he saw Guido's face.

"Put your seatbelt on, chump."

Freddie's chest constricted but he got in and buckled up. The limo rolled forward and headed north to the Trans-Canada.

"Where are you taking me?" Freddie's throat was dry and his voice cracked.

There was no reply.

They motored along the Trans-Canada for about twenty minutes, then Guido swerved off the highway and drove along a county road. A short distance along, he turned into a narrow driveway and came to a stop in front of a rustic wooden shack, standing in the canopy of an umbrella-like tree.

"Get out," Guido growled. He lumbered towards the shack, with Freddie stumbling along behind him. Guido unlocked the door, pushed it open and switched on the lights. Freddie followed him through a galley kitchen to a large sitting room in back. He staggered over to a faded leather couch and lay there, terrified about what would happen next.

Chapter 30

A crazy thing happened today. Jonathan proposed. I didn't expect it. I've been trying to tell him I want to break up. There are things about him that are amazing, but he gets so jealous and I've sometimes seen a spiteful side to him. I should have said no, but I was confused and shocked. I told him I needed time to think about it.
— The diary of Rebecca Sarah Bradley (2003)

Leaving Hound to keep watch at the hospital, Rebecca drove to O'Reilly's house and knocked on the front door. There was no answer. She went to the side door and tried again. No go. She gave up and returned to Maggie's.

Maggie was standing in the hall outside her bedroom, rubbing her eyes. Rebecca hugged her. "Sorry, Maggie, no news about Archie yet." She steered Maggie back to bed and tucked her in, then kissed her on the forehead and turned out the lights.

She stopped outside Freddie's door to listen. All was silent. He was probably asleep. Rebecca decided to question him first thing in the morning. Continuing to her room, she set the alarm for five a.m., but she awoke before it went off. She called O'Reilly's home but got another voicemail. That was strange, and worrisome. Dressing quickly, she went to Freddie's room and knocked on the door. When there was no answer, she opened it and peeked inside. No Freddie. Perplexed, she left Maggie's and drove to O'Reilly's house. Heavy pounding on his front door caused the neighbours to pull their curtains aside and peer out. Rebecca ignored them and kept banging. Finally she heard someone shuffling towards the door.

"Open up, O'Reilly."

"Get lost." His voice was slurred. So that was it. Irish whiskey, no doubt.

"Just unlock it. I'll let myself in. We have to meet DI Sykes in half an hour."

"S'unlocked."

So the stupid door had been unlocked all the time. Rebecca cursed herself for not trying it.

"I'm in."

"Hear you. No need to yell," O'Reilly was in the bathroom. "Make yourself a coffee, whatever."

"Thanks. Take a cold shower and put your uniform on. Don't waste a second. Sykes won't like it if we're late."

"Humph."

She went into the kitchen. To her surprise, it was neat and tidy. The breakfast table was clean, the counters empty of clutter. Maybe he used a maid service.

Rebecca loaded the coffee maker. Curious, she headed to the living room. It was tastefully decorated, furnished with a new couch and matching leather armchair. A finely woven Turkish rug covered the cheap hardwood floor and original artwork adorned the walls. She frowned.

O'Reilly soon emerged fully dressed from the bathroom. Rebecca thrust a mug of strong coffee at him and steered him to her car. As she drove, she told him about the attack on Archie.

O'Reilly groaned. "Why didn't you come in and wake me? Now Cartwright has even more reason to fire me.

Missing during a homicide investigation, and pissed to the gills when Archie was attacked. I'm toast."

"Clam up, O'Reilly," Rebecca said. "Just stay a safe distance from Sykes so he doesn't smell the alcohol."

She pulled up outside the station at six a.m. sharp. Now she had to think up a credible excuse for their absence yesterday, while keeping O'Reilly well away from Sykes. She just wished the chief's eyes weren't so bloodshot.

Sykes was accompanied by his favourite detectives, Chad and Hadi. Five chairs had been arranged in a circle. Rebecca sat O'Reilly down on the opposite side from Sykes.

Sykes regarded O'Reilly and raised an eyebrow. "Cute little town you've got here, Constable." He turned to Rebecca. "Okay, Officer Bradley, start us off. Superintendent Cartwright said you emailed him a report on the McBride investigation last night. I want to see it." He gave her a reproving look. "But first, tell me what you've found out so far, and what your thoughts are."

Why did she have to be so nervous? "S-Sir, I think Herman Vogel's death may be linked to Abigail McBride."

"How so?" Sykes leaned forward.

She told them about the affair between Abigail and Herman, and about the gold mine and land speculation deals. Reluctantly, she mentioned her father's involvement in the mine. She said she hadn't spoken to him recently, so she couldn't provide any details.

Sykes turned to O'Reilly. "Anything to add?"

"Not much, sir. I wasn't aware of Abigail and Herman's affair. I just knew they were good friends." O'Reilly spoke evenly. He said nothing about his own role in Kingsley's deals. It put Rebecca in an awkward position as she could be accused of withholding information. She glared at O'Reilly.

Sykes turned to her. "How did you find out about Abigail and Herman?"

"I was informed by a man named Hound, sir."

"Ah, yes. The elusive Mr. Hound. I need to talk to him, but later. After this meeting, we'll head to the site of the attack. I've called in the Orillia Canine Unit to help track the assailant."

Thankfully, Sykes hadn't queried her on her father's involvement in the gold mine. Rebecca wondered why. Did he know about it?

O'Reilly added, "Sir, I recommend we bring Hound along. He's a brilliant tracker."

Sykes glared at him, and O'Reilly stared right back. Rebecca knew very few people who were able to lock eyes with Inspector Sykes. The chief had guts.

Sykes relented. "All right, as long as he doesn't get in the way." He rose to his feet. The briefing was over.

* * *

Hound arrived at Maggie's shortly after the team. Sykes extended a hand in greeting.

They made an incongruous pair. Sykes was almost a foot and a half shorter. "Mr. Hound, I'm DI Sykes. Chad Williams and Hadi Jafari are on my homicide team. Bob Ward over there is with the Canine Unit. We're about to track Archie MacDougall's assailant. You're welcome to come along."

Hound nodded. "Just Hound, sir, not Mr. Hound."

"Fine." Sykes regarded him closely, then turned to the dog handler. "Bob will lead the search. Nobody get in his way. If you see anything of interest, just tell him. Bob, we're in your hands."

"Thank you, sir. Follow me, please." Bob began by inspecting the area around Archie's chair. It was a confusion of footprints. He shook his head. "The assailant's imprints should be distinguishable in the soft earth inside the woods."

Sykes nodded at him. "Okay, let's get on with it."

Hound raised his hand. "One moment, please."

Bob turned to him. "Yes?"

"What direction did the attacker come from?"

Bob looked puzzled. "The street, perhaps, or the woods. We're trying to find out."

"What about the house?"

"I haven't checked it yet." Bob turned to Sykes, who nodded.

Bob tied Charger to the back fence. After matching Rebecca's shoe prints, and those of Freddie and Maggie, which Hadi had brought from the house, he found nothing else. He shrugged. "Looks like we'll have to search for the assailant's prints in the woods."

Hound cleared his throat.

"Well? What is it now?" asked Sykes.

"The position of Archie's chair suggests he was facing the woods, so the attacker must have jumped the fence farther down, and then struck Archie from behind."

"You're right," Rebecca said. "The chair hasn't been moved."

"Unfortunately the ambulance staff came that way. The whole area's trampled. No way to sort out prints." Bob shook his head.

"All right," Sykes said. "We've accounted for all the shoes." He was growing visibly impatient. "Let's get on with checking the woods."

Bob went to the back fence and examined the ground again. "There's a single shallow footprint leading into the woods from Archie's chair. The assailant must've been light. We should find deeper imprints in the woods."

Sykes rolled his eyes. "Then let's go. Let the dog show his stuff."

Bob patted Charger and gave him Archie's bloodied shirt to sniff.

"This may be difficult," Bob said. "Trail's cold and we don't have anything belonging to the assailant. Charger's not a miracle worker."

"Understood." Sykes pursed his lips.

Charger snuffled about, but couldn't find a scent.

O'Reilly cleared his throat. "Hound? Perhaps you could help?"

Hound hesitated, then stepped forward. "Yes, I can follow the trail."

Bob regarded him skeptically. "How?"

"Slight bends in the grass leading into the woods. They're faint, but I can make them out."

Bob knelt down and peered at the ground. "I can't see anything. You sure?"

"Yes." Hound turned to Sykes, who paused for a second, then waved his hand.

Hound stepped over the fence.

* * *

Hound was at home in the woods. The place was alive with familiar sights, sounds and smells. But there was something new. Alert, almost quivering, he set off, following a trail that was invisible to the others. He led the party on until he spotted a clearly defined footprint in a patch of soft earth. Chad set to work to make a cast.

The group continued through the woods and out onto an overgrown dirt lane.

"I know this place," O'Reilly declared. "Used to be a logging road decades ago. Nobody comes this way anymore. There was a thriving sawmill a short distance from here, but it went out of business."

Hound pointed at a spot not far from where he was standing. "A car was parked over there."

Bob hurried over to examine the place. "You're right!"

"What now?" Sykes asked.

Bob shrugged apologetically. "Charger still hasn't picked up the scent. Maybe we don't need him." He looked at Hound.

"Someone got in the car right here." Hound bent down and pointed at a faint shoe print. "The attacker must have turned his car to face the highway, ready to leave in a hurry. The trail through the woods started to wander, so I figure he was getting tired." He studied the ground. "There's a clump of dirt next to the impression. It might have traces of sweat on it." Sykes took a plastic bag from his pocket and scooped it up.

Hound stood up and stared along the lane. Then he went over to a shallow ditch, knelt, and retrieved a black leather glove. "Maybe this will help."

Bob took the glove and held it out to Charger, who sniffed at it, then yelped and strained at the leash. "That's it," Bob exclaimed. "He's got a scent." He gazed at Hound in admiration.

Sykes beckoned to Hound and they wandered off towards the abandoned sawmill.

* * *

Rebecca watched them disappear behind a line of sugar maples at a bend in the lane. She couldn't help feeling envious of Sykes's evident respect for Hound.

O'Reilly squinted in the bright sunlight. "What's he up to, Rebecca?"

She shrugged. "No idea, but he obviously has a high opinion of Hound. That's not like Sykes."

"Hound's a strange one, all right. But he has an effect on people. I once took him with me to Georgie's, after a biker gang started to get out of hand. He just stood there like an enormous statue and said nothing. They quietened down straight away. It's not just his size either."

Rebecca nodded. "Hound seems like an entirely different person to the one I first met. Remember the milkshake at Duffy's? Have you noticed the change in him?"

"To me, he's always been larger than life. But when we went to that cave, I saw something I hadn't seen before. He seemed to be looking right into me."

"How old is he?"

"Twenty-two, I'd guess."

"When I first saw him at Duffy's, I'd have sworn he was in his teens. Now he seems much older."

O'Reilly looked at her. "You know, I'd say the transformation started when you came to Conroy. You were the catalyst that caused him to emerge from his shell."

Rebecca felt uneasy for a moment. "What does life hold in store for Hound? He can't stay here forever, but he'll never go back to England. Did you know that he's fascinated by mystery books? He has a fabulous collection in his basement library."

O'Reilly nodded. "I've never seen his books, but it doesn't surprise me. He's helped me on a few cases, although only two of them were real crimes. He figures things out fast. But, other than checking Hagger's Creek with me, he steered clear of Abigail's investigation. I wish I'd involved him more. I might've solved the murder a year ago, and by now everything would be back to normal."

Rebecca laughed. "Normal? Has life in Conroy ever been normal?"

O'Reilly's face tightened. "Maybe you're right. But what am I going to do about the mess I've gotten myself into? You'll tell Cartwright about the bribes I took. If you don't, Sykes will find out anyway. Then I'll lose my job. I could get charged and even go to jail." He sat on a rock, with his chin in his hands, and Rebecca suddenly felt awful about her assignment to evaluate his competency.

She looked at him. "I don't know, O'Reilly. I should report you, and I'm planning to. It's my duty. But I've held off so far as I had hoped you would do it yourself. I should've told Cartwright last night, but it wasn't the right time. I could have told Sykes this morning, but it was awkward." She levelled a stern look at O'Reilly. "Will you tell me now how deeply you're mixed up in this deal? It might help me decide what to do about it."

"I shouldn't tell you anything more. It's high time for me to get a lawyer and tell Cartwright myself. I'd rather avoid DI Sykes, if you don't mind. I apologize for not telling him today, but I couldn't muster the courage."

"Understood, I guess," Rebecca said. "In any event, it will go better with Cartwright if you tell him first."

"Thanks, Rebecca. I'll do it right after we return to Conroy. But please believe that I didn't knowingly do anything connected to the murders. All I did was accept money in exchange for keeping my mouth shut about the deals. Kingsley figured I'd find out sooner or later, and he wanted them kept secret. I never imagined Abigail would become a victim. I guess the easy money blinded me. I don't deserve to wear my uniform." He shook his head. "Most frustrating of all is that we can't pin anything on Kingsley. He probably helped Perez with money laundering, but there's no evidence. Sure, he bribed me and Charlie Taylor, but the money was paid in cash. Charlie will deny everything."

"What about Perez?"

"I really cannot understand why Kingsley brought him into it. I've already told you that. I'd gladly give the cash back to get clear of this mess, but it's been spent."

"The furniture and art I saw in your house?"

"Yeah, and a small down payment on a cottage." He hung his head.

"O'Reilly, how could you?"

"Because I'm an idiot. I could walk away from the cottage and forfeit the money. I'll do that anyway, then get rid of the art and furniture. But what's the point? The truth will come out, no matter what I do."

Rebecca clapped her hands over her ears. "I'm not listening." O'Reilly was right. He needed a good lawyer, and fast.

"Sorry. I shouldn't drag you into it. D'you think I can get off without going to jail? If I only lost my job, maybe I could go somewhere far away and try to put this whole mess behind me."

"I don't know. My guess is that if Cartwright believes you're being honest with him, he'll treat you decently. He does have a good side. It's your best chance."

* * *

Sykes and Hound strolled down the lane in silence. They drew near the abandoned sawmill and gazed up at the rusty girders and shattered windows. A musty smell of decomposing wood suffused the area.

Hound took an instant liking to the place. "That's a comforting sight."

Sykes raised his eyebrows.

"This place has a happy feel to it, despite its sorry state. People worked here. They lived good lives as families and friends, all surrounded by beautiful countryside." He sounded wistful.

Sykes regarded him for a moment, then shrugged.

They wandered around the side of the main building.

Eventually Sykes said, "You must know what's going on in this town."

"I thought I did. Now I'm not so sure."

"What do you mean?"

"I have a theory about what happened to Abigail and Herman, but Rebecca thinks there's something missing."

Sykes looked skeptical. "She does, does she?"

Hound stopped walking and peered Sykes. "What's your issue with her?"

Sykes kept moving, as if he hadn't heard the question.

Hound caught up with him. "I never knew the mill was here. I don't know why I haven't been down this lane before. It's almost in my backyard."

"O'Reilly knew it was here." Sykes gazed up at Hound. "He seems to know a lot about what goes on in this area — as he should."

"He's a good man, sir."

"Perhaps, but he's up to something, I'm sure of it. I don't know what it is, and frankly, I don't care, unless it's linked to my case."

"Is Abigail really *your* case?"

Sykes glared at him. "Of course it's mine."

"Isn't it Rebecca's?"

"She reports to me."

"You know what I mean."

Sykes frowned. "You're getting into matters that don't concern you, boy."

"I'm not a boy."

Sykes regarded him for a moment. "Indeed, you're not, but I'll ask the questions, if you please."

Hound shrugged.

They trudged away from the mill. "Why do you believe Abigail's death was a suicide?" asked Sykes.

Hound told him, but Sykes obviously wasn't convinced. He had a sharp mind, Hound could see. He certainly wasn't someone to mess with.

They rejoined the others. Sykes appeared to be lost in thought, only looking up when Bob emerged from the woods, leading Charger.

"I'm going back to Orillia to check out a few things on the computer," Sykes declared. "Constable Bradley, come with me. Thanks a lot, Bob, you can go back now. And thank you, Hound."

Chapter 31

O'Reilly rode into Conroy in Hound's Bentley. He wondered about the vintage beauty. How had Hound come by the money to buy such a treasure?

Sally was waiting for him outside his office. "There you are, chief. Lukas just called. He was asking for Hound. And you."

"What's up?"

"I don't know, but he sounded really distressed."

"He's in Orillia," Hound said. "I sent him there to check on some things for me. Can I use your phone, chief?"

"Go ahead."

He hurried into O'Reilly's office and picked up the phone. "Lukas, I'm at the chief's office. What's so urgent?"

"Thank God you called. I checked the Orillia library for stuff on the abandoned gold mine. Then I went to the registry office to see who holds the deeds to it. Turns out the mine belongs to Jackie Caldwell, not Kingsley. Her husband left it to her, but he inherited it from *his* father. And get this — her father-in-law bought the mine from a man named Steven Bradley, who lived in Conroy decades ago. He owned Maggie's boarding house. Think he's related to Rebecca?"

"Probably. She seems to be connected to this town in lots of ways."

"But that's not why I've been trying to reach you." Lukas's voice was raspy and he was breathing fast. "I just overheard two suspicious-looking guys in a coffee shop. I'm watching them now, from across the street. They work for Marco Perez. I heard them talking about Guido, but they mentioned Freddie."

"Slow down, Lukas. What did they say? Freddie's disappeared. The police are looking for him."

"That's what I'm trying to tell you. Guido kidnapped him. These guys are going out to a shack about half an hour north of Conroy. I've got a feeling something really bad's going to happen. I was three booths away and couldn't hear well, but it sounded like Freddie's going to be disposed of — you know. Killed. They didn't say that exactly, but that's what I think. What're we going to do?" Lukas paused. "Oh God, they're leaving now."

"Follow them, Lukas. But stay well back. See where they're headed. Call me when they turn off the Trans-Canada. If they spot you, drive like hell to the chief's office. Got that?"

"Okay, but I'm really worried about Freddie. These guys are killers. Bring lots of help."

"Will do. And, Lukas? Be careful."

Hound turned to O'Reilly, who was standing next to him, straining to overhear. When the call ended he went around his desk and unlocked one of the drawers. He took out a handgun, and then a key. He hurried to a wall cabinet and retrieved a double barrel shotgun and some shells. This, he handed to Hound. "Know how to use it?"

"Never shot one, but I'll figure it out."

O'Reilly took the weapon and showed him how to load it.

"Chief, what are we going to do?"

"First, call the Emergency Response Team for support."

"What about us? We can't just sit here."

"We won't. That's what the weapons are for. We'll head north on the Trans-Canada and pull off somewhere secluded, then we'll watch for Lukas to go by. If he's right about the shack, Perez's men will soon drive past, with Lukas following them in your roadster. When we see it, we'll pull out and tail the men until they turn off the highway. After that, we'll play it by ear. Hopefully, the ERT will take over."

"Sounds good, chief. I'll call Lukas back and tell him our plan. Can you get Sally to text your cell phone number to him?"

O'Reilly spoke to Sally. Then he called Orillia. "Constable O'Reilly here. Find Superintendent Cartwright . . . No it can't wait. Get him now!" He drummed his fingers on the desk and muttered under his breath. Then he straightened up. "Sir, it's Constable O'Reilly. We've got an emergency situation. I need backup." He listened. "I need help, sir. I can't wait for an hour. It's a matter of life and death . . . Yes, sir. I'm at my office. A man named Hound is with me. Has auxiliary officer training, so I've asked him to help until reinforcements arrive. We're heading out now to see if we can discover where Perez's men are going. Send the ERT as fast as you can."

O'Reilly listened again. His face went red. "I don't agree, sir. If we wait too long for backup, we'll miss them on the highway. And if Lukas can't keep track of them, we'll lose Freddie. We have to get on the Trans-Canada, pronto. I'll call you when we have more information." He clapped a palm to his temple and mouthed a curse. "Sorry, sir, but we're going after them now. We'll do whatever's necessary to protect Freddie." Then O'Reilly shouted, "Do whatever you want to me, but I'm not standing by while another of my townsfolk gets killed!" He slammed the phone down.

Hound opened his mouth, then closed it again.

O'Reilly was glaring at the phone. His hands were shaking.

"Let's get on with it." O'Reilly handed the shotgun to Hound and stormed out of the office. His Chevy spluttered and refused to start. Cursing, he abandoned his car, marched over to the Bentley and plunked himself down on the passenger seat.

* * *

Hound sped through Conroy and onto the Trans-Canada. He guessed that the shack Lukas had spoken of must be somewhere on or around County Road Thirty-Four, about thirty miles away.

They pulled off the highway at the nearest exit. O'Reilly's cell phone rang almost immediately. It was Sykes. "Yes, sir. I'm relieved to hear from you. Thanks for returning. Hound's with me. We're driving north in his Bentley." He told Sykes their plan.

When the call ended, O'Reilly was smiling. "Finally got hold of someone with a brain. Sykes went along with our plan. I'm beginning to like him."

Hound said, "Chief, call Lukas and tell him Sykes is on his way. It might help to calm his nerves."

O'Reilly tried, but got no answer. He tried again, with the same result. "I don't like this, Hound. Lukas isn't responding."

Hound looked grim. He drove a short distance off the Trans-Canada and parked where he and O'Reilly could observe the highway.

Thirty minutes later, his roadster zipped past, with a stranger at the wheel. An old Buick followed close behind, driven by Butch. There were two men in the back seat.

One of them was Lukas.

"Lukas! They've got him," Hound shouted.

"Boot it," O'Reilly bellowed. "Don't lose sight."

Hound swerved out and onto the Trans-Canada. He followed the Buick at a distance, onto County Road Thirty-Four. The Buick travelled a short way and then disappeared down a narrow driveway. Hound drove past it and pulled over.

"I'll call Cartwright and Sykes and give them our location," O'Reilly said. "Looks like we may have to go after them ourselves."

Hound grunted. "Chief, did you notice anything about this place?"

"No. What?" O'Reilly was busy dialling.

"It's close to my cave. The lane to the meadow is just down the road."

But O'Reilly wasn't listening. "Sir," he said to Cartwright, "I think we've found the shack. Hound's friend Lukas is with Perez's men, taken prisoner. Butch Taylor's there too. He's one of them." He stiffened. "Yes, sir, I'll call DI Sykes right away, but we need help now. If there's any further delay, Hound and I will scout out the driveway and see what we can find. If we have to, we'll engage." He listened again and frowned. "I don't agree, sir. We'll hold off if we can, but that might not be feasible. Like I said before, if we have to, we'll engage."

O'Reilly cut the call and thumped his fist on the dashboard. Then he called Sykes and briefed him. He snapped his cell phone shut, cursing loudly. "Cartwright told us to stay clear of Perez's men. Sykes assured me he understood the situation and urged us to proceed with caution. So much for Cartwright."

"We'd better get moving," Hound said. "We can't wait for Sykes to get here. Freddie and Lukas are in big trouble."

"Okay. We'll go down the driveway and find the shack. Maybe we can take them by surprise. Grab the shotgun."

They jogged back to the driveway. There they slowed their pace and crept forward. O'Reilly spotted the roadster sandwiched between a black limo and the Buick. The cars were parked close to a run-down wooden shack with an extension tacked onto the side. Hound and O'Reilly hid in the surrounding bushes.

Hound scanned the area. "We can't reach the shack without showing ourselves. What should we do, chief?"

"Wait here and watch. With luck, Sykes will arrive before they do anything to Freddie and Lukas. I figure they'll take them into the woods to kill them, and then hide their bodies. As long as they remain in the shack, we can bide our time and hope that help arrives."

Just then, the door to the shack swung open and a man in a black suit emerged. A second man, blue-suited, joined him and lit a cigarette. Hound was able to hear what they were saying.

"Time to drag those chumps into the forest and do them. Then we'll get the hell out of here. Place gives me the creeps." The man in the black suit turned back to the door.

"Let's tell Guido to get this over with," said the smoker. "No reason to put it off." He ground out his cigarette butt and followed his companion inside.

Hound whispered, "Chief, we've got a problem. Perez's men are going to come out with Freddie and Lukas, who'll likely be tied up. We won't be able to take the thugs down without the risk of hurting our friends. We have to act now."

O'Reilly heaved a deep sigh. "What do you suggest?"

"Go back and get my car, then race it up the driveway. When you get close to the shack, honk the horn. Make as much noise as possible, then jump out and hide behind the Bentley. Shoot at whoever comes outside to see what's going on. While you're getting the car, I'll go round to the back and wait for the ruckus to begin. The minute you have their attention, I'll rush the shack and burst in, I can ram through any door. I'll blast whoever I find there. With a bit of luck, the men out front will panic and run, but we can't count on it. If they retreat into the shack, you'll have to move fast to help me. The shotgun should do the job for the guards in back, but I may not have time to reload. If they take me out, you'll have to carry on without me. Are you ready for that, chief?"

O'Reilly looked dismayed. "Hound, we could be killed. It's suicide."

"Maybe, chief, but if we don't act, Freddie and Lukas will die. I have to try. It's your call whether you come with me or not."

O'Reilly grunted. "What have I got to lose?"

"Okay, chief, let's go. By the time you return, I'll be in position. Don't waste even a second."

"Good luck, my friend. You're a brave man."

They shook hands, and Hound moved off.

It took Hound no time to circle the shack, but he stopped when he saw the back door. Thirty yards of open space lay between it and the forest. He could see Butch and two of Perez's men through the window, and realized that charging the shack from the back wouldn't work. These men were professional killers. Even with O'Reilly's diversion, there was no guarantee that they would go out front. If not, they would shoot him as he crossed the open space.

He decided to rush the shack from the side, where the men were less likely to spot him. He backed into the woods. But before he reached the shack, he heard the familiar roar of his Bentley. The great machine was barrelling up the driveway, its vintage horn blaring. Hound swallowed hard and braced for action.

Chapter 32

Finally done with basic constable training, although there are still lots of specialized courses I need to take. There's a problem though. For two months now, I've been trying to tell Jonathan I can't marry him, but he won't take no for an answer. He's putting pressure on me to join the OPP. I would love to work there, but I want to win the job on my own merit.
— The diary of Rebecca Sarah Bradley (2003)

Rebecca strained to overhear what Sykes was saying to O'Reilly. She was sitting next to the DI in the back of his car. Hadi and Chad were in front, with Chad driving. They were on Highway Twelve, heading for Orillia.

Sykes ended the call with a frown.

Rebecca looked at him. "What's the matter, sir?"

"Perez's men are holding Freddie Stafford at a shack a half hour's drive north of Conroy. If he's not rescued soon, he'll be killed." Sykes bent forward and tapped Chad on the shoulder. "Go back to Conroy and continue north on the Trans-Canada, full speed. I just hope we arrive in time."

Chad wheeled the car around and they sped along the highway with the siren wailing. Just as they reached the Trans-Canada, O'Reilly phoned again.

"Lukas has been captured," Sykes told his team, after the call was over. "Perez's men are taking him to the shack. Butch Taylor's with them, he's on their side. Hound and O'Reilly are following at a distance. They plan to rescue Freddie and Lukas if we don't get there in time to help."

Sykes called Cartwright. The ERT was on the way, along with Cartwright, but they were twenty minutes behind. Sykes shook his head. "This is bad. We may arrive to find O'Reilly and Hound tried to free the captives and failed. Perez's men won't be easy to take down."

Rebecca gripped Sykes's arm. "O'Reilly and Hound have got to wait for us, sir. If they tackle Perez's men alone, they'll be killed. We have to arrive before the shooting starts."

"We're going as fast as we can," said Sykes. "We'll play it by ear. If necessary, we'll move on them before the ERT arrives, but our main goal will be to pin them down. O'Reilly will have to decide whether to engage before we get there."

"Why didn't you just order him to wait for us?" Rebecca knew she was out of line, but this didn't seem to annoy Sykes.

"Pointless. You didn't hear the way he spoke. He wouldn't have listened. And I couldn't put him in the position of having to refuse a direct order. All I could do was tell him to be careful. Don't underestimate O'Reilly. Cartwright may not like the man, but he strikes me as competent."

Rebecca slumped back against the seat, feeling helpless. Sykes was right. But so was she. O'Reilly and Hound wouldn't be a match for professional killers. The trip seemed endless. She willed the car to go faster. With tires squealing, they finally swerved onto County Road Thirty-Four. Chad switched the siren off.

Rebecca's eyes opened wide. She sat upright.

Sykes looked at her, eyebrows raised.

"This is the road to Hound's cave," she said.

"What are you talking about? What cave?"

"Sorry, sir. I was here yesterday with O'Reilly and Hound. There's a cave nearby that Hound goes to when he wants to be alone. I know we're heading to the shack now, but I have a strange feeling about that cave. Hound told O'Reilly and me to remember the way in case we wanted to use it someday. I'm sorry to bring it up, I just thought you should know."

Sykes grunted dismissively and turned to look ahead. Rebecca felt her cheeks grow hot. Yet again she'd spoken without thinking. But she couldn't shake the feeling that the cave would play a role in today's events.

Sykes spotted a driveway up ahead. "That must be it, Chad. Right where O'Reilly said it would be. Park the car just past the entrance so the ERT can find us. We'll head down on foot. Right. Take your guns out. And, Hadi, call Cartwright. Fill him in, then join us. Rebecca, hang back twenty yards and watch for an attack from the rear. They might be hiding in the woods."

Sykes led the way up the driveway until he reached Hound's Bentley. He motioned for his team to stay put, and he edged past the car towards the shack. He pushed open the door, and beckoned to Chad.

Rebecca inched forward and waited beside the Bentley, alert for any movement in the woods. She heard someone creep up behind her and spun around. Hadi, who raised his hand and whispered, "The ERT will be here in fifteen minutes."

Rebecca nodded, but then she saw bloodstains on the ground. They led away from the Bentley and into the bush. She looked in anguish at Hadi.

He touched her arm. "Stay here. I'll follow the trail."

"Okay, but be careful."

Seconds later, Sykes appeared in the shack doorway. His face was ashen.

Chapter 33

Hound took a deep breath and dashed out of the woods, holding the shotgun in front of him. He made it to the shack and rounded the corner, ready to charge. At the sound of cracking wood, one of Perez's men leapt to his feet. Hound went through the pine easily, as if it were cardboard, but tripped over the door sill and pitched forward. He managed to slide behind a huge leather couch just as three shots rang out, narrowly missing his head. The shotgun went off with a deafening boom and jerked from his grip. He scrambled to his knees.

One of Perez's men was standing above him, aiming a gun at his head. But before he could fire, two loud bangs sounded and his head jerked sideways, splattering blood and brain matter all around. Hound peered over the back of the couch. Lukas was staring down at the body, a gun in his shaking hand. Black electrical tape dangled from his wrists. Suddenly he spun around and raised his gun.

Hound saw Butch fleeing from the room. Lukas's bullet splintered the door frame near his head, but Butch escaped unharmed. Breathing heavily, Lukas kept pulling the trigger until the gun was empty.

Shots rang out from the front of the shack.

Hound bent down to retrieve the dead man's weapon, just as a second gunman burst into the room, firing rapidly. A bullet caught Lukas, and tore into his shoulder. He staggered back against the wall, the gun slipping from his hand.

With a brief glance at Lukas the gunman moved forward to get a clear shot at Hound, who now gripped the dead man's gun. Before Hound could take aim, a bullet grazed his forearm. He dropped to the floor and rolled away, narrowly avoiding another bullet that ploughed a furrow along the floorboards.

Lukas pushed himself off the wall, staggered forward and pawed at the gunman's wrist, forcing his hand down before he could deliver another shot. Hound put his finger on the trigger of the dead man's gun, ready to fire. But he was too late. The second man had broken free of Lukas and shot him in the chest.

Lukas pitched to the floor.

The gunman took aim at Hound. He pulled the trigger, and there was a loud click. The bullets were all spent. He swore and ran off as Hound got to his feet. His hand was growing numb from the wound on his forearm. He swapped hands and held the gun awkwardly. Another volley of shots rang out from the front of the shack.

Hound glanced at Lukas, wanting nothing more than to help him. But there was no time. O'Reilly was in trouble.

Someone called out in a weak voice. "Save me!"

Freddie cowered in a corner of the room. His hands were bound behind his back. Hound ran over and ripped the tape from his wrists.

Hound yelled at him. "See to Lukas! And pick up my shotgun." He ran to the front of the shack but the shooting was already over. He saw O'Reilly disappearing into the trees. Guido, Butch and the gunman stood huddled at the edge of the woods, swivelling their heads back and forth between O'Reilly and the shack. Guido suddenly waved at the gunman to go after O'Reilly.

Hound saw the gunman turning to leave, and he stepped through the door and raised his weapon, but the gunman spotted him and fired before heading into the woods. Bullets tore into the doorframe. Hound ducked back and then peeked out and returned fire as best he could manage. His shots all missed their targets. He returned to the living room and knelt beside Lukas. His friend lay unconscious, breathing raggedly. Hound picked him up and carried him to the relative safety of an adjoining room. He pressed and secured a bedsheet against Lukas's chest to slow the loss of blood. Then he went back to the living room and pulled a rug over the trail of blood. Freddie was lying on the floor, curled up with his arms covering his head.

"Stand up, Freddie!"

Freddie shrank into himself. Hound yanked him to his feet.

"We've got to get out of here. We're sitting targets."

He hauled Freddie through the back door and into the yard. No one shot at them. Outside, Freddie seemed to come to his senses and started to run towards the forest. Hound followed swiftly behind, realizing with a jolt that Freddie had left his shotgun behind. And the handgun was out of bullets, so he tossed it aside.

* * *

Perez's gang regrouped. Guido told the remaining gunman to chase down O'Reilly and kill him.

"Won't get far with that bullet in his leg. Gun's empty — I heard it click. Finish the cop off and come back. I'll find the others. Big man ain't no marksman, and Freddie don't count for nothin'. Skinny guy's dead, right?"

"Right, Guido. Pumped lead right into his chest."

"What about me? You don't need me? I'll just go now, okay?" Butch's voice shook, and beads of sweat dotted his forehead.

Guido snorted. "No fuckin' way. You're coming with me."

"I'm no killer," whimpered Butch.

"Soon will be, dog turd." Guido gave him a dull stare. He beckoned to Butch and headed for the shack.

Butch stood still for a second, and then followed Guido.

Guido entered the back room. "Freddie and the big guy scarpered." He pointed at Hound's shotgun lying on the floor. "Forgot about that. Heard it out front. Good thing he left it." He looked around the room. "Where's the skinny guy?"

"How would I know?" Butch whined.

Guido cuffed his head. "Don't piss with me, jerk. Move it, outside. You go first."

"Why me?"

Guido cuffed him again. "Because, fool, if anyone's nearby, they'll shoot you first." He grabbed Butch by the collar and flung him through the shattered door. Butch stumbled into the yard, with Guido behind him.

"Big guy and Freddie won't get far. Took the skinny guy with them, so he must be alive. Good. It'll slow them down. The cop will call for backup, so we need to work fast."

Right now, though, there was this idiot to deal with. Perez should never have recruited him. Guido thought for a moment, and smiled.

He set off after Hound and Freddie.

* * *

O'Reilly hopped a short distance and then had to stop and rest. His wounded leg was stiff and painful. Breathless, he scanned the area. As far as he could tell, no one had followed him, and Sykes should be arriving soon. He felt a glimmer of hope, then wondered whether Hound was okay. At least part of his plan must have worked, because Butch and the other thug had fled from the shack. On the other hand, why were they still alive?

O'Reilly wiped his forehead with the back of his wrist. He had no ammo, so his only chance was to try and make it to the road, where he might run into Sykes.

He heard more gunshots coming from the shack. What did that mean? O'Reilly prayed that Hound was still alive. He hobbled on, hoping no one would come after him.

The woods seemed to go on forever. With no idea where he was, O'Reilly ploughed on until he saw sunlight filtering through the treetops and the woodland thinning out. At last! The county road. Then his heart sank. He'd travelled in a circle and was heading back to the shack. There was a black-suited man ahead of him, searching the bushes. The man hadn't seen him yet, but he soon would.

O'Reilly turned and hobbled away.

This time he headed in the right direction, and had almost reached the county road when he heard footsteps right behind him and his pounding heart sank with dread.

The man knocked O'Reilly to the ground. "Time to die, copper."

O'Reilly squeezed his eyes shut and braced himself.

Then he heard someone shout, "Drop the gun!"

O'Reilly stayed still and half opened his eyes.

"You heard me. Drop it!" Hadi Jafari strode forward, pointing his regulation SIG P229 at the gunman.

After a moment's hesitation, the man threw down his weapon and raised his hands.

* * *

Hound and Freddie were easy to track. Guido followed a swathe of broken branches and trampled bushes. He'd been here before. Perez had shown him a stream he could use as an escape route if things went

189

wrong. And they sure as hell had. Hound was heading towards the stream now, and Guido figured he'd catch him near the waterfall. Then he could put an end to this miserable venture.

He was spitting mad. Why couldn't they just have killed Freddie? Instead, the whole thing was a mess, and one of their best men was dead. Perez would be furious, and even Guido didn't care to be around an enraged Perez. The witnesses would all have to be eliminated, and one of them was an OPP officer. That upped the stakes. To make things worse, there wouldn't be time to hide the bodies before the cops arrived. If they caught him, he'd be arrested and thrown in jail for a very long time.

No more branches snapped. The woods were silent. The trail of blood became indistinct. Guido halted and listened.

Butch ran up against him. "What's happening?"

Guido seized his arm. "Shh! They've gone to earth."

"What're we going to do?" Butch's eyes bulged.

"Go forward, idiot. What else? We'll find them soon enough."

"They have a gun."

"One I gave you, right? Imbecile." Guido's dark eyes flashed.

"I don't know," Butch mumbled.

Guido regarded him with contempt. "How did we bring an asshole like you onto the team? Didn't you count the shots? Big guy has a round or two left, tops."

"That's enough to kill us," Butch whimpered.

"Not us. You." The side of Guido's mouth rose in a crooked grin.

Butch swallowed audibly. "What?"

"Don't get it, do you? Useless piece of shit. You're the bait. That's why you're with me. Big guy will use his bullets on you, then I'll finish him off."

"No damn way. I'm out of here." Butch turned to run.

Guido grabbed him by the hair and jerked him back. "Listen, moron, if you don't flush them out, I'll shoot you." His grip tightened. "Anyway, there's no worry. Big guy's wounded. Can't shoot straight. And Freddie? Piss his pants before he'd shoot anything. Your chances are good."

He seized Butch by the shoulders and shoved him forward. Butch dug his heels into the ground and began to blubber. A wet patch appeared at the front of his jeans.

Guido bared his teeth. He jammed his gun against Butch's face and slid the barrel under his upper lip. "Move! Count of three, or you're dead. One. Two. Three . . ."

Butch stumbled through the tangled bush and out into a clearing. "They're gone, Guido. Let's get out of here before the cops catch us."

Guido pushed into the clearing and looked around. "Don't make sense. They can't just disappear into thin air." He tramped about, ending up at a thicket of bushes abutting an enormous rock face. "Must have went in here. Best place to hide. Get your ass in gear." He grabbed Butch by the collar and flung him at the thicket.

Butch lurched forward and stopped. "Please, Guido, let's just get the hell out of here."

Guido pointed his gun at him. "Move it, asshole."

Quaking, Butch ploughed into the thicket, until he reached an open space next to the rock. A narrow cleft penetrated the wall. "I've found something. Could be a cave."

"Wait," Guido said. "I'm coming in."

Chapter 34

I've told Jonathan it's over between us. I had to. I've been offered a job with the OPP in Orillia. No help from him that I know of. I sure hope not. He denied it when I asked. He also said he can't accept that our relationship is over. He asked me to give it another chance. I said no, but he hasn't given up. I could see the determination on his face. I just hope he's not going to make my life difficult.

— The diary of Rebecca Sarah Bradley (2003)

Sykes went inside the shack. He found one dead man, and Lukas, unconscious and barely alive, hidden in the bedroom. He called the ERT.

When he re-emerged, Rebecca told him Hadi had gone into the woods, following a trail of blood that led from the Bentley.

Sykes thought fast. "Chad, go find Hadi and help him. Rebecca, come with me. We're going after whoever fled from the shack. Keep your gun at the ready."

He took off and jogged into the woods with Rebecca following. They hadn't gone far when she dashed past him, calling, "I know where they are."

"Where?" Sykes ran after her.

"I told you earlier. The cave." Rebecca sped up.

Sykes was struggling to keep up. "Tell me more," he panted.

Rebecca slowed to a trot. "Hound's cave. It's near here. I recognized the woods up ahead. If they were being chased, they'd go there for safety."

"Let's see if we actually find it," Sykes gasped.

"Please, sir. Just trust me." Rebecca took off again.

The sound of gunshots echoing through the trees brought them to a halt.

"The cave. I'm sure they came from there." Rebecca sprinted forward.

"Wait!" Sykes ran after her. When they arrived at the clearing in front of the cave they heard thudding noises, like fists on flesh.

Rebecca crossed to the thicket, parted the branches and plunged inside.

* * *

Freddie was wheezing and wide-eyed with panic. Hound put his hands on his shoulders and pushed him down onto the cot. "Sit there and be quiet, or they'll hear you."

Freddie looked tearfully up at Hound and whimpered. "They're going to kill us."

Hound left him there and went to a cabinet bolted to the cave wall. He took out a first aid kit and extracted a roll of gauze, binding his wounded forearm as sweat poured down his face. Perez's men were close by, and the cave was their only hope. Why hadn't Freddie picked up his shotgun when he told him to? They had no weapons to defend themselves with, beyond a dull table knife, which would be useless.

Hound heard a noise just outside the cave entrance. Butch, arguing with Guido. They'd found them. Hound groaned softly.

"Freddie, you have to help." He shook Freddie, then slapped him.

Freddie's eyes half-opened.

"If you want to live, you'll have to act." Hound's voice was a whisper. "They're here. There's only two of them, so we have a chance."

Freddie collapsed sideways.

"Stop that!" Hound pulled him upright and shook him. "You tackle Butch when he comes inside. He'll be first, and easiest. I'll take Guido." To his relief, Freddie's foggy eyes cleared. He opened his mouth to speak, but Hound put a finger to his lips. He pointed to the opening. "There. Crouch down and hold still. Do not make a sound. If we surprise them, we stand a chance."

Hound dimmed the light.

Freddie got to his feet and stumbled to the tunnel. If he didn't help, there was no hope for them. Butch might not be armed, but Guido would have a gun. Hound grabbed a wooden stool and stood at the cave mouth behind Freddie. They didn't have to wait long.

Butch squeezed inside. Hound lunged forward and shoved him at Freddie, who wrapped his arms around Butch's neck, the two of them falling to the floor. Almost immediately, Guido poked the barrel of his gun through the tunnel opening and opened fire randomly. Pressed flat against the wall, and close to the tunnel, Hound avoided getting hit. He counted seven shots in total. But how many bullets were left?

Then Guido charged into the cave, and Hound pounced, using the stool as a shield. Two bullets slammed into the thick wooden seat. He thrust the stool at Guido's face, but Guido quickly raised his fist and smashed the stool from his grasp.

Hound knew he couldn't escape Guido's next shot. From the corner of his eye, he'd seen Butch shake off Freddie. His stomach knotted. He would have to face Guido and Butch alone.

"Kill him, Guido!" Butch screamed. "Kill the bastard."

Guido bared his teeth. "You stupid shithead."

He swung around and shot Butch three times in the chest, punching him against the wall. Echoes of the deafening explosions died away, and the room filled with the smell of spent gunpowder.

Hound snatched up the stool again, but to his surprise, Guido aimed his gun at Freddie and pulled the trigger. *Click*. *Click*. It was empty. Guido tossed the gun aside. "Fuckin' Glock. Counted wrong." He advanced on Hound, rolling his shoulders. Hound thought fast. Guido was a formidable and vicious opponent, trained to kill. Hound flung the stool away then stood absolutely still, facing Guido.

With a mighty roar, Guido charged at Hound. Just before he reached him, Hound dropped to the ground on all fours. Guido tripped over him and crashed to the floor. He lay half stunned for a moment, and then struggled to his feet.

Hound rose upright and shoved Guido into the narrow tunnel opening, trapping his right shoulder and arm. He struck again and again at Guido's head until blood gushed from his nose and his rotting teeth cracked. But Guido wasn't finished yet. With a jerk that ripped his shirt open and tore the skin off his shoulder, he broke free of the tunnel and launched an uppercut at Hound's unprotected jaw. Hound staggered back.

Guido stepped forward and pushed him to the centre of the room. He punched the wound on his forearm, and Hound cried out and clasped it with his good arm. Guido emitted a low growl, blood dripping from his ruined mouth, and slammed his fist into Hound's head, knocking him to the floor. Gasping for breath, Guido stumbled forward and kicked him in the ribs. Guido slumped over, breathing hard, while Hound rolled over and got to his hands and knees, swaying precariously. Guido grinned and raised his foot above Hound's exposed neck.

"Sayonara, big man."

Before Guido could drive his leg down, Hound reared up. His shoulders rammed into Guido's raised foot, and he fell backwards.

Hound pushed to his feet, screaming like a wounded elephant. Guido managed to get up too, and stood facing Hound. Both men were exhausted and injured, their chests heaving like giant bellows.

Before either of them could make a move, a voice yelled, "Freeze!"

Rebecca burst through the tunnel entrance and pointed her gun at Guido. Sykes came in right behind her. He stood at her side and sneered at Guido. "It's over, schmuck."

Guido's battered face sagged. His hands fell to his sides. He looked beaten.

Then he thrust out a bloodied arm and pointed at the tunnel entrance, yelling, "Shoot them!"

Rebecca and Sykes turned, and Guido sprang. They whirled about and fired in unison, catching Guido in mid-stride. His knees buckled and he crashed to the floor, where he lay motionless.

Hound cast Rebecca a weak smile. "I knew you would come."

Rebecca nodded slowly. She went over and dragged Butch off Freddie, who was conscious, but his eyes were glazed.

Sykes bent down and examined Guido. "Dead." He looked up at Rebecca. "Cool under pressure, DC Bradley. I'm impressed."

She nodded and turned to Hound. "Where's Constable O'Reilly?"

"The last I saw of him, he was hightailing it into the woods. Lukas is still at the shack, in the side room. He was

shot in the shoulder and chest. He needs help, fast."
Hound pressed a hand to his own injured ribs.

Rebecca went to him and touched his arm. "Hound, we know about Lukas. The medics should be with him by now."

Hound's voice shook. "He saved my life. I've been very lucky. Could've died twice today, maybe three times. But O'Reilly may need help."

Sykes pulled out his cell phone and called Chad. "Sykes here. Have you found O'Reilly?" He listened and turned to the others. "O'Reilly's safe. Flesh wound in the leg. He should be fine. Hadi's taken one of Perez's men into custody. He caught up with the gunman and O'Reilly in the woods near the county road."

Next, Sykes called Cartwright, who confirmed that the medics were tending to Lukas.

With Rebecca's help, Hound limped to the oak stool and sat down. Gradually the strength returned to his legs. He focused his mind, and the pain in his ribs subsided to a dull ache.

Sykes looked at him. "Wait here. I'll bring help."

Hound stood up. "No need. I can make it on my own."

"And me!" The sound of Freddie's feeble voice echoed across the cave. "I can walk." Using the wall for support, he pushed himself upright.

Sykes studied them both closely. "Okay, we'll go back together. You can get treated at the shack."

They left the cave and made their way slowly back through the woods.

* * *

Cartwright was waiting for them outside the shack. An ambulance, numerous squad cars and two ERT vans were there with their lights flashing. The scene had been taped off. In the bedroom, the medics were working on

Lukas. He was alive, but barely. The ambulance was waiting to rush him to the hospital in Orillia.

O'Reilly had a large bandage wrapped around his leg. He seemed to be doing well. He climbed unaided into a squad car that would take him to a medical centre a few miles south of Conroy. He waved to Rebecca and Hound, and the car sped away.

One of the medics examined Hound, and then Freddie. He cleaned and dressed Hound's forearm and put it in a sling. Hound held his free arm against his injured ribs. His jaw was bruised and his right eye was swollen almost shut.

Sykes glanced at Hound, and then went over to Cartwright. They moved a short distance away and began talking in low voices. From time to time, Sykes could be seen pointing at Hound, who was sitting on a tree stump beside the shack.

"There's something strange about that man," Sykes stated flatly.

Cartwright frowned. "What do you mean?"

"I don't know, but he recovered from his fight with Guido way too fast, and he's handling the pain in his side too easily. He should be bent double, groaning, not sitting upright like that. And there are other things about him that puzzle me. I'm asking for your permission to look into his past."

Cartwright shrugged. "Okay, if that's what you want, although you don't need my permission. I don't see why you're so interested, but let me know what you find."

The three of them drove Hound and Freddie to the medical centre. Freddie was in fine form — he complained the entire way. Rebecca sat in the front seat, sandwiched between Cartwright and Sykes. She was thinking about the cave and the uneasy feeling it gave her. It was certainly no safe haven.

Chapter 35

At last, I'm a constable with the OPP, at the central region office in Orillia. DI Cartwright heads up the Criminal Investigation Branch. He insists he had nothing to do with me getting the job, and he still wants to get together again. That's impossible now, even if I did want to give things another try. My goal is to become a detective in his Branch, but only after he leaves it. I've heard he's on the fast track list for future promotion.
— The diary of Rebecca Sarah Bradley (2003)

The following morning, O'Reilly lay in bed in the medical centre. Rebecca stood beside him, relieved to learn that his wound wasn't too serious. The bullet had passed right through the fleshy part of his thigh. He was going to be moved later today to the hospital in Orillia for rehab work on his leg.

Freddie Stafford had been treated for head wounds and shock. The police had questioned him about the attack on Archie and released him on his promise not to leave the area without notifying them first. Lukas was in the Orillia hospital in intensive care. Archie was there too, still in a coma.

Rebecca smiled at Hound, who was occupying the bed next to O'Reilly. She knew he was anxious to leave the centre, but the medical staff had insisted he stay the night. His ribs were cracked, not broken. The doctors planned to x-ray his jaw later today.

Cartwright and Sykes arrived, followed by Chad and Hadi, who beamed at Rebecca. She'd grown to like Hadi a lot. He was a decent man and a clever detective. She could learn a lot from him.

Rebecca cleared her throat. "I'm certain Kingsley McBride is the key to the homicides, although I can't prove it. I should've caught onto him sooner, but he came up clean in the investigation last year. Anyway, I was searching for new leads . . ." She tailed off, aware of making excuses for herself.

Sykes grunted. "I interrogated him yesterday. He came to Orillia, at my request. He brought along Clayton Metcalfe, a sleazy Toronto lawyer, who made sure he said nothing useful. And Freddie Stafford gave us a whole lot of drivel. It's possible that McBride attacked Archie, and killed Herman. He has no alibis for either incident. But I doubt that he'd do it on his own. He's too smart to expose himself in that way. It's more likely he's the link to Perez, who could have done the dirty work. There's a small chance that Freddie attacked Archie, and he might even have killed Herman, but I don't believe it for a minute. He couldn't step on a spider without seizing up. So that's it, the entire list of suspects."

"What about the mayor?" Rebecca asked. "He's involved in the land deal."

"Disappeared without a trace. Like Perez. But I interviewed him when I arrived in Conroy. He had rock-solid alibis for both murders." Sykes shrugged.

Rebecca looked at O'Reilly, who was lying with his head towards the window. He saw her reflection and rolled over. She gave him an encouraging nod.

He drew in a deep breath. "Okay. I'll tell you everything I know."

They all stared at him.

"What!" Cartwright spluttered. "What haven't you told us? I knew you were holding something back last year." His hands balled into fists.

O'Reilly's voice was resigned. "Now you'll get the opportunity you've been waiting for. You'll be able to pack in my job."

Cartwright folded his arms.

O'Reilly told them about the gold mine and land development deals. Rebecca noted with appreciation that he didn't try to play down his own role.

Sykes nodded from time to time. Rebecca guessed that he'd already figured out O'Reilly's connection to the affair. Rebecca had changed her opinion of Sykes. Her respect for the DI had grown rapidly during the brief time she had spent with him. He still set her on edge, but now she believed he was fundamentally a good man.

When O'Reilly finished, Sykes turned to Hound. "Has anything happened to change your thoughts about who killed Abigail and Herman?"

Hound regarded him in silence. Then he looked at Rebecca. An awkward silence settled over the group.

Sykes waved his hand in the air. "All right. The floor is all yours, DC Bradley." He'd called her DC! Rebecca's entire body tingled. Her coveted CIB job was getting nearer.

Cartwright stroked the scar on his cheek and frowned.

"Okay, here goes." Rebecca went on to tell them what she had learned about Abigail, Kingsley and the gold mine.

"Kingsley hooked up with Jackie Caldwell many years ago when he found out she owned the rights to the mine. More recently, he brought in my father as a partner, which puzzles me. My father's no fool. He knows more about goldmining than anyone. But I won't talk to him without DI Sykes's permission." Rebecca glanced at Sykes, who said nothing. She was convinced that something bad was going on, or had gone on in the past between Sykes and her father. A definite enmity existed there, although she had no idea what could have caused it. Sykes seemed to freeze up whenever her father was mentioned, and he'd shown no interest at all in talking to him. She filed away that thought for now and moved on.

"I believe Kingsley ran out of money, so he approached Perez. Then he bribed Mayor Taylor and Constable O'Reilly to keep quiet and act as covers for the deals. They would have learned about them anyway so he had to bring them in. Finally, I believe Kingsley had Abigail and then Herman murdered, to stop them from revealing his plans. It's possible he brought Perez on board for that purpose."

Cartwright looked baffled. "If you're right, it's McBride we're after. But what evidence can we use to indict him?"

Hound turned to Sykes. "I have an idea. If we can't get at Kingsley directly, maybe we can make life miserable for him. Force him to make a mistake."

"How?" Sykes asked.

"By asking George Bradley and the van Rijns to convince Kingsley that his deals are no longer viable. The van Rijns do business with my family. I could talk to Mr. van Rijn and let him know what's happening. I'm sure he'll help us if he believes Kingsley had something to do with Abigail's murder. And there's Constable O'Reilly. He can tell Kingsley he'll testify that he took a bribe. And Freddie will testify too, so that only leaves Mayor Taylor. I don't know if he'll come clean, but we can try."

"Forget it," O'Reilly grunted. "Believe me, Charlie won't say a word."

"Okay. But we can still put pressure on Kingsley."

Sykes added, "And on Perez — if we can find him." His expression hardened. "I'll take care of that."

"Okay," said Rebecca. "I'll talk to my father, with DI Sykes's permission."

Sykes nodded. "It's time for us to take the initiative."

* * *

"Rebecca. Wonderful to hear from you." Her father sounded pleased, and surprised. They didn't often speak over the phone, and never during the day.

"Dad, I'm sorry to disturb you at work, but there's something important I have to talk to you about. I'm conducting a homicide investigation in a small town in central Ontario. It's called Conroy. You know it, I believe." She heard a faint intake of breath.

After a moment, he said, "Yes, and I know you've met Archie MacDougall there. He called and told me about it."

Very interesting. So Archie really is working for him.

"Have you heard what happened to Archie?"

"No. What? Tell me."

He sounds very concerned. Doubly interesting. So Archie's more than just another employee.

"His neck was slashed two nights ago, and he was slugged on the head. He's in intensive care in the Orillia hospital, in a coma. His condition's stable, but the doctors don't know when, or if, he'll wake up, although they sound quite positive."

She heard him breathing hard. "That's awful, Rebecca. I'll call there right away. Who did it?"

"We don't know, Dad. It's under investigation."

His tone stiffened. "Let me know when you find out."

"Of course, Dad, I promise. But right now I need you to tell me about the abandoned gold mine north of Conroy. And Kingsley McBride, the man who's planning to develop it. You're his partner, I've heard. Is that true?"

There was a long silence.

"Dad? Please speak to me. This is important."

His voice turned cold. "Are you investigating me?"

"Not specifically, Dad, but that mining deal may be central to the investigation. The police are keeping Kingsley McBride under observation. They may watch you too, eventually. Right now, I'm asking you to help us with Kingsley. It will go down well if you do."

More silence.

"Dad?"

"Okay, Rebecca. What do you want from me?"

"We — I mean the police — need you to tell McBride that his mining deal stinks, and you're pulling out."

"Oh, that's all, is it?" He sighed heavily. He went silent for a few seconds, and, to her surprise, capitulated. "All right, Rebecca, I'll do it. For you. But only if you stop asking me questions about the mine. You don't need to know anything about my business. If you recall, you passed on the opportunity to run it with me when you joined the OPP."

She heard the familiar bitterness in his voice.

"Okay, Dad. Thanks. I'll sign off now. Maybe we can talk about my job another time, when I'm in Prospect."

"Don't count on it." The line went dead.

Chapter 36

What the hell was going on? Kingsley was worried. First George Bradley, then Nicholas van Rijn, had told him they were backing out of the mining and land deals. And that jerk, van Rijn, even had the cheek to ask for his money back. As far as Kingsley was concerned, it was a dowry, and he intended to keep it, despite Abigail having died. Anyway, he'd forked out a fair chunk of it to Bradley, who had refused to return it. Then O'Reilly called him and said he'd spill everything he knew to DI Sykes, adding he'd also get Charlie Taylor to talk. To top everything off, that loose-mouthed chimp, Freddie Stafford, was still at large.

Kingsley called Tony Albertini and told him what had happened.

"What should I do, Tony? Please help me."

His half-brother laughed. "Time to clean up your house. And mine. Now here's what I want you to do . . ."

Kingsley listened to the instructions and hung up, shocked. He was in really deep now.

He decided Charlie Taylor would be the first to go. He called Charlie's home number, using a disposable cell phone that Tony had given him. "Charlie, we need to meet. I'll explain later. I'll pick you up in exactly one hour, outside of town. Wait in the bush at the south end of Main. Make sure no one sees you there, or sees you get into my car. And tell no one about it, not even your wife. Don't ask questions. Just do it."

* * *

Charlie paced back and forth in front of Kingsley, wringing his hands. "Kingsley, I can't waste time on this. My son was killed yesterday. The police are climbing all over me. We shouldn't be seen together. And why did we have to drive out here? Why couldn't we talk in the car?"

"I'm sorry, Charlie, but it was necessary."

"My son's dead, Kingsley. My wife's hysterical. I have important things to attend to."

"I too have important things to do." Kingsley glanced at a large tree behind the mayor. He raised his hand. "Regrets, Charlie, but we can't take any chances." Then he stepped aside.

Charlie swivelled round to see what Kingsley was looking at, just as Marco Perez stepped from behind the tree and aimed his Glock. He fired twice. Charlie staggered back, his hands pressed to his chest. Blood squirted between his fingers. He turned and stared at Kingsley, then dropped to the ground.

"One problem solved." Perez's face twisted into an evil grin.

Kingsley sighed. "Charlie was a friend." He stared off into the woods.

"Leave no witnesses, that's my policy." Perez trained his gun on Kingsley, but before he could pull the trigger, a shot echoed through the woods. Perez fell to his knees, with a bullet in his back. His startled look up at Kingsley was almost beseeching. Then a second bullet slammed into his head, splattering blood and brain matter everywhere. He crashed to the ground and lay face down over Charlie's corpse.

Kingsley edged forward to confirm that Perez was dead. He began to laugh hysterically. "Leave no witnesses, eh? I checked with your boss, asshole. It was time to let you go." His grin matched that of Perez.

Jackie Caldwell emerged from the forest and leaned against a tree trunk, cradling her hunting rifle like a baby.

"Good girl." Kingsley's knees were shaking. He smiled faintly at her. "Your shooting skills are as good as ever."

He was amazed at Jackie's nonchalant pose. "You've just murdered a man. How can you be so calm?" He wiped sweat from his forehead.

"It was a pleasure." She glanced sideways at him. "What would you have done without me?" Her eyes narrowed. "I'll bet you couldn't have pulled the trigger."

Too right, thought Kingsley. His hands were trembling, but Jackie appeared calm, almost serene. She seemed to relish the kill, maybe it had turned her on. He shuddered. Then he started to worry.

Jackie stalked over and nudged the body with her toe. "I never liked Perez and his bully boys. So what do we do now, Kingsley?"

"Perez's associates will take care of the corpses. Nobody will find Charlie, or this scumbag." He snorted derisively. "Anyway, it's time to get back to town. Nice day for a drive in the country, don't you think?" Kingsley was amazed at how little remorse he felt at having Charlie murdered. And as for Perez — good riddance.

Jackie took hold of his arm and gave him a sultry smile. They strolled to his car and drove south along the Trans-Canada. Kingsley stared fixedly at the road ahead. To his relief, Jackie ceased making amorous overtures. He could only hope.

Now that Charlie and Perez had been taken care of, Kingsley's mood lightened. Archie MacDougall was dangerous, but Tony's men would deal with him tonight. O'Reilly too. Lukas wasn't a threat. All the loose ends would be tied up by tomorrow, except for Freddie, but Kingsley had a plan for him, and this time it would be permanent. The gold mine and land deals would have to be put on hold, maybe forever, but that Dutch shyster, van Rijn, wouldn't get a penny of his money back. And Kingsley's cozy relationship with Tony guaranteed him a bright future in Hamilton. At last, he would finally escape from Conroy, and Jackie.

A black Lincoln Continental zipped past them in the opposite direction.

"The clean-up team," Kingsley declared, and he began to whistle. He wondered if there was anything Jackie wouldn't do for him. Then he worried about the price he'd have to pay.

Jackie snuggled closer, and laid her head on his shoulder. Kingsley stiffened. She closed her eyes and hummed contentedly. Kingsley began to sweat. Sure enough, a short while later, she said, "Kingsley, take me to your house. I can't wait any longer."

His whistle withered on his lips. It dawned on him that he might be saddled with this python for life. Could he drum up the courage to kill her? Boy, did he ever want to. But then he'd have to give up the gold mine forever, and he wasn't ready to do that — yet.

Maybe it wasn't such a great day after all.

Chapter 37

When he heard the news about Lukas, Shorty blamed himself for chickening out of their spying escapade. He couldn't bear to face Hound. So, with nothing better to do, he set off for Duffy's.

On his way to the coffee shop, he saw Kingsley McBride drive past in his Crown Vic, heading north. Jackie Caldwell was sitting next to him in the passenger seat.

Shorty entered Duffy's and eased himself into a window booth. Daisy brought him a soda and sat down opposite. "Can I do anything for you, Shorty?"

"No thanks, Daisy. I just want to be left alone." He fought back tears.

"Okay, but if you need someone to talk to, I'm here." She squeezed his hand and returned to the front counter.

He was still at Duffy's an hour later, gazing forlornly out the window. He saw Kingsley go past the shop again, heading south, alone in his car. Minutes later, he rumbled by once more, going north. Someone was crouched low in the passenger seat, but it wasn't Jackie. Shorty craned his neck but he couldn't make out who it was. His curiosity piqued, he kept a watch on the street. After another hour,

Kingsley passed the shop a fourth time, heading south. Jackie Caldwell was back, leaning against him.

Shorty left Duffy's and hurried in the same direction, figuring Kingsley might be going to his house a few blocks away. Sure enough, the Crown Vic turned off Main and pulled into the driveway of Kingsley's two-story Tudor-style house.

Shorty paused to consider what to do next. The simple answer was nothing. Go home and forget about Kingsley. Instead, he decided to wait and see what was going on. Hound might want to know what Jackie and Kingsley were doing together. Things seemed pretty cozy between them. And they *had* been hanging around each other a lot since Abigail's death.

Kingsley's house was surrounded on three sides by a thick hedge that blocked it from the neighbours' prying eyes. Shorty pushed through a gap and snuck in back. Underneath a second-floor window, he stopped and listened. He heard grunts and moans, and then a woman's voice cried out. Shorty was sure it was Jackie. A few minutes later he heard the sound of water running. He waited. The shower stopped, and Jackie's shrill voice sliced through the air. "Again!"

"I can't. I'm done for." Kingsley sounded like he was begging.

"You're getting weak, darling. Is it the stress?"

"I'm taking you home. Right now." Shorty detected revulsion in Kingsley's voice. "If the police come around, remember the story we agreed upon. You're my alibi, and I'm yours. Got it?"

"Yes, dear. I *so* enjoyed today." Jackie didn't seem to be offended by Kingsley's tone. Maybe she hadn't noticed. "Wasn't it thrilling, Kingsley? Much more fun than hunting lousy deer."

"No, and keep your mouth shut. Don't speak of it again, even to me. You'll get us put away for life."

"Yes, my love."

Shorty backed out of the bushes and sprinted away. He had no idea what Kingsley and Jackie were talking about, but he had to tell the police. Not Sykes, who terrified him, but Rebecca. She'd know what to do. But — dammit, he didn't have her cell number. Maggie's would be the best place to check. He arrived at Maggie's house to find the front door ajar, and the sound of voices coming from inside. There seemed to be an argument underway. He tiptoed down the hallway and heard Maggie in the parlour, shouting at someone. The target of her anger was trying to defend himself, but not doing a very good job. Shorty tiptoed forward.

"Tell me everything, Freddie. Just what have you been up to?"

"You don't need to know, Maggie. And believe me, you don't want to."

"I'll be the judge of that. Archie was almost murdered, and in my own backyard. You know who did it, don't you?"

"No! I swear I don't."

"It was you who cut his throat."

"No, Maggie, never. I wouldn't hurt anyone. I couldn't. Certainly not Archie. He's my friend."

"I heard them talking," Maggie fired back. "Detective Sykes and that tracker, Bob. They said the attacker wore small shoes, like yours. You tried to kill my Archie!" Her voice rose. Shorty heard glass shattering, and someone running through the house.

He ducked into a closet, narrowly avoiding Freddie, who dashed into the hall and raced past him, with Maggie close behind. Freddie sped from the house. In a flood of tears, Maggie stumbled back along the hall and up the stairs.

Shorty guessed Rebecca wasn't here.

The plot thickens, he mused. Had Freddie tried to kill Archie? He couldn't believe it. He crept from the house and followed Freddie.

Freddie headed directly to Kingsley's house, stuffing Valium tablets into his mouth as he went. At least the police were wise to Kingsley's whole shady scheme now. He hadn't told them much, but at least they knew Kingsley was behind it all. After his row with Maggie, Freddie became convinced that he had to set the record straight. He was willing to help them bring Kingsley down. His drug-addled brain came up with an idea. He would tell Kingsley that he'd taken copies of his correspondence with Perez and turned them over to the police. It wasn't true, but it would really upset the two-faced weasel. He smiled, eager to see Kingsley's reaction when he told him.

Freddie arrived at the house, out of breath. The Crown Vic was in the driveway. Kingsley never walked anywhere, so the skunk must be at home. Freddie inhaled deeply and marched up the front steps.

* * *

Shorty peered around the trunk of a large tree and watched Freddie hammer on the front door. As soon as it opened, Freddie shoved in past Kingsley, who peered up and down the street and disappeared inside.

Shorty waited a few seconds. Beneath the dense cover of some garden shrubs, he crawled towards the house. He could hear the sound of raised voices coming through an open window.

"I've had it with you, you bastard!" It was Freddie.

"Shut up, fool."

"They'll nail you," shouted Freddie. "And I'll be first in line to help them."

Kingsley's voice was even. "Calm down, Freddie. Go to the liquor cabinet and pour yourself a drink, there's a good boy."

"Piss off!" Freddie yelled. "I'm calling the police and telling them to come here. See how you like that." Shorty heard the stamp of feet as someone crossed the room.

Another set of footsteps followed, and then a thud. Everything went quiet.

Shorty's heart thumped. He backed out of the shrubs and scrambled through the hedge, fumbling for his cell phone as he went. O'Reilly was laid up at the medical centre. No help there. The OPP in Orillia? But they would take too long to get here. Shorty wondered where Jackie Caldwell had disappeared to.

Reaching Main, Shorty peered up and down the street. He saw Rebecca's Mercedes in O'Reilly's parking lot.

* * *

Shorty crashed through the station door, making Rebecca jump.

"Shorty! What's the matter?"

"Kingsley McBride," he gasped. "Freddie's at his house. He threatened to send Kingsley to jail. I think Kingsley slugged him."

"Quick. Jump in my car." As soon as they were seated in her Mercedes, Rebecca thrust her cell phone at him. "Call Superintendent Cartwright. His number's in my contacts. Tell his assistant you're with me and it's an emergency. Say I'm at Kingsley's house, and going straight in without a warrant. I don't want him ordering me to stay put until reinforcements arrive. Freddie's in grave danger."

Shorty hit the call button. By the time he got Cartwright on the line, they were at Kingsley's house. But it was too late. The Crown Vic had gone.

Rebecca leapt from her Mercedes and rushed to the front door, which was unlocked. Inside, there were fresh bloodstains on the study carpet. She scrambled back into her car and snatched the phone from Shorty.

"Sir, Rebecca here. Looks like McBride knocked out Freddie Stafford and took him away in his car. I'll see if I can find them, but I need backup. O'Reilly's still in hospital. Is Sykes in town?"

"He's back in Orillia."

"Damn. Then I'm on my own. I'll call when I catch up with Kingsley, *if* I do. You should alert all patrol cars to watch the Trans-Canada. Shorty will describe his car." She passed the phone to Shorty while she turned the Mercedes around. When she was on her way, she retrieved the phone. Cartwright warned her to be careful.

She looked at her companion. "Any ideas where Kingsley might go?"

"None."

"Okay, I'll just have to ask people if they've seen him." She felt like shaking the steering wheel. They must have just missed him.

Shorty turned to her. "I have an idea. Call Hound."

"Why?"

"Just do it. He'll think of something."

"All right, but he's at the medical centre. What can he do from there? I'll call DI Sykes too, but he's in Orillia. What about you, Shorty? Are you willing to help? Things could get rough, you know."

Shorty looked through the windscreen, his chin thrust forward. "I'll give my life if I have to."

Rebecca stopped to question a couple of townsfolk along Main. They hadn't seen Kingsley.

"Where could they have gone?" she muttered.

Shorty turned to her. "Kingsley was with Jackie Caldwell today. He could have gone to her house."

Rebecca followed Shorty's directions while he told her what he'd overheard between Kingsley and Jackie. When he'd finished speaking Rebecca slammed on the brakes, grabbed the phone from Shorty and found the medical centre number. She hit dial and handed the phone back to Shorty.

"Ask for Hound."

The receptionist put him through.

"He's on the line." Shorty returned the phone.

"Hound, there's an emergency." She told him what had happened.

Hound said, "Rebecca, whatever you do, don't try to rescue Freddie on your own. You'll be killed if you tackle Kingsley and Jackie without assistance. Wait until support arrives. I'm heading there now."

"No, Hound. You stay at the centre. We can handle it."

"I'm on my way. And no, you can't handle this one. Take my word for it. Keep away from Kingsley, and at all costs avoid Jackie. I'll be there in twenty minutes." He ended the call.

When they got to Jackie's, the Crown Vic was there, parked close to the house. Rebecca looked at Shorty. "Hound said to stay put. He doesn't want us going after Freddie. Says it's too dangerous. What do you think?"

"I may have lost my best pal because I wasn't around when he needed me. We can't leave Freddie alone with them." Shorty balled his small hands into fists.

"We don't know for sure that they're going to kill him. They wouldn't do it here anyway. My guess is they'll take him out of town."

"What if you're wrong?"

She shrugged. "I think Hound was right. There's two of them and they could be armed." Rebecca drove her car farther up the street and parked where they couldn't be seen from the house. The trouble was, they couldn't see Kingsley's car either.

Rebecca called Sykes and reached his voice mail. She left a message telling him the situation, and that she intended to rescue Freddie. Next, she called Cartwright. While she waited for him to answer, Rebecca wondered why Hound had told her to avoid Jackie *at all costs*.

Chapter 38

Hound struggled to pull on his clothes. Every movement made him cry out in pain. He woke O'Reilly, who raised himself on an elbow and rubbed his eyes.

"Hound, what are you up to?"

"Rebecca and Shorty are outside Jackie Caldwell's house. She and Kingsley have taken Freddie prisoner."

"Why? What's going on?" O'Reilly sat up and yawned. Hound figured he was still on sedatives, although he was scheduled to be moved to Orillia in an hour or so.

"I reckon this is the final piece of the puzzle." Hound slipped on his shoes, but he couldn't manage the laces. Using the bed frame, he hauled himself to his feet and hobbled from the room.

He spoke to the receptionist. "Call a taxi, would you?"

She shook her head. "Mr. Hounsley, you know you're not allowed up. Get back to your room."

"Just call the taxi. Now. It's an emergency."

While she hesitated, Hound leaned over the desk, pressing a hand against his cracked ribs. With a loud yelp, he snatched the phone from its cradle.

The receptionist shot to her feet. "You can't take my phone like that. I'm getting the charge nurse, right now." She hurried away.

Hound had just finished the call when the charge nurse stormed into the hall, the receptionist in tow. "Mr. Hounsley, you're to stay in bed. Get back there this minute." She folded her arms.

"Just Hound, ma'am. Sorry, but I can't do that. I'm needed elsewhere, urgently. I'd appreciate it if you could get my painkillers for me."

"Certainly not. Whatever it is, it can wait. You need rest. Come along with me." She grabbed his arm and tugged, but Hound stood firm.

She let go. "Have it your way. But you'll be back, and in excruciating pain. Don't expect any sympathy then." The thought seemed to please her.

Hound ignored her and hobbled out to the parking lot, where the cab was waiting.

* * *

Swearing volubly, Sykes stalked out of Cartwright's office. How did he always manage to be away from Conroy just when something was happening? The McBride and Vogel cases were about to come to a head, but here he was, miles from the action. He checked his voicemail and heard Rebecca's appeal for help. He cursed again.

Chad was coming down the hall towards him.

"Things are heating up again," Sykes yelled. "Get my car. And find Hadi. We're going back to Conroy."

"Why don't we just move there, boss?" Chad grunted, and ran off to find his colleague.

Why not? thought Sykes. There'd been more action in tiny Conroy in a week than he'd seen all year — two killed, and another at death's door. There might be more bodies if they didn't get there soon. Cartwright had been handed a plum case last year with the Abigail McBride case, and made a mess of it. Sykes had let him have it, and now he regretted stepping aside, even if he'd had a good reason for it. He might have prevented Herman's murder. To make things worse, he was being outclassed by an inexperienced constable, and a complete amateur. Rebecca and Hound had been a step ahead of him all the way.

Chad and Hadi pulled up, and Sykes got in. He tried to call Rebecca but her number was busy. Muttering imprecations under his breath, he leaned back in his seat while they raced towards the Trans-Canada.

* * *

Kingsley and Jackie threw the bound and semi-conscious Freddie into the crawl space under Jackie's house. They went upstairs and stood facing each other in her living room.

"Now what, Kingsley?" The corners of Jackie's mouth were slightly upturned.

Right now, all Kingsley wanted was to put his hands around her neck and squeeze. Real hard. "You're enjoying this, aren't you?" he said. "Well, you're in it too, you know, up to your ears, so there's no reason to smile like that." And what the deuce *were* they going to do? "I wonder where Perez made people vanish."

"It's too late, Kingsley. Whatever you do now, the police will find out about your little schemes. That filthy little girl detective is on to you. Hound too. They won't give up." Her black eyes glittered.

"And what about you?"

Jackie smiled. "They'll never get me. After all, what have *I* done wrong?"

"You murdered Perez, for a start."

"Who's to know? It's your word against mine, and it's you they're after." That irritating little smile played about her lips.

"Then help me." Kingsley ground his teeth. Oh, if only he could finish her off now. What a relief it would be.

"Of course, Kingsley. I've always helped you, haven't I?"

"Huh?" Kingsley glared at her.

Jackie began counting on her fingers. "First of all, Abigail. I took care of her, and no one was any the wiser — including you. Then I was forced to kill Herman. That was her fault, the Bradley bitch. Archie should have been next, but I slipped up there. Now it's Freddie's turn. Then I can deal with the Bradley whore once and for all. Hound too, if he gets in our way. After that, we'll be safe."

Kingsley stared at her, incredulous. This wasn't possible. His head spun. If she had indeed murdered Abigail and Herman, the implications were staggering.

"Come on now, Jackie. You're joking." Kingsley blinked rapidly. "Aren't you?"

"I did it for you, Kingsley. You wanted me to, you know you did. You just didn't have the courage to ask. I'm very strong. Abigail didn't struggle at all when I strangled her, and then I strung her up to make it look like a suicide. I think she wanted to die. You betrayed her, Kingsley, with your shady deals and your scummy friends."

Kingsley was stunned. He groped for the nearest chair and sat down heavily. This changed everything. He would have to get rid of Jackie. She was insane.

Suddenly it all became clear to him.

He remembered when they were in high school. She'd stalked him then. She was always there, sidling up to him and offering to help with whatever he needed. He went off to university and forgot all about her. After graduation, he found a job in Toronto.

One day, out of the blue, Jackie wrote to him about the gold mine. Her husband, Paul, had inherited the rights from his father. When Paul died a short while later in a hunting accident, the rights and all his shares passed to Jackie. They were worthless, then, and remained that way until the price of gold started to rise, many years later. In her letter, Jackie told Kingsley she would transfer a quarter of her shares to him, but only if he returned to Conroy and developed the mine. He checked the assays and consulted experts at the Bradley Gold Corporation. They confirmed that the ore was of high quality. George Bradley himself vouched for it. So Kingsley moved to Conroy and began his affair with Jackie, well before he met Abigail and married her. Jackie had seduced him with a promise of additional shares, although he would only get them after the mine was fully operational. He found the vile woman repulsive, but there was so much to gain.

These thoughts brought him back to Paul's death. Where it all started.

"What about your husband, Jackie?"

"Yes, Kingsley. Paul was in the way, just like his father."

"What? Your father-in-law too?" His mouth opened and closed like a landed fish.

Jackie's face shone with pride. "The old man went first. Poisoned, like a garden pest. Nobody suspected a thing. Everyone blamed his weak heart. Steven Bradley — the lousy crook — stole all the money Paul's father had invested in the mine. But he still got the rights after Bradley was murdered." She laughed out loud. "Well, that cheating pirate reaped what he sowed."

Kingsley lurched to his feet and stumbled about the room, shaking his head. "You've murdered five people, counting Perez, and tried to kill one more . . ." He stopped in his tracks. "You killed Steven Bradley, didn't you?" He slumped against the wall.

"Don't be silly, Kingsley. I was a teenager back then. Someone else killed Bradley. But I would have, eventually." She sniffed.

Kingsley massaged his temples. His head was throbbing so hard that he feared he might have a stroke.

Jackie's voice lacked all emotion. She might have been talking about an afternoon's housework, a trip to the supermarket. "Don't worry, dear. All we have to do is kill

Freddie Stafford and the Bradley bitch. Hound too, I guess. Then we'll be safe."

Kingsley began to laugh, hysterically. "What about O'Reilly? And Sykes? I mean, where the hell is this going to end?"

Jackie glared at him. "You're mocking me, Kingsley. Don't mock me. I can't stand that." She plucked at the buttons on her blouse.

Kingsley stumbled to the liquor cabinet. With a shaking hand, he filled a whiskey glass with vodka and gulped it down like water. He poured a second glass and swallowed that too. He poured another.

Jackie's eyes were nothing but slits. Her lips curled, revealing sharp yellow teeth.

Kingsley's blood ran cold. What if she decided to kill *him*? He realized she could easily dispose of both him and Freddie and get off scot-free. Even if he told the police that Jackie was the killer, they wouldn't believe him.

He downed his third vodka. His head was spinning, but he knew what he had to do. He would drive Jackie and Freddie somewhere deep in the countryside and get rid of both of them.

He darted a furtive look at her. Flecks of spittle had gathered at the corners of her mouth. He must calm her down.

"Jackie, there's no need for us to fight, darling. Let's get Freddie. It's time we took care of him. Bring your rifle and we'll head north. We'll haul him into the woods and finish him off there."

Her face lit up. "Now you're talking. We're in this together, you and me, aren't we? Just like Bonnie and Clyde."

"You bet." Kingsley shuddered.

"I know a place where we can dump his body. No one will ever find it." Jackie headed towards the stairs. "I'll tell you about it on the way."

* * *

Shorty kept watch while Rebecca called Sykes. He answered immediately and told her that the ERT had been mobilized, but it would take them at least thirty minutes to reach Conroy. He was on his way. He warned her to be careful, and ended the call.

Rebecca turned to Shorty. "We'll wait here until Hound arrives. The Emergency Response Team is on its way, and DI Sykes will be here soon. It would be crazy to enter the house without backup. We might be captured or shot."

"Okay, Rebecca, but I'm afraid for Freddie. They'd better get here fast."

Then they saw the Crown Vic back down the driveway. Kingsley was behind the wheel, with Jackie beside him. They couldn't see Freddie.

"Crap." Rebecca pounded the dashboard. "Freddie must be on the back seat, or stashed in the trunk. We'll follow them and see where they're going. Hound doesn't have a cell phone, so I won't be able to tell him. I'll call Sykes again."

"Don't worry. Hound will find us." There was no doubt in Shorty's voice.

Rebecca nodded. She followed the Crown Vic through Conroy, and then north on the Trans-Canada.

Chapter 39

Hound arrived at Jackie Caldwell's house to find the driveway empty. There was no sign of Rebecca and Shorty. He told the taxi driver, whose name was Arthur, to wait. Then he sank back into the seat and emptied his mind. He came out of his brief trance convinced that Jackie Caldwell was the missing piece in Conroy's murder puzzle. He recalled O'Reilly telling him that Jackie had shot her husband somewhere in the woods off County Road Thirty-Four, which placed the shooting in the vicinity of his cave. She claimed she'd tripped over a root and accidentally pressed her rifle trigger. Her husband was standing in front of her and the bullet struck him in the back. He died instantly. The police investigation found no motive for murder, so they deemed it an accident and closed the file. At the time they didn't know that Paul Caldwell owned the gold mine, or that it might be viable someday. The question still remained of how Kingsley became involved, but Hound now knew that Kingsley and Jackie were long-time lovers. She must have used the mine as bait to ensnare him.

Hound struggled to sit upright and tapped the elderly driver. "Arthur, go along Main."

"Sure thing, Hound. What're you looking for?"

"Kingsley McBride's Crown Vic and Rebecca Bradley's convertible."

"You mean the red Mercedes she keeps at Maggie's?"

"Yes, that's the one. You seem to know everything, Arthur. I need to find her. Shorty's with her."

"Then let's go to Duffy's and ask there. People watch the street. Someone might've seen them go past."

"Good idea."

Arthur drove to the shop and waited while Hound went inside and spoke to Daisy.

"Morning, Hound. That Arthur I see outside? Why don't you—?"

"Sorry to cut in, Daisy, but I need to ask people here if they've seen Kingsley drive by. And Rebecca, in her convertible."

"No need. I saw them myself ten minutes ago, heading north. Jackie Caldwell was in Kingsley's car. Rebecca went past less than a minute later, with Shorty. What's up?"

"Sorry, Daisy. Gotta go." He returned to the taxi.

"They drove past here ten minutes ago, Arthur, heading north. Try the Trans-Canada. Maybe we can catch them."

* * *

Chad took a deep breath and asked, "Sir, what's going on? Why are we chasing the town accountant and a librarian like there's no tomorrow? And what's McBride up to anyway?"

"This whole case bugs me, Chad. How come a small-town chump like McBride suddenly turns into a wheeler-dealer linked to a southern Ontario crime syndicate and a moneyed family in the Netherlands? Cartwright should've caught on to that last year, and Constable Bradley hasn't even got around to interviewing him yet."

"Speaking of Bradley, what's the story with her?" Hadi chimed in. "Her father's in on the mining deal. She said she wouldn't talk to him until you approved it. Why didn't she call him right away when she found out he was involved? And how did she persuade Cartwright to hand her the McBride case?"

"It's no surprise that George Bradley's involved," Sykes replied. "He's involved in numerous goldmining ventures across Canada and around the world. He even collects gold artefacts. But Cartwright tripped up badly last year. He didn't find out about the mine or the land speculation deals. As for Rebecca, she was right not to contact her father without checking with me first."

Chad gave a grim smile. "Why don't we just ask Mr. Big what's going on? Maybe he's not so lily white himself, if you know what I mean."

"Leave him to me," Sykes snapped, and then felt badly about it. "Sorry, Chad. This whole case is making me touchy."

"Sure, boss. No problem. Can I ask another question?"

"Shoot." Sykes raised his eyebrows.

"It's awkward, sir."

"Go on. What is it?"

The big detective squirmed in his seat. "Well, sir, Hadi and I have been wondering what your problem is with Rebecca Bradley. I know it's none of our business, but we think she really does belong in the CIB, even if she has some rough edges."

Sykes took a while to reply. "Let's just say I've been wrong. I take it you would both agree if I asked Cartwright to transfer her to our branch?"

Chad and Hadi smiled and nodded.

"Good. I'll submit the request when we return to Orillia. But I'm not one of her favourite people, so it might help if the two of you talked to her first. Tell her I've been impressed with her investigative work.

Encourage her to come and see me when we're back in Orillia."

Chad looked pleased. "Now, one more question, sir. A personal one this time." He glanced in the rearview mirror.

"You guys are doing a lot of thinking. You sure you have enough cases to work on?" Sykes tilted his head.

"Sorry, sir. Maybe this isn't the right time to ask."

Sykes stared at Chad's eyes in the mirror. "This was your last question, right? So let's have it."

Chad took a deep breath. "Well, sir . . . why haven't you left Orillia for a better position? You're the top homicide detective in the country."

Sykes grunted. "Thanks for the vote of confidence, guys. But the problem with a promotion is that I would no longer be on the street, which is where I want to be."

"Fair enough, sir. It's none of our business anyway. We're proud of you. You've taught us a lot. We just think you should get more recognition for your achievements. Look at the way Cartwright's been promoted, and it was you who solved most of his cases for him."

Sykes laughed. "If that's what's eating you, forget it. I'm happy with where I am. I don't need any more accolades, but I do appreciate the respect my colleagues give me. And I'm proud of both of you. That's enough for me."

"Well, sir, we didn't tell you, but Chad and I have both turned down offers from elsewhere. Not that we'll stay in Orillia forever, but it's hard to leave while you're around."

Sykes leaned forward and patted both men on the shoulders. Yes, he had been content — until he saw Archie, and was reminded of George Bradley. He would never tell anyone what had happened between him and Bradley, but it had ruined his friendship with Archie. His thoughts turned to his former close friend, still lying in hospital in a coma.

Sykes's focus then shifted to Rebecca, and the reason he'd kept her at a distance. It was her father, and not her lack of ability that had caused him to block her transfer to the CIB. Now that he'd seen her work on the McBride case, he realized her talent should be nurtured. Her burning desire to bring criminals to justice reminded him of himself. So to hell with George Bradley. Let him find out that his daughter was moving to the CIB to work for him. If Bradley wanted another confrontation, he was ready to meet that formidable man head-on.

Sykes checked his watch. No call from Rebecca. Ten minutes was far too long. He took out his cell phone.

* * *

Rebecca tailed Kingsley's car along the Trans-Canada until it veered off the highway onto County Road Thirty-Four. So far she'd kept her distance and was confident that Kingsley hadn't seen her. Now came the dangerous part. If he noticed her following him, he might turn off and lie in wait for her. She couldn't risk that. And what if he was heading for Hound's cave? The thought made her stomach tighten. Something about that place seemed to attract trouble.

Rebecca slowed to a crawl. She would wait until Kingsley's Crown Vic was out of sight before she got off the Trans-Canada.

Shorty turned to her. "What're you doing? Why are you going so slow?"

"Don't worry, we won't lose them."

Shorty watched Kingsley's car disappear from view, and then he pounded his fists on his thighs. Rebecca felt sorry for him. Only a week ago he was sitting in Duffy's, trading insults with his best buddy. Since then, his sheltered world had fallen apart. Now he was risking his life to save Freddie.

Rebecca sped up and spotted Kingsley's car turning onto the dirt road leading to the meadow. He was definitely heading towards Hound's cave. A feeling of dread overtook her.

She eased her Mercedes onto the road. Kingsley's Crown Vic had rounded a bend and was out of sight. She knew she had to time her arrival carefully or Kingsley might get to the meadow and travel too far into the woods for her to find him. She was counting on the element of surprise. If she could creep up on them in the forest and catch them unawares, she might find a way to save Freddie.

She cruised up to the meadow and saw Kingsley's Crown Vic parked beside it, empty. She took in a deep breath.

"This is it, Shorty. We'll trail them through the woods and look for a way to free Freddie. You still with me?"

Shorty wore a glazed expression, but he said, "Let's go." He opened the car door.

"Right. Off we go." Rebecca took out her cell phone, which rang before she could make the call to Sykes. He was only a few minutes away. She told him what she was doing and gave him directions to the meadow, and then the cave, in case the chase ended there.

Rebecca unclipped her holster and drew out her gun. She got out of the car and started to jog across the meadow, listening for telltale sounds. Shorty followed close behind her. There were no promising noises to guide them, and Rebecca soon realized that she'd lost track of Kingsley. The cave was her only hope now, so she got on the trail that led towards it and continued through the bush until she was almost there. Her gut wrenched. If she was wrong about the cave, Freddie would die, and she would bear the guilt for the rest of her life.

Shorty was puffing at her heels. "It's okay, Shorty," she reassured him. "We'll find them."

Then a single gunshot pierced the silence of the forest.

Chapter 40

Kingsley reached the end of the meadow road and brought his Crown Vic to a stop. He turned to face Jackie.

"Now what? Is this where we get rid of Freddie? Not here, surely?"

Jackie ignored him and got out of the car. She gazed slowly about her.

"We have to get moving. There's no time to lose." Kingsley wanted to get this over with. "Come on. Just tell me where to go." He opened the trunk and hauled out the bound and gagged Freddie.

Kingsley fumbled with the rope around Freddie's ankles. He glared at Jackie. "Get over here and help me."

"Yes, dearest." She hovered at his shoulder while he released Freddie's feet.

He sighed. "Okay then, just get your rifle."

Jackie grinned happily and removed it from the car. Kingsley peered at the safety catch. It was off. Good.

"Take me to this secret place you told me about, and hurry," he snapped.

Jackie pivoted and started to tramp across the meadow. Kingsley followed, dragging Freddie along with him.

Jackie led the way to the end of the trail, and then pushed through a stretch of bush. She entered a clearing and halted. She closed her eyes for a moment, and a blissful expression settled over her face.

"This is where my husband met his end, near the thicket by the rock wall over there. That was the moment the gold mine came to me, and you did too, Kingsley." She sighed. "Freddie will rest peacefully here. We'll bury him in the thicket. No one will ever find him."

Freddie sank to his knees, weeping. Jackie cuffed his head.

It was time to make his move. Kingsley edged closer to her and held out his hand. "Give me the rifle, Jackie. Let me do it."

Freddie struggled against his wrist restraints, but Jackie ignored him and said, "Why, Kingsley?"

"Because I've never killed anyone before. I want to know what it feels like. I want to be able to talk to you about it. Please, dear, give the gun to me." His hand was almost on the barrel, but Jackie stepped back a pace. She gave him a puzzled look, and then her face contorted with rage.

She'd figured it out. Kingsley panicked. He lunged at her and seized the rifle with both hands, but she held onto it. They fought for control of the weapon, Jackie twisting and yanking on the butt while he clung desperately to the barrel. Freddie was staring at them. Then he seemed to wake up. He backed slowly into the thicket and through the narrow cleft in the rock leading to Hound's cave.

Meanwhile, Jackie gave a final wrench to the rifle butt and tore it from Kingsley's sweaty palms. Her finger hit the trigger. Kingsley spun around and dropped to the ground. He rolled on the grass, bleeding from a graze on his shoulder. Jackie watched him, wide-eyed. She moved closer.

Kingsley groaned. "Bitch! You murdering bitch. See what you've done."

"Not me, Kingsley. It was you. You did it to yourself." The sight of fresh blood had a strange effect on Jackie. Her eyes went glassy. But then she stiffened. She whirled about.

"Where's Freddie?"

Kingsley looked at the spot where Freddie had stood just a few seconds ago.

Jackie put a hand to her forehead. "He's gone, Kingsley. It's your fault. I'll find the little rat and blow his brains out." She ran around, looking into the bushes. Then she stopped and tilted her head. She strode to the edge of the clearing and peered into the dense foliage. To the sound of rustling leaves and snapping twigs, Rebecca Bradley burst out in front of her and froze, staring straight down the barrel of a rifle held inches from her face.

* * *

"Drop the gun." Jackie's voice dripped with venom.

Rebecca opened her mouth. She dropped the weapon close to her feet, just as Shorty crashed through the bushes and came to a stop beside her. Across the clearing, Rebecca saw Kingsley McBride swaying on his knees. He was clutching his shoulder and wheezing, and one arm of his shirt was covered in blood.

Jackie fixed her glittering eyes on Rebecca. A triumphant smile spread across her face. "I've saved a special bullet for you, vixen."

Finally Rebecca understood everything.

"You're the one. *You* murdered Abigail and Herman."

Jackie bared her teeth. "Yes, I killed them. And now I'm going to kill you." She stepped back and pointed the rifle at Rebecca's heart.

Chapter 41

Hound directed Arthur to turn onto County Road Thirty-Four. A few miles later, he pointed to the right. "Take the dirt road just ahead. Drive until it ends at a meadow." He slumped back in the seat, moaning.

"Yes, sir, Hound. I take it you're going somewhere in the woods. Sorry to be nosy, but I'm guessing you'll be wanting me to wait for you?" Arthur sounded hopeful.

"Yes, please. And stay near the car. I may need you in a hurry. If I'm not back in an hour, you can go. Mind if I pay you later? I didn't bring any money."

Arthur chuckled. "No problem, your credit's good with me."

They pulled up at the meadow. "Looks like you have company," said Arthur.

Rebecca's Mercedes was parked behind Kingsley's Crown Vic. Hound's pulse quickened. He got out of the taxi and staggered. Sweat dripped from his chin. With a supreme effort, he fought down the pain and pushed himself away from the car.

"I'm off." He limped across the meadow and into the woods. He'd feared that Rebecca wouldn't heed his warning. And when Daisy told him she'd seen Kingsley and Jackie heading north, he knew where to look for her. Jackie had shot her husband in the vicinity of his cave, so the chances were good that she would go there again to kill Freddie. If not, then Hound didn't have a clue where else to look.

This whole tragic business had started near his cave. Hound prayed it would end there.

Chapter 42

Sykes urged Chad to drive faster. He tried calling Rebecca's cell phone again, but got no answer. He had an uneasy feeling she was heading to Hound's cave. He decided now to approach it using the shack route, rather than from the meadow. He was worried that he might not find her in the woods around there, and he wasn't certain he could find the cave from that direction. Using the shack route was a gamble too, but lives were at stake and he couldn't afford to get lost. He called the ERT and gave them directions to the meadow as well as the cave. They would check the woods near the meadow first, and then head to the cave if they found nothing there. That way both areas would be covered. Then he called Cartwright and briefed him.

"Are you mad?" Cartwright bellowed. "You're going on guesswork. What's got into you?"

"Sorry, sir, but time is tight. We need to check both possibilities, without delay."

Cartwright spluttered. "If you're wrong, Sykes, I'll have your ass. And if Rebecca gets hurt and you're not there to help . . ." His voice faded.

"I understand, sir, but it's the best plan I can think of. If you have a better one, tell me now." He waited.

Hearing nothing, Sykes cleared his throat. "We're at the shack, sir. I have to go." He cut the call and got out of the car. "Let's hustle, guys. And don't ask questions."

They raced past the shack, in the direction of the cave. A shot rang out. Sykes grimaced. Freddie? Or Rebecca? He burst into a sprint. They were drawing near to the cave when they heard a second shot, and then a third. Sykes pulled out his gun and pushed through the bush until he was just outside the clearing. A shrill voice pierced the air.

"I'll kill you all!" Jackie Caldwell was almost hidden by the surrounding bush, but Sykes made out the rifle butt pressed against her shoulder.

"Stop! Drop the rifle."

Jackie twisted around, aimed and fired. Sykes dove to the ground. A bullet whizzed past his ear. He waited a moment, then raised his head. Jackie had turned back and was pointing her rifle again. He raised his gun and shot twice. The second shot winged her. She dropped to her knees, and the rifle slipped from her hands.

Sykes pushed to his feet. He needed to get to her before she could recover. He kicked Jackie's rifle away, and almost recoiled at the look she gave him.

Seconds later, Chad and Hadi arrived and put her in handcuffs.

Sykes looked around and saw Hound lying sprawled on the ground. Beneath him were two bodies. He raised his head and rolled onto his back. The right side of his shirt was soaked in blood. Rebecca struggled to her hands and knees and crawled over to check his wound. Shorty got up and stood staring down at his friend.

Hound tried to sit up. "Hold still," Rebecca urged. "Let me stop the bleeding first."

"I'm fine," he said. Then he fainted.

Rebecca looked over her shoulder at Sykes. "We need help, right away."

Sykes nodded. "The ERT should be at the meadow by now. Medics are with them. I'll direct them here. Tend to Hound. It could take a few minutes for them to arrive."

Chad and Hadi were trying to minister to Jackie's wound, but she bit at their hands like a trapped animal.

Sykes heard Kingsley cry out from across the clearing. "Help me!"

Sykes ignored him and nodded towards Hound. "Can he hold on for a while?"

"I think so," Rebecca said. "I've slowed the bleeding."

"How did he find you?"

Her forehead wrinkled. "I don't know. He must have guessed that we'd be here. I was staring down the barrel of Jackie Caldwell's rifle when he crashed through the bush and jumped in front of me. She shot him in the shoulder. She fired a second time, but he twisted around and knocked Shorty and me to the ground. He fell on top of us to shield us. She would have shot him again, and us too, but then you showed up." She turned back to Hound.

Sykes pulled out his cell phone and called the ERT. They had found the meadow, but weren't sure where to go from there. He told them to follow the trail leading into the woods. "Listen for shots. Hadi and Chad will fire their guns every minute or so to guide you to the clearing." Then he called Cartwright and told him what had happened.

Next, Sykes turned his attention to Kingsley McBride. He was on his knees, and stared up at Sykes.

"She tried to kill me," Kingsley moaned, and pointed a shaking finger at Jackie. "She's the murderer. She killed my wife. Herman Vogel too. She attacked Archie MacDougall. Thank God you got here in time. She was going to kill us all."

Sykes was skeptical. There was something about Kingsley McBride that disturbed him. Jackie, too, was peering at Kingsley with a strange look on her face. Sykes sensed a deep hurt beneath her fury.

Freddie Stafford shuffled out of the thicket on his knees. His hands were bound behind his back and a gag hung loosely around his neck. "Kingsley's a liar," he gasped. "He was going to murder me. They're both murderers."

Chapter 43

O'Reilly sat up in his hospital bed in Orillia. He glanced at his watch. It was 04:03 in the morning. He should be asleep, considering the sedative the charge nurse had made him take, but something had woken him. He looked around the room, which glowed faintly with monitor lights.

He held his breath and listened. The ward was silent. Too silent. The charge nurse and at least one orderly were always on duty at night, moving unobtrusively about. Now, even the computer and the supply cart were quiet. O'Reilly took hold of his crutches, hobbled to the door and peered along the corridor. Two men in trench coats were approaching his room, their fedoras pulled low. Both carried guns. His stomach dropped. They must be Perez's men, searching for him, and Archie too. Where the hell was their police protection? And where were the charge nurse and the orderlies?

O'Reilly backed into the room and looked around for something to use as a weapon. All he found was an aluminum cane. It would have to do. He picked it up and went to the telephone. He dialled 911, aware that pushing the help button beside his bed would alert the men to his location. He whispered to the operator, "Send the police, urgently, and tell them to call hospital security. Two men with guns are on the second floor, west wing, searching the rooms." He hung up, feeling sick. Help wouldn't arrive in time.

He went to the door, took another peek and jerked back immediately. The men would be here in seconds. The cane wouldn't be much use against guns. He scoured the room again, but all he could add to his armament was a metal bedpan. An image passed through his mind of his photo in the *Orillia Packet and Times*, a bullet hole in his forehead, the cane and bedpan clutched in his outstretched arms. He shook his head, grabbed the bedpan and hid behind the door.

Just as the men reached his room, the swing doors at the end of the hall opened and a medical team came in, wheeling a hospital cart with a patient on it. The men jumped into the room without seeing O'Reilly. One of them stuck his head out to see where the cart was heading. Seizing the moment, O'Reilly swung round the door and slammed the bedpan into the back of the nearest man's head. The blow propelled him into his colleague, who tumbled to his hands and knees in front of the cart. His Glock fell from his grip and slid across the hall.

The other man whirled about, his gun held in both hands. O'Reilly rammed the cane into his stomach. The man doubled over and O'Reilly brought his knee up into his face. The blow knocked the man backwards into the door frame and he slid to the floor, stunned. O'Reilly bent over and snatched the weapon from his hand, cursing his wounded leg.

Meanwhile, the other man had scrambled to his feet and was fleeing down the hall, leaving his gun and his companion behind. He crashed through an emergency exit door and set off the alarm.

The medical team stopped outside O'Reilly's room and stared at the scene.

"Send a security detail to Archie MacDougall's room, quick." O'Reilly gave them the number and said, "Police are on their way. Everything's under control here."

The woozy gunman stared into the muzzle of his own Glock, blood streaming from his shattered nose. Hospital guards arrived and took charge of him. O'Reilly heard sirens wailing, followed soon after by heavy boots tramping along the corridor. While a policeman snapped cuffs on the gunman, O'Reilly told them what had happened. He hobbled off to check on Archie, and found him wide awake, and confused.

"Officer O'Reilly. Good to see ye here, wherever 'here' is. One minute I'm out back at Maggie's, smokin' a wee cigarette, and now I'm lyin' on this bed with a bugger of a headache and a line o' stitches in my neck."

O'Reilly limped over and placed a hand on his shoulder. "It's great to see you, Archie. I have a lot to tell you, but I'll hold on that until you're feeling better."

"Aye, that can wait a bit, I reckon. But I had the strangest dream, I can tell you. Floatin' I was, and I met Hound and Rebecca holdin' hands and floatin' too. Now what do ye make o' that?"

O'Reilly embraced him. "Welcome back, Archie. You gave us quite a fright."

Chapter 44

Another terrible Christmas in Prospect. Dad hasn't forgiven me for becoming a cop. I pressed him again about my mother's death, and we had a nasty fight. He still won't talk about it. I'm sure he knows something he won't tell me, but he will someday. I'll make him.
— The diary of Rebecca Sarah Bradley (2004)

Two weeks later, Rebecca, Hound, O'Reilly, Shorty and Archie met at Duffy's. Daisy had reserved a booth for them in a quiet corner of the shop. When they had settled, a pretty young girl rushed over to serve them. Rebecca recognized Bridget, and gave her a big smile. Bridget smiled back. She looked happy.

After the news broke of a second murder in Conroy, followed by the shootout at the shack and the dramatic cave fight, traffic along Main Street had mounted to city rush-hour levels. Many tourists and vacationers had diverted from their usual routes northward, in order to visit this 'Wild West' town. Some of them stayed overnight. The Royal Oak was booked solid for the first time in more than a decade.

Rebecca glanced at O'Reilly. "It didn't take you long to sort out Bridget's father, did it?"

He grinned broadly. "Indeed not. I took Hound with me at a time when I knew her father would be alone. I grilled the man something fierce, with Hound towering beside me, glaring down at him. He denied everything, but we put a scare into him. Now he scrambles to the opposite side of the street whenever he sees Hound."

Rebecca looked at Hound, and an intriguing thought struck her. He was actually attractive, in his own way. Not handsome, but he radiated an inner power that complemented his enormous size. For the first time since they'd met, she could imagine him with a girl beside him. The thought made her smile.

She hadn't felt this good in a long time, sitting here with the first true friends she had ever had.

Hound lounged across from her in the booth, one massive leg stretched out into the aisle. A super-sized milkshake sat on the table in front of him. Daisy had made it especially for him. His shoulder was bandaged and he wore a sling, but he seemed content. He winked at Rebecca, then reached into his pocket and took out a cell phone, which he pressed to his ear. Shorty gave him a thumbs-up.

Hound smiled at Rebecca over the top of his glass. "So what next, Madam?"

She sat upright and smiled at her companions — Shorty, O'Reilly, and to her delight, Archie, who had been discharged from hospital on condition that he take a month's rest. Lukas was still in Orillia, but was out of intensive care and on the mend. He'd been near death for a week, and it would take a long time for him to recover. Sadly, his lungs would be scarred for life.

"Right now," Rebecca said, "we digest the feast we just devoured at Maggie's. The banquet she served would bring in a thousand hungry tourists. In fact, I believe it already has." She waved her hand at the packed booths and the throng of tourists meandering along Main.

"I'll second that." O'Reilly licked his lips. "That meal was worth getting shot for. I mean . . . oh dear." He put a hand over his mouth.

Hound patted his arm. "We know what you mean, chief."

Shorty raised his soda in the air. "Here's to Lukas, the best friend anyone could ever have. May he join us soon at Duffy's."

They all raised their glasses.

"What about you, Rebecca?" Hound asked. "What comes next?"

She gave them a big smile. "I have an announcement. I've been transferred to the CIB. I can't believe it yet. I'm on track to become a bona fide detective, working for DI Sykes. Acting DC Bradley, officially, at your service." They all congratulated her. "And you, Constable O'Reilly, or should I call you chief? Have you settled things with Superintendent Cartwright?"

He cleared his throat. "I see you've heard the news. Turns out he's not such a bad guy after all." Everyone burst out laughing. "And I won't stand for any of you taking cheap shots at him."

"But what's the news?" asked Rebecca.

His face turned pink. "Okay. It seems Cartwright wants me to stay on and run things here, at least for the time being. I won't say we're exactly cozy yet, but we'll get along for a while, provided he doesn't spend too much time in Conroy." He grinned sheepishly. "Oh, and Sally stays on."

"No kidding." Shorty said. "Then things will be back to normal."

"Not a chance!" Rebecca and Hound yelped together.

"There's no such thing as normal in this town." Rebecca lowered her voice. "I have a feeling there's more to come."

Hound glanced quickly at her, and then turned to O'Reilly. "Chief, what about the charges against you?"

"What charges?" O'Reilly's face wore an innocent expression. "The lawyers agreed to leave me alone, probably because I saved Archie's life. And my own, mind you. I'm a hero now. Haven't you read the papers? I've got articles from the *Toronto Star*, *Globe and Mail*, and *National Post* framed and hung on my office wall. *Orillia Packet and Times* too." Oh, and I've been nominated for the Ontario Medal for Police Bravery, by DI Sykes no less. Keep that to yourselves, please. I'm not supposed to know." O'Reilly broke into a huge grin.

Archie spoke up from the corner of the booth. "Aye, a hero, for sure, Constable O'Reilly. Congratulations." He spread his fingers in a victory salute.

"There you go," O'Reilly said. "Sometimes having police avoid asking awkward questions can be very helpful," he grinned. "It's such a strange world." He tilted his head at Rebecca. "I only wish I'd been born smarter."

She raised her glass. "To O'Reilly, hero of Conroy."

They all followed her lead.

Hound asked, "What will happen to Freddie Stafford?"

"Nothing," Rebecca said. "His role in Kingsley's schemes was trivial. He packed his bags and left town a few days ago. He said not to expect him back in Conroy, or anywhere near it. He'll be in Toronto, though, testifying at the trials of Kingsley and Jackie. I have nightmares about that woman."

"And Mayor Taylor? What happened to him?" Hound queried.

"Nowhere to be found," O'Reilly said. "Same as Marco Perez. DI Sykes is all over it, but there's no leads. Shorty overheard a few words between Kingsley and Jackie that suggest they might have killed poor Charlie, but they didn't mention any names. We believe either Kingsley or Perez killed him. Or Jackie might have done it for Kingsley. But if so, where did they hide his body? And Sykes figures we'll never find Perez. It's likely he's sipping piña coladas on a Caribbean island or hiding out somewhere in South America."

Rebecca turned to Hound. "Please tell us what you plan to do, Hound, if you know. We're so grateful for the courageous role you played in this whole affair. I've never met anyone like you in my entire life."

Hound stared at them, as though seeking the answer in their faces. He didn't speak. After a while he shrugged his shoulders and leaned back in the booth.

"There's no need to tell us now, but I'll pass along a compliment I heard from an unimpeachable source." Rebecca watched him while she spoke. "I was reviewing the McBride and Vogel cases yesterday with my new boss. We talked about your help in solving them. Without thinking, Sykes referred to you as Inspector Hound, I swear he did. He seemed amused at first. Then he looked at me and asked, 'What do you think? Would he consider it?' I can tell you for a fact that Sykes doesn't praise anyone lightly. He has the greatest respect for you. I'll just leave it there. It's something to consider as you think about your future." She gave him an encouraging nod.

"Thank you," Hound mumbled.

Not long afterwards, the group prepared to leave. They hugged each other and agreed to get together soon.

Chapter 45

I couldn't sleep last night. I broke into a sweat and shook all over. The thirteenth anniversary of my mother's death is coming up this month — on my twenty-first birthday. I'll be going to Prospect to celebrate with Dad. Things will get really tense. I'll make him tell me about her. I'm in the OPP now. I need to start investigating her murder in earnest.

— The diary of Rebecca Sarah Bradley (2004)

Rebecca watched her pals leave Duffy's and go their separate ways. She had no special affection for Conroy, but she'd made her first real friends there. As she left the shop, Daisy pulled a long face and waved goodbye.

Rebecca went to the parking lot and climbed into her Mercedes. She opened the rooftop. The thought of the drive to Orillia was inviting, with the warm sun on her face and the fresh wind blowing through her hair. It would be August soon, three or four months before the arctic air masses moved south and snow carpeted the ground.

Winter was her melancholy season, the time of year when she huddled indoors at night, and when her mother's unsolved murder weighed most heavily on her mind. It was getting harder every year to put that tragedy behind her. She just *had* to find a clue before winter set in. She needed something to give her hope. And that something might exist in Conroy. It always came back to that town. The McBride investigation had unveiled disturbing links to her family, though not to her mother's murderer. But she would come back and do some personal sleuthing as soon as she had free time. Her dodgy grandfather had left a big footprint on Conroy — one that she was ashamed of. For the time being, however, Sykes had loaded her down with work. Mostly tedious interviews and fact checking, but she didn't mind. One of her goals had been achieved. She would be a real detective soon. Next was to become the best homicide detective in the OPP, DI Sykes notwithstanding.

She drove slowly out of Conroy, past the stand of white pine that had greeted her on first trip there, and headed south on the Trans-Canada. Then her thoughts turned to the mysteries that had not yet been solved, especially Maggie and Archie's links to her tight-lipped father. Her dad had a pile of explaining to do. She still needed to have a private chat with Archie about him, and another with Maggie. And there was the question of why her grandfather had promoted a gold mine near Conroy in the first place. Had it just been a scheme to bilk money from the townsfolk, or was there more to it? Solving that mystery might yield clues to his murder.

Also, how had the mine suddenly become viable in Kingsley McBride's hands, nearly two and a half decades after her grandfather left Conroy? Rising gold prices couldn't be the only reason, she was certain of that. There couldn't be much gold there. And why had her father partnered with Kingsley? She *had* to find out, even if it meant discovering that her father was a crook, like Steven Bradley. And, just maybe, her mother's murder was linked to that cursed gold mine. If it was, and her father knew something about it, her world would fall apart.

As Rebecca eased back into the soft leather seat of her Mercedes and drove away, a solitary tear rolled down her cheek.

Chapter 46

Twenty-one years old. Thirteen years to the day since I found my mother dead in my home. I'm just a few miles from Prospect, and my father. I'm ready to have it out with him. I've waited a long time for him to tell me what he knows about her murder.
— The diary of Rebecca Sarah Bradley (2004)

Rebecca pulled into the parking lot at the OPP office, just as the day-shift officers and staff were heading out. Inside the entrance to the admin building, she ran into DI Sykes.

"Good day, DC Bradley. Back from your Conroy reunion, I see. I trust your battered friends are on the mend?" He sounded as if he meant it.

"Yes, sir, thank you for asking. Lukas had a really tough spell. He's still in the hospital, but the doctors say he'll recover further. The others are doing fine."

"Good to hear that, and I mean it. As you've no doubt guessed, though, I'm here for a reason. I need to talk to you. Can you spare the time?" His face was unreadable.

"Of course, sir." What now? Sykes never engaged in idle chatter.

"What I have to say is best done in private. Please follow me." He led the way to his office on the second floor. Passing Cartwright's closed door, Rebecca recalled their Sunday meeting just over three weeks ago, when she had manipulated him into giving her the lead on the McBride case. So much had changed since then, it felt as if years had passed.

The lights in Cartwright's office were off. He must have left earlier than usual. Had Sykes planned their meeting so as to avoid him? She still didn't know what made them detest each other so much. On the other hand, she was beginning to understand what an extraordinary detective Sykes was. No wonder Cartwright acted skittish around him.

"Take a seat." Sykes gestured to Rebecca, and then sat on his worn office chair, which creaked as he settled in.

She dragged a metal folding chair in front of his desk.

Sykes observed her for a short while, and said, "There are things about Jackie Caldwell that I believe you should know."

"Yes?" Rebecca pressed her hands onto her lap. Her mouth was dry.

"The psychiatrist said she's delusional. She even believes she wields some sort of magical power. But more to the point, she has a pathological hatred of you. Do you understand what that means?" He peered into her eyes.

She wasn't really sure, but she nodded.

"I think I've found out why," Sykes said, and Rebecca leaned forward.

He took a deep breath and placed his palms on his desk. "Her father-in-law was a partner in Steven Bradley's goldmining scheme. He lost a pile of money when it went bust. He ended up owning the mining rights, which were worthless after the gold price fell in the early eighties. Jackie's father also invested in the mine, but as a silent partner through her father-in-law. When the hoax was uncovered, her father lost everything he owned and was forced to declare bankruptcy. He lost his house and had to close the sawmill he'd run for more than twenty years. You remember the abandoned mill we found outside Conroy?"

Rebecca nodded.

Sykes's lips compressed. "Jackie was a teenager when it happened, a top student at the county high school. Her father's ruin destroyed any hope she had of going to college or university. She quit school and took local jobs to help pay the bills. In her interviews, she claimed her mother couldn't cope with the humiliation of being poor, as well as the loss of her position as the wife of a successful businessman. She fled town and never returned. That, on top of everything else, was too much for Jackie's father to handle. He never recovered. Jackie was left with no money, no mother, and a wasted father."

Sykes stopped speaking.

Rebecca leaned back in her chair and stared out the window at the station parking lot. She hadn't considered Jackie's past during the entire investigation. But there was always a reason why things turned out the way they did, and suddenly she felt sorry for Jackie. It was hard to believe such a terrible woman had been a child with dreams of her own, but of course she had, just like her. She felt ashamed for not even thinking of it. The worst part, though, was that Steven Bradley had ruined Jackie's life. Her grandfather had helped to turn Jackie into the hateful woman she became. So he had Abigail's blood on his hands, and by extension, Rebecca did too. And Conroy had turned from being a triumph for her into a disaster founded on greed and hate. And now an awful thought struck her. Was Jackie any different than she was, with her mission of revenge? What would *she* do when she came face to face with her mother's murderer? How far would she go? Would she kill, or attempt to kill, as Jackie had done? Failing that, would she become twisted and hateful if she couldn't catch the murderer? Her obsession with revenge had already harmed her personal relationships. She had even used Cartwright to get what she wanted. She wondered now if it was it worse to lose a mother at the hands of a murderer, or to be abandoned by her? At least she had the memory of a mother who'd loved her. Jackie had nothing to look back on except rejection.

So Jackie hated her because Steven Bradley had destroyed her family and her future. Years later, when *she* showed up in Conroy, Jackie sought revenge. Could she be blamed for that?

Through the second-floor window, Rebecca watched two teenagers walking together, hand in hand. She thought about a life filled with love and caring, goodness and light. But that life had died for her when she was eight years old, and it had died for Jackie too. Was she doomed to live a life of misery in a hopeless quest for something she would never accomplish? And if she did find the murderer, would it just lead to further complications and heartbreak?

She heard papers shuffling, and her mind returned to the present.

"Thank you for telling me, sir." She tried to hide the tremor in her voice. "I wonder how many people in Conroy know what you've just told me, and what they think of me. If they find out, I'm sure they won't welcome me back."

Gently, Sykes said, "That's why I told you, Rebecca. I would advise you to think twice before going back there. But that would be pointless, wouldn't it?" His grey eyes had a softness that she had never seen before.

"Yes, sir, it would." Rebecca took a deep breath, rose slowly to her feet, and left the room.

THE END

Author's Note

Her Dark Path is a work of fiction, with license taken to fit the geographical setting to the storyline. A small town named Conroy was created, located on the eastern side of Georgian Bay, Ontario, and just off the Trans-Canada Highway. County Road 34 (also known as Muskoka Road) has been used imaginatively, with other settings added as needed to suit requirements of the novel.

Acknowledgements

It would be impossible to acknowledge all the people who took personal time to read and review various drafts of the novel, but a special thank-you is given to my wife, Elizabeth Everhardus, and my Sisters in Crime (Toronto) critique group, which in past years included Patricia Kennedy and Karen Blake-Hall, and currently includes Lesley Mang, Terri Dixon and Susan Daly. Another special thank-you for reviewing the entire novel is given to Michael Sears (co-author with Stanley Trollip of the wonderful Detective Kubu series set in Botswana), Ed Seaward, Senator Elaine McCoy, Jane Pagel, Gord Miller, Paul Griss, David Pollock, Paula Bryan, Joanne Brown, Linda Ogilvie, and Norma Duncan (Sisters in Crime, United States, with whom I did a productive manuscript swap). To the many others whose names I haven't mentioned, and who offered comments and kind words of support, thank you all.

Professional reviews and editing of early to late-stage novel drafts were done by Cheryl and Elaine Freedman, Aviva Layton, and Tom Willkens, all of whose edits and advice were invaluable in improving the novel and teaching me how to write better. A very early draft was also reviewed by author Elizabeth Duncan through the Humber School for Writers, Creative Writing Course, and a later-stage draft was evaluated by Sara Saddington through Humber Publishing Services.

The final thank-you goes to Joffe Books and its superb editors, Anne Derges and Sophie Wilson, who put the novel thorough very substantial edits before it was finalized and published.

Thank you for reading this book. If you enjoyed it please leave feedback on Amazon or Goodreads, and if there is anything we missed or you have a question about then please get in touch. The author and publishing team appreciate your feedback and time reading this book.

Our email is office@joffebooks.com

www.joffebooks.com

ABOUT THE AUTHOR

Her Dark Path is Ken Ogilvie's first novel. Prior to taking up writing, Ken worked in a variety of roles in the environmental policy domain, including positions with three governments in Canada (Federal, Manitoba and Ontario) and as the Executive Director of Pollution Probe, one of Canada's premier environmental groups. He remains active as a consultant on energy and climate change, and sits on the boards of two national non-profit organizations – the Pembina Institute for Appropriate Development, and Quality Urban Energy Systems of Tomorrow. He is well known across Canada for his environmental work, and has received two honorary doctorates from the University of Waterloo, Ontario, and Thompson Rivers University, British Columbia.

More info at www.kenogilvie.com

Made in the USA
San Bernardino, CA
22 November 2017